SOME DAYS ARE LIKE THAT...

I walked, and Lord! the sands shifted beneath my feet to the point where I stumbled and fell several times. Through the thickest of fogs the sea roared like Leviathan a-dying, slapping intermittently with the force of a hurricane, tearing chunks of the shore line away and swallowing them in its agony.

Once I learned its direction I scrambled for higher ground, and the beach was eaten behind me as I climbed. Grasping at shrub, root, and rock, sliding back, catching hold again, I pulled myself at length above its reach, achieving, however, as I did so, a region where the winds swelled and howled their answer back to the sea-beast below. And Lord! the tumult of the elements' divorcement! Earth, air, and water strove, then fled one another in heartbeat pulses!

And then—as I raised myself those final feet— a gout of fire fell the welkin's course to fry a tree before me, last element joined in gasping image cast upon my streaming eyes. I lifted my arm in moment shield and when I let it fall, the tree smoked and flickered in the wind and the figure of a man stood, almost unconcerned, nearby, staring past me toward the raging invisible sea, dark cloak flapping.

"Allan!" I cried, recognizing him as I drew near; and then I added, "Poe!"

Baen Books by Fred Saberhagen
The Dracula Tapes
Vlad Tapes

Pilgrim

Baen Books by Roger Zelazny
Forever After *(editor)*

THE BLACK THRONE

**ROGER
ZELAZNY
&
FRED
SABERHAGEN**

THE BLACK THRONE

Copyright © 1990 by the Amber Corporation and Fred Saberhagen

A Baen Books Original

Baen Publishing Enterprises
P.O. Box 1403
Riverdale, NY 10471
www.baen.com

ISBN: 0-7434-3579-6

Cover art by Patrick Turner

First printing, October 1990
Second printing, November 2002

Distributed by Simon & Schuster
1230 Avenue of the Americas
New York, NY 10020

Production by Windhaven Press, Auburn, NH
Printed in the United States of America

The Black Throne

I

She sang beyond the genius of the sea, and he heard.

Walking on that gray, warm morn through fogs which entombed his world in near-viscous whiteness, perfect as snow, quietening as cloak or shroud, the boy moved with a certain deliberation, wordless voice within his head, veiled forms swaying about him, avoiding cobble and branch in passage through the wood behind the school, oddity back of a place once known well, occurring mystery somehow situated to hold his soul chrysalis for a vital season, somehow special, personal, and marking a passage distinctive as scar or tattoo upon his life and forever.

It was more than the dark voice of the sea that made the world acutest at its vanishing. And the sea, for that matter, the sea ought not to be this close, ought it? Nor in this direction. No.

1

Yet sea must there be. Somehow the song told him this, wordless though it ran. Sea must there be, and to it hieing on this day, he, day embedded in cotton, warm, salt tang within it, like the interior of vein or artery, song throbbing through.

Brittle fingers brushed his shoulder, leaves kissed moistly. He drew back from a dark treeform, stumbled against another, recovered. One grows accustomed to fog in London. Even an American child comes quickly to understand it, to separate caution from fear, to appreciate the distortions of distance, the slippery footing, the dearth of echoes. He moved in half-conscious quest of the singer—a quest which might have commenced before his awakening. Indeed, this seemed, somehow, but a continuation of a peculiar dream.

He did remember getting up, dressing, departing. But that had almost been an interlude. This had been going on before that. Something down on the strand. . . . Beach? Strand. Same thing. He had to go and find it now. He knew it would be there. The singing had been present on both sides of sleep. It had told him, it led him. . . .

He walked on, his clothing grown clammy, beginning to cling, a feeling of dampness coming into his shoes. The way sloped downward, and as he followed it the trees retreated, though shadows still formed within the fog; and a bell—somewhere a bell was ringing, just at the edge of awareness, slow, earthy, full-throated counterpoint to the ethereal song.

The first sea salt smell reached his nostrils as he began the descent, and he increased his pace. Soon, soon. . . .

The trail steepened abruptly. From somewhere there came the calls of gulls; their dark shapes slid above the overhead whiteness. The faintest of breezes drifted past him then, bearing even stronger sea smells than he had noticed earlier.

The trail widened, losing its steepness. Suddenly, there was sand underfoot, and smooth pebbles clicked and bounced. The sound of the sea came to him. The gulls continued their calling. The sounds of the bells began to fade.

The singing, hardly louder than before, seemed nevertheless nearer. Turning left, he followed it, passing about the squat form of a final tree—a palmetto, it would seem. But it shouldn't be growing here.

The fog became more active, drifting in from the apparent direction of the water. In places the whiteness broke, giving him glimpses of pebbles and sand. In other places it writhed, serpent-like, near to the ground, or was blown into grotesque shapes which faded almost as quickly as they formed. Advancing till he came to the water, he halted, stooped, let the sea run into and out of his hands. He raised a finger to his lips.

It was real. Warm and salty as blood.

A wave slopped over his shoetops and he backed away. He turned and began walking again, certain now where he was headed. He increased his pace. Before long, he was running.

He stumbled, picked himself up and kept going. Perhaps he had somehow crossed over and was back in his dream. The tinny sound of a buoy bell came to him now, marking some channel far to the right. The sea itself seemed of a sudden louder. A vast flock of birds passed overhead, uttering cries unlike those of the gulls or any other birds he had ever heard. The bells—somewhere behind him now—took on a new voice, answering the random notes of the buoy with something patterned, something deeper. And the singing. . . . For the first time the singing grew louder. It seemed very near.

A dark form appeared suddenly in his path. A small hill or—

He stumbled again, trying to avoid it. As he fell, the singing ceased. The bells ceased. He looked upon bleak walls and vacant eye-like windows—battlemented, turreted edifice emergent from duneside—drear, dark, partly crumbling, beside a gray, unruffled tarn. He was falling—somehow too fast—toward it. . . .

Then the fog swirled and the veil fell away. What had seemed a distant prospect was almost within reach, as an instant rearrangement of perspective showed it to be a castle of sand constructed on a slope above a tidal pool.

His outflung arm struck a wall. A tower toppled. The great gateway was broken.

"No!" came a cry. "You mean thing! No!"

And she was upon him, small fists pummeling his shoulder, head, back.

"I'm—sorry," he said. "I didn't mean—I fell. I'll help. I'll put it back—the way—it was."

"Oh."

She stopped striking him. He drew back and regarded her.

She had very gray eyes, and brown hair lay disheveled upon her brow. Her hands were delicate, fingers long. Her blue skirt and white blouse were sand-streaked, smudged, the hem of the skirt sodden. Her full lips quivered as her gaze darted from him to the castle and back, but her eyes remained dry.

"I'm sorry," he repeated.

She turned her back to him. A moment later her

bare foot kicked forward. Another wall fell, another tower toppled.

"Don't!" he cried, rising, reaching to restrain her. "Stop! Please stop!"

"No!" she said, moving forward, trampling towers. "No."

He caught hold of her shoulder and she pulled away from him, continuing to kick and stamp at the castle.

"Please . . ." he repeated.

"Say, leave the poor fellow's castle alone, would you?" came a voice from behind them both.

They turned, to regard the figure which approached through the fog.

"Who are you?" they asked, in near unison.

"Edgar," he replied.

"That's *my* name," said the first boy, staring, as the other drew nearer.

The newcomer halted a pace later and they both stared. The boys resembled each other to the point of twindom. Hair, eyes, pigmentation, physiognomy seemed identical. The resemblance extended to posture, gestures, voice, and the school uniforms they wore.

The girl, halted in her rampage, turned her head slowly from side to side.

"I'm Annie," she said softly. "You could be brothers, or—something."

"I guess so," the newcomer acknowledged.

"So it might seem," said the first boy.

"Why were you breaking his sand castle?" the second Edgar asked.

"It's *my* sand castle, and *he* broke it," she said.

Edgar Two smiled at Edgar One, who shook his head and shrugged.

"Uh, why don't we all put it back together?" the

other boy said. "I'd bet we could do an even better one than what was there—Annie."

She smiled at him.

"All right," she said. "Let's."

They dropped to their knees about the disheveled sand heap. Annie took up a stick and began tracing new outlines. "The central keep will be here," she began, "and I want lots of towers. . . ."

They worked in silence for a long while, both boys soon removing their shoes, also.

"Edgar . . . ?" she asked after a time.

"Yes?" the boys answered.

They all began to laugh.

"There's got to be more to it than that," she said to the first boy, "if I'm to tell you apart."

"Allan," he replied. "I'm Edgar Allan."

"I'm Perry—Edgar Perry," said the second boy.

The boys stared at each other again.

"I've never seen you anywhere around here before," Perry said then. "You visiting or something?"

"I go to school," Allan replied, gesturing with his head in the direction of the small bluff he had descended.

"What school?" Perry asked.

"Manor House School. It's just up that way."

Perry's broad forehead creased and he shook his head slowly.

"I don't know it," he said. "But I don't really know this area. I go to a school called Manor also— though I don't know you from there. I was just out walking. . . ." He glanced at Annie, who had turned her head as Allan spoke, as if noticing the hill for the first time. "Do you?" he said to her.

"I don't know either school," she said. "But this area is mine—I mean, it's very familiar."

"It's interesting you both have American accents," Allan observed.

At this, both of them stared at him.

"Why shouldn't we?" Annie said then. "You do, too."

"Where do you live?" Perry asked suddenly.

"Charleston," she said.

He shifted from foot to foot.

"There's something peculiar about this," he said. "I was having a dream this morning before I came walking here, before I found this place—"

"Me, too!"

"Me, too. . . ."

"—almost as if I were already here with someone: You two."

"Yes, so was I."

"I was, too."

"I hope I'm not still dreaming."

"I don't think so."

"It feels a little strange, though," Allan said, "as if it's real in a very special way."

"What do you mean?" Perry asked.

"Dip your hands in the water," the other boy told him.

Perry leaned to the side and obliged.

"Yes?" he said then.

"Sea water is never that warm," Allan answered.

"Well, it's been sitting in this pool for some time, and it had a chance to heat up."

"The sea's the same way," Allan answered. "I felt it earlier."

Perry rose to his feet, turned away, began running toward the water. Allan glanced at Annie, who laughed. Suddenly the two of them were running after.

Before long, they were splashing about in the ocean, laughing, dunking each other, waves boiling about their legs.

"You're right!" Perry called out. "It's never been this way! Why should it be like this?"

Allan shrugged.

"Perhaps it's warm because the sun's shining on it hard someplace we can't see. Then the waves are bringing it to us that way—"

"That doesn't sound right. Maybe it's a current— like a river in the sea—"

"It's warm because I wanted it to be," Annie interrupted. "That's why."

The boys looked at her and she laughed.

"You don't think this is a dream," she said, "because it's not your dream. It's *mine*. You remember getting up this morning and I don't. I think it's mine, and this is *my* place."

"But I'm real! I'm not a dream-thing!"

"So am I!"

"I invited you, that's why."

Both boys laughed suddenly and splashed her. She laughed, too.

"Well—maybe . . ." she said, and then she splashed them back.

Their garments grew wet and were dried several times over, as they felt compelled to verify the sea and its moods on several occasions. Slowly, between baths, a new castle grew beneath their hands. This one, larger and more ambitious than that with which Allan had collided, sprouted towers like asparagus branches, its thick walls climbing and descending the rolling sandscape, rippling inward and outward, sprinkled and dampened from the pool where small crabs, bright fish, and hidden molluscs dwelled amid the glitter of stone, shell, and broken coral. Impulsively, Allan reached forth and took Annie's gritty hand within his own. "It's a wonderful castle you thought of," he said. Even as she began to blush Perry had hold of her other hand. "It is," he said, "and if it's a dream, you're the best dreamer yet."

He could never be sure how their time on the beach ended. There was a great sense of amity with Perry, as if the two were—somehow—brothers, though his feelings for Annie were different and he was sure that Perry loved her, too. The light around them was gray, and sea-green, and pearly with the mist. The sun rarely appeared. The sea and the air were timeless, throbbing warmly beside and about them.

"Oh, my God!" said Annie.

"What's the matter?" both boys shouted, turning in the direction of her wide-eyed gaze.

"In—the—water," she said. "Dead—isn't he?"

The fog had parted. Something wrapped in tangles of seaweed and a few tatters of cloth lay half in and half out of the water. Here and there a patch of swollen, fishbelly white flesh showed. It might have been human. It was difficult to say, wrack-decked as it was, tossed by the surf, strands of fog drifting past it.

Perry rose to his feet.

"Maybe it is and maybe it isn't," he said. Annie had covered her face by then, and was peering between her fingers. Allan stared, fascinated.

"Do we really want to know?" Perry continued. "It may just be a mess of weeds and trash with a few dead fishes caught in it. If we don't go and look, it can be whatever we want it to be. You know what I mean? You want to tell your friends you saw a body on the beach? Well, maybe you did."

The fog moved between them, hiding it again.

"What do *you* think it is?" Allan asked him.

"Seaweed and rubbish," Perry replied.

"It's a body," Annie said.

Allan laughed. "No, you can't both be right," he stated.

"Why not?" Annie said suddenly.

"The world just doesn't work that way," Allan said.

Allan rose and began walking through the fog in the direction of the body.

"I think that sometimes it can," he heard her say, somewhere behind him.

The fog churned, parted once more. Through a sudden rift Allan caught sight of the heaving mass, now drawn entirely back into the water a few paces offshore. This could be resolved in a matter of moments.

He strode forward, simultaneous with the shifting of a wall of fog to a position directly before him. But he was not about to let the vision escape. He plunged ahead. Any moment now he should feel the water swirl about his ankles—

"Allan. . . ." Her voice seemed distant.

"Where are you . . . ?" Perry called, also, it seemed, from afar.

"A moment," he answered. "I'm near it."

It seemed that they called again, but he could not distinguish the words. He pushed on. Suddenly, he seemed to be moving uphill. There were dark shapes about him once again. The ground seemed to have grown harder. From overhead came that strange bird cry.

"E-tekeli-li!" it seemed to sound. He began to run. He stumbled.

✧   ✧   ✧

And then. And then. And then.

Bright splash in the pool of my vision, up from the sand, against my brow, falling, fallen, then.

I was on my way back to the fort when it happened, returning from Legrand's hut. I did not even suspect that my life had been permanently changed. Not that my life before had been devoid of visions. Far from it. But this time I experienced none of the premonitory sensations or perceptions with which the visions were wont to announce themselves.

When the golden beetle flew up from somewhere and struck me in the face I could not have known that this signaled a change in everything for me, forever. I sought it as it lay on the sand before me, a remarkable and brilliant gold in the lowering October sun. I knew that certain chafers had something of a metallic color, gold or silver, and might be very beautiful. But this. . . . This was an unknown species, unknown at least to me. As I knelt to regard it more closely, I was amazed by its markings. The black spots on its back, I suddenly realized, were so situated as to result in its likeness to a golden skull.

I pulled a large leaf from a nearby plant, brushed the gleaming insect onto it, wrapped it carefully and put it into my pocket. Legrand, I was certain, would be extremely interested when next I visited him. If not a disquisition, an intriguing speculation would doubtless result.

I trudged on along the sandy beach, depressed despite a pleasant afternoon, an interesting find. I studied the dark cloud formations on the horizon while petitioning an inordinate boon of destiny, all unknowing that it had—in a way—already been granted. Just inland, to my right, a dense, almost impenetrable thicket of evergreen myrtle covered most of the ground. Graveyard flowers, I've heard them called, giving full and easy coverage. It was such a strange thing—to see a dream after years of dreaming, to realize of a sudden that it was, somehow, of a piece with life. Then, at the instant of the spirit's triumph, to have it snatched away before any understanding might follow. Left, left and bereft then, mystery proved but reason fled, a piece of my own life seen, as it were, for the first time, in a new light, then torn from me with no means of recovery. What evil hap might grant one's fondest wish against all odds, then snatch it away but moments later? I kicked at a stone, listened to a distant roll of thunder far out over the water. It was not only that my entire view of life had been altered in a few minutes—I am not so introspective and inclined to metaphysic as to be paralyzed by this—but that it should occur in such a fashion as to portend a doom and me powerless to defend the beloved ghost against it.

After I'd gone perhaps another mile my path turned inland, penetrating the thickets. This way took one across the island. The shadows were struggling to unite as I passed within, for now the sun was setting.

I halted a bit later as I emerged on the inland side of the island. Something was very wrong. I rubbed my eyes and shook my head, but the vision did not change.

They stood inland, beyond the tidal creek and a mile or so of marsh—tall in the reddish dusk, a pair of wooded bluffs, where I would take my oath none had stood before. Something was wrong, very wrong, and I'd no idea what it might be. I doubted my staring would alter the vista, however, and I turned again upon my westward path. Shortly thereafter, I was able to see the lights of distant Charleston twinkling across the harbor, some already masked in part by the rapidly accumulating fog. The fog seemed to approach with an uncommon swiftness, and I halted for some while to regard its performance.

The disposition of the city seemed slightly different than the last time I had studied it from this vantage, though my mind was troubled and the fog moved too quickly for me to be certain of anything. For with fog I could see her again with the eyes of memory, Annie, dream child, dream girl, dream lady, Annie, she whose existence I had counted over the years as some recurrent fantasy, a child's imaginary playmate who had, somehow, grown up along with him, who, somehow, summoned me, or I her, to realms of hysterical vision, usually upon a seashore, Annie, my dear hallucination, my lady of the fog. . . .

And that was all. For what more could she be— my secret aberration, dream companion, somehow friend or even more . . . ?

Annie. Not real. Of course not. All those times we had met, no more substantial than the fog I now considered. Or so I'd thought. Until the day before yesterday when my world was broken.

I had been walking in the town, prompting digestion following dinner. Then as now a bit of fog had drifted on the sea breeze through lengthening shadows. Autumn matched the sea with a dampness of its own. Storefronts mixed darkness with reflections. A patient spaniel awaited his master before a public house. Dust glistened on the roadway. Several dark birds passed seaward, uttering raucous notes. At this, I was overtaken by a great feeling of uneasiness. Moments later, I heard the cry.

That seems the best way to put it, though upon reflection it does not seem I actually could have heard her just then. For the coach was not yet even in sight. It was more that *there was a cry and I apprehended her presence.*

A moment later the coach careered around the corner—a tall, black affair—springs protesting, horses all lathered, its swart driver wrestling with the reins, lips curled back in something near to a snarl. The vehicle swayed dangerously, straightened, and plunged ahead, passing me in a swirl of dust. But I saw her face at its window—Annie. Our gazes met for but the briefest of moments, and she started and I heard her cry out again, though I was not certain that her lips had moved, nor did any of the several other pedestrians near me show any signs of having heard.

"Annie!" I shouted back, and then she was by me and gone away down that street that took her to the sea.

I turned and I began running. The dog barked a few times. Someone shouted something I could not understand and followed it with a laugh. The coach rumbled on its way, gaining on me, and I found myself racing through a cloud of dust.

I began to cough before I reached the corner, and my eyes were brimming, I moved back to the side of the road as the coach pulled away, regaining the boarded walk I had departed. I continued to follow, though at a slower pace, concerned more with keeping track of the coach than catching up with it immediately. I was, in this fashion, able to keep it in sight for some while, increasing my pace as the dust settled. When it turned, I ran again, to the corner in question, and I caught sight of it once more.

Eddie, I seemed to hear her say. *Help me. I fear that I have been drugged. I believe they mean me harm. . . .*

I began another dash, this time downhill. The coach seemed headed toward the harbor, was almost there, actually. I ran on, oblivious to everything but the plight of a woman whose very existence had been a thing of ambiguity to me but moments before. My lady of dreams and shadows, of beaches and mists, was somehow trapped in the real world, confined to a coach rushing toward the docks. She needed my help and I'd some fear as to my ability to reach her in time to provide it.

Nor was this fear unjustified. As I pounded down the street her captors must have been transferring her to a boat. By the time I reached the pier upon which the coach stood abandoned, door flung wide, the boat was already drawing alongside a black ship of somewhat unusual construction, sails raised and bulging—a frigate or brig perhaps (I'm a soldier, not a sailor)—which looked swift, and possibly well-enough armed, to be a privateer. I'd swear I heard her call one more time then, though the distance was great, and as I uttered an oath and looked about for some means of transport for myself the boat was grappled to the ship's side where its crew commenced transference of a burden which had to be an unconscious woman.

I shouted, and none of them paid me the slightest heed. Nor did anyone appear in the vicinity to see what prompted my cries. I was tempted to plunge into the water and swim out, though common sense warned me of the foolishness of putting myself into such a weak position. Then—for an instant—I thought that my shouts had been answered. A series of cries were uttered aboard the vessel. But moments later these were followed by sounds of the anchor winch. It was sailing orders that I was hearing.

Powerless, I watched as the vessel turned slowly to begin a tacking sequence which bore it into the line of a breeze which quickly took it seaward. There was no one about who might assist me, no vessel I might appropriate in which to give pursuit—and, of course, no chance of achieving anything by myself even if I did possess a small, fast boat. I could only stand and curse and watch my Annie being spirited away to the ends of whatever perverse destiny had ruled our association.

And so the coming and going which had ruled my thoughts these two days, casting a pall that even an afternoon with Legrand could not lift. And now, as I made my way back to Fort Moultrie, I'd a premonition I would not be returning to the service this night, for riding at anchor perhaps a quarter of a mile out from shore was a ship, a black ship of somewhat unusual construction. I would swear it to be the vessel into which I had seen Annie being taken.

Later. Later. Much later. Walking. Staggering, really.

And he staggered through the fog, seeking her, uncertain how he had returned from Fordham to the kingdom by the sea. Perhaps the air would clear his head. There was a gap somewhere between events. The Valentines had been kind, as had Mrs. Shew. But the break in consciousness between that then and this now was so strange a thing as to deny the touch of reason. There was a gap—yes! a black chasm— somewhere at his back, a thing profound as death or sleep. Yet he could not be dead, unless to be dead was to feel as if one had been drinking. He massaged his heavy brow, turned slowly and looked back. The fog prevented his seeing where he had come from, beyond a half-dozen or so irregular tracks. And he knew as he considered them that he was incapable of retracing them. He stood swaying, listening to the sea. At length, he turned again, continued what he knew to be his course. This was a special place, a place where holidays of the soul were celebrated. Why now? What now? Something was denied, something withheld. Like a word at the tongue's tip, the harder he tried the more difficult it was to recall.

He reeled; once, he fell. Truly, he could not remember whether he had taken a drink. He suspected that he had, though its occasion eluded him. The waves came louder of a sudden. The sky was darker than it usually was here, behind the fog. He brushed sand from his trousers. This was the place, yes. . . .

Stumbling forward now, his head cleared and the grief assailed him, fresh, heavy, overwhelming. And with it, he suddenly knew what he would find, with but a little more persistence. He turned inland, and after but a few paces a dark bulk loomed.

The ground rose, grew less sandy though the voice of the sea lost nothing of volume. His step grew steadier as he exerted his will. The massive shape before him diminished somewhat. Its lines grew clearer. Eyes blazing, jaw tightening, he hurried.

Arriving, he put forth his shaking hand, slowly, to touch the cold, gray stone. Then he sank to his knees there on the threshold, and for a long time he remained unmoving.

When finally he rose the sea was sounding even

more loudly at his back and its crumbling fingers had touched his boot. Without a backward glance he reached for the black iron gate, unlatched it. He pushed it open and entered the place's damp interior. He rested long amid the shadows then, listening to the sea, to the sounds of birds in their passage.

It was later, much later, in another place, in something like tranquility, that he wrote, "I was a child and she was a child, in a kingdom by the sea. . . ."

Downward to the shore. . . .

> We walk about, amid the destinies of our world existence, encompassed by dim but ever present *Memories* of a Destiny more vast—very distant in the bygone time and infinitely awful.

> We live out a youth peculiarly haunted by such shadows; yet never mistaking them for dreams. As memories we *know* them. *During our Youth* the distinction is too clear to deceive us even for a moment.

> *Eureka*, Edgar A. Poe

II

A wisp of fog rode the evening wind by me as I approached the shore. The vessel was too far off to hail. I began a quick search of the darkening beach hoping for some small boat that might take me out to her. Minutes passed, and the futility of the enterprise asserted itself.

I turned my attention once more to the ship. Despite the oncoming night and the fog, I realized that I was going to swim out to it. There was no other way to get there. Though I had been skilled at rough-and-tumble even before I'd joined the army, I had no illusions concerning my ability to defend myself against an entire ship's crew. My speed as a boxer, my expertise at wrestling would hardly serve me against a dozen sturdy sailors with belaying pins and boat hooks. Yet I could not let the black ship sail away again, taking Annie out of my life for what was likely the last time. I would have to take any chance, run any risk rather than let her get away.

But even as I knelt to unlace my boots, I heard the creaking of a winch. It came from the ship, where moments later I saw that a boat was being lowered into the water. My boots remained laced and I stood slowly, squinting. Obviously, the ship was not about to sail away this instant. With a party about to disembark from it, I might stand to increase my chances of helping Annie by observing rather than splashing my way out to the sinister hulk. It was also possible that the entire affair might be handled with less risk than I had first anticipated.

After all, could I be certain that there was something nasty afoot? Might I not have misunderstood a situation wherein Annie had been hurrying of her own volition to keep a pressing shipboard engagement? Could I not be projecting my own fears and apprehensions onto an innocuous event—turbulent emotions bred of our mysterious relationship?

The perverse imp which invariably appeals against my reasonings shouted *No!* It is unfortunate how often that imp seems possessed of the greater part of wisdom. I felt this minutes later, after the rowers of that boat had commenced their way shoreward through the deepening fog. For I hailed them, and they corrected their course, coming in my direction.

There were eight or ten men in that longboat, headed toward me with rapid, powerful strokes. I wondered just then what their purpose might be in coming ashore here, at just this time. Then I caught clearer sight of their leader, an evil-looking ruffian. The man was staring at me, grinning, rubbing his knuckles. Somewhere, my imp chuckled.

It bothered me, the way the man stared—not so much his general mien and apparent intent, as the fact that I seemed the object of his entire attention. I could not help but feel that their purpose in bringing the boat ashore, right now, right here, was only to do me some strange harm. A feeling—irrational, yet unshakable—filled me: They wanted me, and they had somehow known that this was where I would be this evening.

Fog blew between us as they reached the shallows, and I heard them shipping oars, splashing over the gunwales, heard the grating of the boat's bottom as they drew it landward over pebbles and sand. I turned and bolted.

A cry went up at the fog's next parting, and I heard the sounds of pursuit. I turned inland, crashing through a thicket. The landing party followed, nearer now, trailing me easily.

"Hold up or we'll go harder with you!" called one of the men—the leader, I believe. This was all the inducement I needed to double and redouble my effort to escape.

Something grazed my shoulder—a thrown stone most likely—and the next cry sounded even nearer. I kept going, aware that someone was gaining on me. From the sounds of his breathing, the sounds of his passage, I could tell that he would be upon me in a moment.

I turned quickly and faced my pursuer, a swart, wiry fellow with a club in his right hand. He halted and drew back in apparent startlement at the unanticipated confrontation. I kicked immediately at his nearest kneecap, missed and struck his thigh. The leg gave way, and I stepped in, punched his throat and snatched away the club. Another, a shorter man with

a nasty scar running from mouth to ear was rushing toward me, and I knew I could not escape him.

I waited, hands low. He was unarmed and I let
him swing at me without interference, stepping back,
leaning a bit. His fist shot by me and I clubbed
his elbow. He howled and I stepped in immediately,
swinging toward his temple, missing and clipping the
hinge of his jaw. He was pushed aside by a large,
black-bearded individual who swung a dagger at my
stomach. I dodged the stroke, struck at his arm and
missed. His left hand caught me beside the head
then, knocking me against a tree. I saw his teeth and
two gaps through his beard as he slid forward, the
knife beside his hip, left hand extended to clear the
way.

Too stunned to move, I watched him come on.
Then an unnaturally long hairy limb crossed his breast
from the right, jerking the knife arm back up against
his body. A misshapen hand appeared upon his left
hip. He was then raised high into the air and hurled
back among his fellows.

I shook my head, clearing it somewhat as I beheld
what I knew, from pictures, to be an ape; as to what
sort, though, I was ignorant. It was difficult to tell its
true size because of its slouch and its shambling gait.
Its advent and action produced considerable conster-
nation among my pursuers, however. Two of them had
been knocked down by the hurled man. At that
moment a brace of pistols was fired from behind me,
to the left. One man fell, another clutched at a suddenly incarnadined arm.

"This way, mate!" came a raspy voice from the rear
and my arm was seized in a powerful grip. "C'mon,
Emerson! Move it!" he cried, and the ape turned
toward us and followed.

I allowed myself to be led, through the brush to
a cleared area which took us to the beach. We commenced running then. I'd no idea where we were
headed but the short man at my side moved with a
definite purpose. There were sounds of pursuit, but
the fog muffled them more than a little and it was
difficult to tell whether they were on the right track.
My first glance at my rescuer had made me think
him, for a moment, to be a child, as he was no more
than four-and-a-half feet tall. But then I glimpsed his
strange ruddy face beneath an unusually coarse shock
of dark hairs, and I realized simultaneously the width
and thickness of his shoulders and upper arms.

He ran, I jogged, the ape lurched and sprang along
the shore. At length, we halted beside a pile of brush
which the man immediately attacked. I gave him a
hand as soon as I realized that a small skiff was
concealed beneath it. Before we had done with it,
however, one of our pursuing sailors stumbled toward
us out of the fog. He held a cutlass in his right hand
and he raised it high when he beheld us.

"Damn!" he cried, rushing forward.

The small man stood between us. His left arm
went up as the blade was swung toward his head. He
caught the wrist of the man's swordarm, halting its
descent entirely. Then, without particular haste, he
reached forward with his right hand, catching hold
of the fellow's belt around its buckle. At that moment,
I heard a crunching sound, as of grating bones, from
the vicinity of the wrist he was still squeezing. The
swordsman repeated his earlier observation, but he
was already off his feet by then, raised into the air
by the small man, who turned and cast him out over
the waters. Immediately, the short man caught hold
of the skiff, which he pushed, effortlessly, seaward,

having paused only to give me a wink and an evil grin.

"All aboard, Mr. Perry! Emerson—you, too! Come on!" he said. Then, in afterthought as we boarded, "It is Perry, ain't it?" he asked.

"It is indeed," I said, taking up one of the oars. "I never saw any of those men before. I've no idea why they attacked me." As we commenced rowing I added, "I must thank you for your intervention. It was most timely."

He snorted something resembling a laugh.

"Aye. It were most necessary," he said. "And almost too late."

We drew heavily upon the oars, and after several minutes I could discern nothing but fog in every direction. The ape pushed its way between us, moved forward into the prow and crouched there. Every now and then it made a gesture which seemed to mean something to my rescuer, and he corrected our course slightly on these occasions.

"Peters," he said suddenly. "Dirk Peters, at your service. We can shake hands another time."

I grunted. Then, "You already know my name," I said.

"True," he acknowledged. I waited for several strokes, but he did not elaborate. The fog remained heavy. The ape gestured again.

"Hard to port. A pair should do it. I'll ease up and you pull," Dirk said then.

I complied, and when course was corrected, we resumed our normal rowing, I asked, "Where are we headed?"

Following a two-stroke pause, he replied, "There's a gentleman aboard a certain ship as has expressed a devout wish to see you. The same gentleman as sent me and Emerson ashore to look after your interests."

"It seems an awful lot of people know who I am, knew where I was going to be and knew when I'd be there."

He nodded slowly.

"So it seems," he said.

A little later, the ape uttered a low sound and bounced several times in place.

"What's that, Emerson?" Dirk asked. Then, "Oh. Oh-oh," he uttered and suddenly we were backing water.

There followed some eerie echoes, and then a great dark shape loomed ahead and sliding to starboard. It was the ship from which my pursuers had come. Even as we turned we drew nearer, and I was able to make out her name. She was the *Evening Star.*

Nearer still. Then through a lighted port above the poop deck, I saw a dear, familiar form: Annie. She stood gazing out into the fog, not even turning her head in my direction. In fact, something about her demeanor and her mien gave me the impression that she was sleepwalking, entranced, drugged. A slowness of movement, an air of detachment—

A hand fell upon her shoulder and she was jerked away from the glass. Immediately, a heavy drape was drawn and the light was gone. And Annie was gone.

I uttered some sound, released my oar, and began to rise.

"Don't even think of it!" Peters snarled. "Yer a dead man if you set foot on her! Emerson, hold 'im if he tries to go overboard!"

And the creature actually did take hold of my collar. It could have weighed no more than I did, but having seen what it could do to a man I knew I should have no chance of escaping.

In a moment I realized that Peters must be right. Dead, I would be of no use to Annie. I slumped. Then I took hold of my oar again.

We rowed on, for some considerable distance. The fog broke and re-knit itself several times, though there was nothing to see but water and a few stars on those occasions when it opened. For a time I wondered whether we might have become lost, rowing in a great circle, or out to sea, or about to run aground. Then the shape of another vessel came into view—as mysterious and formidable-appearing as the first.

"Ahoy!" Peters shouted.

"That you, Peters?" came the response.

"It is, and I've brought company."

"Come alongside," called the other.

We did, and shortly thereafter a rope ladder was cast down near us. Emerson snagged it immediately. Before we climbed to its deck, I caught sight of the vessel's name: *Eidolon*.

The man looked frighteningly distinguished, with his dark hair light at the sides, gray mustache neatly trimmed, impressive brow, jawline rugged as he clenched a delicately carved pipe between perfect teeth. His well-tailored uniform was impeccable. He was tall and slender within it and his smile inspired confidence.

"This is Captain Guy," Peters said.

The man removed his pipe and smiled.

"Edgar Perry . . . ?" he said.

"Yes."

He extended his hand. I took it.

"Welcome aboard the *Eidolon*," he told me.

"Thank you. Glad to meet you," I said. "Everybody seems to know who I am."

He nodded.

"You have been the subject of some attention."

"Of what sort?" I asked.

The captain glanced at Peters, who looked away.

"Um, I'm not certain it is my place to say," he stated.

"Is there anyone around who might be able to say?"

"Of course," he said. "There is Mr. Ellison."

He looked to Peters once more, and Peters looked away again.

"Mr. Seabright Ellison," he said then, as if that explained something.

"Do you think I might be able to make the acquaintance of this gentleman?" I inquired.

Peters snorted and took hold of my wrist.

"Come along," he said. "We'll be about that business right now."

"Just what sort of vessel is this?" I asked then.

Captain Guy paused in the process of replacing his pipe and said, "Why, this is Mr. Ellison's yacht."

"Come along," Peters repeated, and we left the captain puffing in the fog.

He led me below, and had I not already been informed I should have guessed from the fine woods and the high level of craftsmanship employed in facings and moldings that the ship must be a pleasure craft devoted to private use rather than a commercial vessel. And as we made our way, I wondered that Dirk Peters rather than Captain Guy was conducting me to my visit with the owner. Might he be somewhat more than the common seaman I had taken him for?

He halted before a door carved with swimming dragons and rapped sharply upon it.

"Who is it?" someone called from the other side.

"Peters," he replied. "An' Perry's with me."

"A moment."

Shortly, I heard a chain fall and the door was opened. I beheld a large man—over six feet in height and of great girth. He had on a dark green and black dressing gown over an unfastened white shirt and trousers. A white fringe was all that remained of his hair, and his eyes were bright blue.

"Mr. Perry!" he greeted. "I cannot say how delighted I am to see you in good health!"

"It appears that I have you to thank for it, sir," I told him.

"And you are most heartily welcome. Come in, come in!"

I did that. Peters—at my side—gave a small salute, which Ellison returned, and departed.

"Pray be seated," the big man said. "Are you hungry?"

I thought back over the supper of marsh-hens which Legrand's slave Jupiter had fed me only a few hours ago.

"Thanks, but I've eaten," I told him.

"Something to drink, then?"

"Can't say as I'd have any objection to that," I answered.

He went off to a cabinet from which he returned with a squat decanter of ruby fluid and a pair of shot glasses. He filled the tiny things, raised one and said, "Your health." I nodded and watched as he took a small sip. I sniffed it. It smelled like wine. I took a sip. It seemed a Burgundy. I took the rest in a single swallow, wondering at the eccentricity which prompted the man to drink in this fashion. His eyes widened slightly, but he refilled my glass immediately.

"Good man, that Peters," I said. "He timed his intervention perfectly, moved strongly, efficiently. Got me away against strong opposition. I confess I still haven't the least idea why those men attacked me, though. Or why—"

"Yes?"

"There is someone aboard their ship—the *Evening Star*—someone with whom I have an intimate connection. I'd be grateful if you could tell me anything of their purposes. Or simply who they are." I drank my other tiny portion of wine in a quick swallow, and went on, "How did you know I was going to be where I was? And that I'd need rescuing?"

He sighed and took another sip of his own drink, then refilled my own again.

"Before going into that, Mr. Perry," he said, "there are a few details about your background concerning which I'd like to be certain. I must be sure—absolutely sure—that you are the gentleman I think you are. Have you any objection to answering a few questions?"

I chuckled.

"You saved my life and you're buying the drinks. Ask away."

"All right. Is it or is it not a fact that your mother was an actress," he began, "and that she died in poverty."

"Damn it, sir!" I responded, then got hold of myself. "Those are the facts," I said more softly, "as I understand them. I was not quite three years old when her death occurred."

His expression did not change, and his gaze fell upon my wineglass for the barest instant. Almost as

a cue, I felt obliged to raise it and drain it. I did
so, and he refilled it immediately, following this with
but the smallest sip from his own.

"She died of consumption?" he went on. "In the
city of Richmond?"

"That is correct."

"Satisfactory," he replied. "And what of your
father?"

"'Satisfactory,' sir?" I inquired.

"Come, come, young man," he said, touching my
arm. "Sensitivity must wait. Matters of great moment hang in the balance here. I meant only that
it was the answer I hoped to hear from you. Now,
your father?"

I nodded.

"He was an actor, also, by all reports. He vanished
from my mother's life and from mine, a year or two
before she died."

"Indeed," he muttered, as if that, too, were satisfactory. "And you had the good fortune, upon your
mother's death, to be adopted by a prosperous Richmond merchant," he continued, "John Allan, and his
wife?"

"I would say rather that Mrs. Allan took pity on
an orphan, and took me in. I was never formally
adopted."

Seabright Ellison shrugged.

"Still, as a member of the Allan household, you
enjoyed advantages denied to many," he observed.
"For example, your four years in a private school in
England—Manor House School, in the north of
London, was it not?"

"It was," I admitted. "Your knowledge of my life
astonishes me."

"And I suppose," he said, "it might have been at

about that time when, in some—shall we say dream, or vision—you first encountered Annie?"

I stared at him. No one in waking life could know of her. I had never spoken of her.

"What do you know about Annie?" I whispered hoarsely. "What *could* you know about her?"

"Not a great deal, I assure you," he answered. "Certainly not all that I should like to know. Still— more than you do, I dare say."

"I have seen her," I said. "Two days ago, in Charleston—and again, within the hour. At this moment she is aboard—"

He raised his hand.

"I know where she is," he told me. "And while there is some danger involved, nothing threatens her at the moment. I can quite probably help you to reach her—eventually. But things will really proceed more swiftly if you will permit me to take things in my own order, at my own pace."

I nodded.

"Very well," I said, and I drained my minuscule wineglass once again. He refilled it, shook his head and muttered something that sounded like "Amazing."

Then, "Are you familiar, Mr. Perry, with the name of 'Poe'?" he asked.

"There is an Italian river, I believe," I stated.

"Really!" he hissed. "P-O-E. A man's name. Edgar Poe. Edgar Allan Poe."

"Sorry . . ." I said, then, "Ah. A confusion of identity. Is that it? Those men on the beach— They really wanted to kill this Edgar Poe."

"No." Ellison raised his hand. "I beg of you, be of no illusions on that score. I've no doubt those men knew exactly whom they were to kill. It was you, Sergeant Edgar A. Perry. I will not say that Edgar

Poe is in no danger. Far from it. But his fate will be more subtle, I suppose . . . and it need not directly concern us."

He sighed, regarded his drink, then raised it, and finished it.

"There is," he began slowly, "a confusion of identity, certainly. Yes, you are confused with Edgar Poe, in such a way as two human beings have rarely been confused in all the history of the word. But—I repeat—there is no confusion in the minds of those from whom I saved you tonight, and who will certainly seek your death again. No. It is certainly Edgar Perry they want dead."

"Why?" I asked. "I don't even know them."

He drew a deep breath, sighed again, refilled his own tiny glass.

"Do you know, sir, where you are?" he asked, after a time. "The question is not rhetorical—and I do not mean it in the sense that you are in my cabin or aboard my ship. Pray, think in larger terms than that."

I stared, studying him, I suppose, trying to decide what he was getting at. But I felt too buffeted by events to be particularly creative. So, "Charleston Harbor?" I suggested, to keep up my end of the conversation.

"True. Quite true," he replied. "But is this, indeed, the Charleston harbor with which you are familiar? Have you seen nothing, during the past few hours, to suggest that this is a Charleston harbor which you have never seen before?"

I saw again those wooded bluffs at sunset, and I recalled that strange golden beetle, hopefully still in my pocket. I reached inside and felt around. Yes. The leaf was still there. I withdrew it.

"I've something here," I began, as I unwrapped it.

The golden beetle was still present. It moved slowly upon the leaf which I placed atop an adjacent table. Ellison donned a pair of spectacles and studied it for several moments. Then, "A beautiful specimen of *scarabeus capus hominus,*" he remarked, "but not, I think, that unusual. You find it truly remarkable, however?"

"I have a friend on Sullivan's Island who collects insects, extensively," I explained. "His collection contains nothing remotely like this. Nor have I seen anything like it anywhere else."

"But in this world, Mr. Perry, it is most common."

"This world. Meaning—?"

"Meaning the world where Charleston Harbor has bluffs and ravines just inland," he stated. "Where this beetle is common. Where a certain sergeant serving at Fort Moultrie *ought* to be named Edgar Allan Poe—but now is not."

I raised my wineglass and stared at it. I drained it. He chuckled.

". . . Where wine is commonly served in glasses no larger than the ones we have before us," he went on. "Yes, pour yourself another, please." He took a sip from his own as I did so, and I extended the decanter in his direction. "No, no more for me, thank you. My tolerance for alcohol is not remotely the equal of yours, I am sure."

"I still do not understand," I said, "about Poe, and why he's not at the fort, where you say he should be. Where is he? What has become different?"

"He has gone to the world you came from," he said. "He has taken your place in your world, as you have taken his in this." He paused, studied my face. Then, "I see that you do not find the idea completely unbelievable."

"No," I told him, "I do not. I have—known Edgar Allan for most of my life, through a series of strange encounters—as I have known Annie." I could feel my palms growing moist as I spoke. "You seem to have some idea what's going to happen to her aboard that ship. What do they want with her? What are they going to do to her?"

He shook his head slowly.

"She is not in danger of immediate bodily harm," he said. "In fact, her health is probably a matter of considerable concern to her captors. It is her mental and spiritual powers they wish to exploit."

"I must get to her, find a way to help her," I said.

"Of course," he agreed. "And I intend to show you how. You and Annie and the man you knew as Edgar Allan have met many times over the years, you say, under unusual circumstances . . . ?"

"Yes—sort of dream-like encounters. Real enough, but with a special feeling to them."

"Beyond the experiences themselves," he said, "have you any understanding as to what they represent?"

I shrugged.

"Impossible to say, sir. We've discussed it occasionally but never found any satisfactory answers."

"You and Poe inhabit separate worlds, similar yet different," he said. "As for Annie, though, I am not certain which might be her true home—possibly yet a third alternate Earth. I see you nod, sir—as if the notion of other versions of your world were not unfamiliar."

"The possibility was discussed—once, briefly," I said.

"Oh? Poe's idea?"

I nodded.

"Interesting mind there," he remarked.

I shrugged.

"I suppose so," I admitted. "A trifle melodramatic, and inclined to take off after chimera, though."

"He was right."

"Really, sir."

"Really. I am telling you the truth, as I understand it."

"I can follow you," I said. "I can even believe you, I guess. But I suppose it bothers me a bit to see the man right again—and in such a bizarre matter."

"He was often right in odd matters?"

"Yes. As you say, interesting mind, interesting ways of thinking."

"Imaginative," Ellison supplied.

I finished my drink.

"All right," I said then. "Premise accepted. What follows?"

"You, Edgar Poe, and Annie constitute a sort of psychic unit transcending the several worlds," he began. "It is Annie's exceptional abilities along these lines which provide the motive force of your connection. A number of people who see a way to profit by her mesmeric talents have kidnapped her and confined her in this world. It could only be done by switching around everyone in your triad. Hence, it was necessary that you and Poe also be exchanged—"

I snorted.

"Mesmerism, sir! Really!" I said. "This sounds to me like the makings of a hoax."

His eyes widened and he smiled. He shook his head.

"You have no trouble with alternate realities, yet you balk at the notion of subtle influences? Between people, between people and nature? Indeed, you are an amazing man."

"I have seen something of alternate realities," I explained, "yet I have never seen this so-called animal magnetism in operation."

"I have reason to believe it operates in all affairs to some degree, mainly beneath the level of our attention—though I do believe its effects to be much more potent in this world than in your own. Anything which affects the psychic faculty seems particularly strong here. Were I to consume as much alcohol as you have this evening I should be ill for days. This, I believe, is why her captors desired your Annie's presence here. Wherever she was, her abilities were considerable. Here, they will become even greater. If you truly do not believe, you need but wait. I will show you evidence before too long."

I wiped my palms again.

"Enough," I said. "I spoke hastily. I accept it, *arguendo,* as I want to know where this takes us. Who are these people who have Annie? What are they doing to her? What is it they want her powers for?"

He rose, and clasping his hands behind his back, paced a few paces.

"You've heard of the famous inventor, Von Kempelen?" he said at last.

"Yes," I answered. "Of course. I believe he even had something to do with the creation of the famous mechanical chessplayer I saw in Charleston a while back."

"Possibly so," Ellison replied. "Have you heard it said that he has gone more deeply than most into the writings of Sir Isaac Newton, Father of Alchemy?"

"No," I said.

"There are stories," he continued, "rumors that he'd transmuted lead into gold and grown homunculi."

I chuckled. "Human gullibility being what it is—" I began.

He chuckled, also.

"Of course," he said. "I doubt he succeeded with the homunculus."

I waited for him to continue, and he did not. I glanced at him.

"As to the transmutation," he finally said, "I speak as one who knows that he succeeded."

"Oh," I answered, both out of politeness to my host, and out of a sudden realization that in *this* place such a thing might actually have happened. "A useful skill, to say the least."

My gaze followed Ellison in his pacing, which had taken him to the far end of his quarters. I noticed for the first time that a low bench he was passing bore various pieces of arcane equipment. Noting my attention, he smiled wistfully and flipped a hand in that direction.

"Alembic, retort, distillator, furnace," he announced, in passing. "Yes, I dabble a bit in these matters myself—which is why I understand both the achievement and the conspiracy." He picked up a small burnished object, held it for a moment. It emitted a high-pitched shriek, lowered its voice to a growl, grew silent. He set it aside casually, shifting his attention to something floating in a green liquor within a helical vessel. "Von Kempelen found the secret," he continued, "then fled back to Europe when he realized the Unholy Trinity had discovered him out and was after it. They feel that Annie can be used to run him to earth and to force the gates of his mind."

"Can she?" I asked.

"I believe so," he replied. "By all reports she is a formidable lady."

"Whose reports?"

"Yours, and that of a thing which came into a mirror at my command, to advise me. And there is yet another—"

I felt momentarily dizzy, and I knew it wasn't the wine because the total of all those little glasses hadn't even equaled one good goblet of the sort to which I was accustomed.

"I'm trying," I said, "to understand. I repeat, who are these people who have Annie and wish to use her to steal Von Kempelen's secret?"

"Goodfellow, Templeton, and Griswold," he replied. "Dr. Templeton—a somewhat elderly and mysterious individual—is their mesmerist. I believe they are employing his powers to control Annie in the tracking of their prey. Then there is old Charley Goodfellow— a hearty, good-looking honest seeming fellow as ever slid a knife between a man's ribs. And, finally, Griswold. He is their leader and is considered rather a ruthless gentleman."

"And these men are aboard the *Evening Star*?" I inquired.

"So I believe," he answered.

" . . . Where this Dr. Templeton is attempting to place Annie in a trance, so that she can divine Von Kempelen's whereabouts for them?"

"So I fear."

"If she is as strong as you think he may not succeed."

"Most likely they would drug her first. I know that I would."

I studied him, his back against the laboratory table, and he gave me more than casual scrutiny in return.

"So," I said after a time, "I thank you again for

the timely rescue, and for the information on Annie. . . ."

He smiled. "And you're asking me 'Why?'" he said then.

"It's not that I disbelieve in altruism," I told him, "but you have gone to a lot of trouble on behalf of strangers."

"I'm prepared to go to a lot more," he said, "to thwart these men. And you are correct. There is a measure of self-interest involved, as in most human affairs."

I shrugged. "Results leave more of an impression than motives," I said. "I'm grateful, whatever your reasons."

"I'm a rather wealthy man," he said then.

"I'd guessed as much," I replied, sweeping my gaze significantly over the handsomely carved furniture, across the oriental rug and over a number of tasteful paintings. "So if it's not love or money it must be revenge, right?" I asked. "I'd guess one or all of these fellows did you a very bad turn at some point—"

He shook his head.

"A good guess, but wrong," he said. "It *is* money. I know sufficient of the area to believe the story of Von Kempelen's success, and I know sufficient of Annie's strength to believe that she will succeed in discovering his secrets. And I am sufficiently wealthy to have my own affairs disposed in such a fashion that any serious disturbance in the price of gold could be disastrous to me. I am uniquely positioned both for being harmed by them, and for anticipating them and thwarting them. So your reason is love, mine is money, and we can leave revenge out of this. We are therefore, as I see it, natural allies."

"It does look that way," I said. "And I'm certainly willing to go with you against them."

He pushed himself away from the workbench, smiling.

"Good, that's settled," he remarked.

He crossed the room to a small writing table, seated himself, took out stationery, ink, a pen, and began writing even as he continued speaking: "Shortly, I must introduce you to my own chief mesmeric consultant, Monsieur Ernest Valdemar."

"I should be happy to meet him," I stated.

"To be sure, to be sure," he replied. "You are to take command here, to pursue these men, to thwart them, to recover your lady."

"Me? Take command?" I inquired.

"Yes. Good that you're a military man, isn't it?"

"I don't understand. What of you?"

"Long sea voyages upset me in the extreme these days," he replied, "and I believe that Griswold and company will be heading for Europe shortly, since that is where Von Kempelen's fled."

"Where in Europe?"

"You'll have to apply to Monsieur Valdemar for that information."

"When might I get to meet him?"

"His nurse, Miss Ligeia, will introduce you at some point."

"The man is an invalid?"

"Oh, he has his problems. But his virtues more than compensate."

He completed a page, began another.

"Yes," he went on, "this ship will be at your disposal, captain and crew. And that includes Peters and his 'orang-outang,' Emerson, as he calls the beast. I will provide you with letters of introduction and credit for people and banks in any of a variety of places in which you might find yourself, before I leave."

"And where might one get in touch with you?" I asked.

"I suppose it is possible that you have never heard of the Domain of Arnheim?" he said.

I shook my head.

"It lies in New York state. I will include directions," he stated. "Hopefully, you will be by to report the complete success of the enterprise. And a trio of obituaries would make me a very grateful man."

"A moment, sir," I stated. "My intent is to rescue Annie. I'm not enlisting to kill anyone."

"Of course not," he replied. "What I said was merely that their obituaries would please me, for these are ruthless men and I see the possibility of a confrontation in which you—a professional soldier— might be forced to employ violence in self-defense. In such an instance I would be very grateful.

"Trebly so, in the best of all possible worlds," he added, smiling.

I nodded.

"Lives are but dice in the hands of the Almighty," I observed, which seemed sufficiently ambiguous to keep him happy without committing myself to anything. At least his smile broadened and he returned my nod as if we had an understanding.

I rose, turned away, did some pacing of my own, trying to order my thoughts. Ellison went on writing.

"You would give me command of this vessel?" I inquired, after a time.

"Captain Guy will continue in command," he replied without looking up. "He is the sort of man who would not dream of overruling the ship's owner. He will obey your orders."

"Good," I replied. "I know nothing of the actual management of a ship's affairs."

"All that would really be necessary would be for you to tell him where you want to go, and when."

"And this I am to discover from Valdemar?"

"By way of Ligeia, yes." He stopped writing for a moment and looked at me. "If you have any problems," he said then, "I recommend you talk to Dirk Peters. While it is true that his manner is rude, his formal education nonexistent, and his appearance uncouth, he is totally trustworthy and very shrewd. No one aboard this ship would dare to cross him."

"I can well believe it," I said.

I returned to the decanter, bore it across the room to the workbench, where I appropriated a decent-sized glass. I filled it and took a drink. I saw then that Ellison had paused in his writing and was watching me. He shook his head and looked away.

"Amazing," he said. I took another swallow. Then he asked, "Is there some problem?"

"Yes," I replied. "This means I'll be taking off without leave from Fort Moultrie."

"So it does," he said. "Do you really think they would grant you leave for an enterprise of this nature? Or that you'd even have time to request it?"

"No," I answered. "I understand the situation. But I've enjoyed my service, in the main, and I don't want to end it looking like a deserter. I want to write a letter to my Commanding Officer, requesting leave and explaining how I've serious personal matters to attend to."

He appeared to ponder it for a moment, then smiled again.

"Very well," he said. "Compose your letter and I will take it with me when I go ashore and see that it is delivered. Of course you must sign it 'Edgar Allan Poe.'"

"I didn't think of that—" I began.

"On the other hand, I can speak to a senator of my acquaintance and arrange for your immediate discharge."

"Perhaps that would be preferable. . . ."

"Settled then. I'll have the papers waiting for you at Arnheim when you return with the good news."

He winked and returned to his writing. I paced, sorting my thoughts. After a time, I cleared my throat.

He glanced up again. "Yes?" he asked.

"Where are my quarters to be?" I inquired.

"Why, right here, this stateroom," he responded, "as soon as I vacate the place." He blotted his letter, folded it, put it aside. "And that will be very soon," he added.

I fingered my shirtfront. I was wearing civilian garments fit for rambling in the wilds, and looking the part.

"Pity I've no chance to obtain a change of clothes," I remarked. "Feels strange to be taking off on something like this with just what I have on my back."

"Rummage through the sea chests," he said, with a gesture which took in a big one at the foot of the bunk, another in a corner, and a large armoire across the room. "They've all manner of garments in 'em."

So I did, and as I was about it he inquired, "You're a Master Sergeant, I believe?"

"Yes," I replied.

"So you've had more than one tour of duty?"

"Yes."

"Ever do any time in the cavalry?"

"I did."

"Then you know how to use a saber."

Memories of sweaty saber drills—stamping and cutting under an afternoon sun—returned in detail.

"Yes," I replied. "The guard makes a good knuckle-duster."

He squinted, as if trying to decide whether I were making some sort of joke. Actually, I was, though I was also speaking the truth.

"A good weapon," he said at last, "for its silence—however you use it. I just wanted you to know that Captain Guy has many in his armory, in case you've a desire to practice with one."

"Thanks."

I studied him. Finally, I could not resist asking, "Ever use one yourself?"

"Oh, yes," he replied, "in my younger days, in the Caribbean."

"What part?"

"All over, aboard ships," he answered.

"I thought you'd a tendency to seasickness."

"Not so much in those days," he said.

"What sort of ships?" I could not resist asking.

"Oh, merchantmen, of course," he replied, as if awakening from a reverie and realizing the line of my questioning. "Merchantmen, naturally."

"I guess a little practice wouldn't hurt," I said then.

Was that twitch to his left eye something of a wink? For a moment I covered it with an eyepatch, grew him a black beard and wrapped a red bandana around his skull. I tried to see him that way perhaps forty years ago, swinging a cutlass. I wondered. . . .

"Good idea," he said.

I turned up several trousers and shirts of medium to high quality, as well as two jackets, one light and one dark, which looked as if they would serve me.

The russet shirt and black trousers I tried fit well, and I decided to keep them on.

"Well enough done," Ellison observed, glancing my way as he put his signature to the last of the letters. "I'll show you my hidden safe, where we'll file these. Then I'll introduce you to Miss Ligeia before I take my leave."

"Very good, sir," I replied.

And these things were done. Thus did I make the acquaintance of Seabright Ellison, master of the Domain of Arnheim.

He wrote, as the fog crept up to the window, pressed against it:

> I have spoken of Memories that haunt
> us during our Youth. They sometimes
> even pursue us into our Manhood:—
> assume gradually less and less indefinite
> shapes:—now and then speak to us with
> low voices. . . .

A wind stirred the fog, a slice of moon found its way through the parting. He thought ahead to the end.

III

I walked, and Lord! the sand shifted beneath my feet to the point where I stumbled and fell several times. Through the thickest of fogs the sea roared like Leviathan a-dying, slapping intermittently with the force of a hurricane, tearing chunks of the shoreline away and swallowing them in its agony. Once I learned its direction I scrambled for higher ground, and the beach was eaten behind me as I climbed. Grasping at shrub, root, and rock, sliding back, catching hold again, I pulled myself at length above its reach, achieving, however, as I did so, a region where the winds swelled and howled their answer back to the sea-beast below. And Lord! the tumult of the elements' divorcement! Earth, air, and water strove, then fled one another in heartbeat pulses! And then as I raised myself those final feet—a gout of fire fell the welkin's course to fry a tree before me, last element joined in ghastly image cast upon my streaming eyes. I lifted my arm in moment shield, and when I let it fall, the tree smoked and flickered in the wind, and the figure of a man stood, almost unconcerned, nearby, staring past me toward the raging, invisible sea, dark cloak flapping.

I rose into a crouched position, shielding my face with my arm, and I moved in his direction.

"Allan!" I cried, recognizing him as I drew near; and then I added, "Poe!"

He inclined his head slightly in my direction, something like a wistful smile occurring as he responded. "Perry. Good of you to stop by. I knew, somehow, that you would."

I came up beside him, his cloak striking me about the right thigh and hip.

"What the hell's going on?" I asked.

"It is but the perishing of the Earth, dear Perry," he replied.

"I do not understand."

"The Art-scarred surface of the Earth is purified as the physical power of a word is withdrawn from its atmosphere," he said. "The passions of the most turbulent and unhallowed of hearts are unleashed. A welter of unfulfilled dreams dies about us."

I brushed my hair from my eyes. The tree crackled at our back, lighting the fog most balefully. The seas boomed like thunder.

"The memory of past joy—is it not present sorrow?" Poe went on.

"Well—could be," I replied. Seeing him more clearly now, I realized that he—who had always seemed of an age with me—appeared considerably older, his face more heavily lined than my own, dark pouches beneath his eyes. It was almost as if we

viewed each other from different times in our respective lives. "The thought of future joy," I suggested,
"might sort of balance things out. Isn't that the
meaning of hope?"

He considered me for several seconds and then
he shook his head and sighed.

"Hope?" he repeated. "That word, too, has been
withdrawn from the atmosphere, the ether, the land.
Things fall apart, dear Perry. For all that, you are
looking remarkably fit."

"Allan . . ." I began.

"Let it be 'Poe,'" he said, "between us."

"Damn it then, Poe!" I cried. "Just what is it you
are talking about? I truly do not understand you!"

"The beloved spirit is departed," he answered. "In
this absence the shell of our world crumbles. She is
gone, my other self. Alas! most evil of all evil days!
That which pervaded this place pervades no longer—
and you know the name as well as I.

"Annie . . ." he sighed, and he raised his arm in
trembling gesture. I turned my head in the direction
he indicated, seaward, and the fog parted to where
I beheld upon the sea-chewed strand the form of a
gray mausoleum, so slickly drenched by the assaulting
waves as to appear masked in glass. "Her tomb," he
said then.

"I don't believe you!" I cried, and I drew away
from him. Turning, I rushed back toward the cliff.

"Perry!" he called after me. "Come back! It's no
use! I do not know what will happen to me if something ill befalls you!"

"She's not there!" I shouted back. "She can't be!"

I was descending, scraping my arms, tearing my
garments.

"Perry! Perry!" he wailed.

I saved my breath, half-sliding, half-falling the rest of the way to the sand. Immediately, I was on my feet, fighting heavy winds and knee-high waves as I crossed to the shining monument. I could still hear Poe before the burning tree on high. I could distinguish no words, but only a baying sound now.

I caught hold of the black iron gate, lifted its latch, flung it open, and entered. I crossed its murky length, black water swirling about my ankles. A stone sarcophagus lay upon a ledge before me.

It was empty. I wanted to laugh and cry simultaneously. Instead I lurched to the entrance, where I cried, "Poe! Poe! You're wrong! She's not here! Poe! Poe!"

A great dark wave came rushing toward me and it smote me back into the tomb.

I awoke upon the stateroom floor, though I recalled having cast myself the previous evening across the big bunk which had been Seabright Ellison's. I did not recall having fallen from it, nor any means by which my garments could have become soaked and torn. There was sand in my shoes and a series of tracks led back from where I lay to a location near the center of the room, where they seemed to begin. I rotated a knuckle in my right eye then sat up. On removing the ruined russet shirt I discovered a number of abrasions on my forearms. Then I recalled the storm, the mausoleum, the wailing form of Poe beneath the burning tree.

I hunted up fresh garments in the sea chest, changing into them as I reflected upon the experience. I hoped that Poe was all right. I had been unsettled as much by the seeming strain of madness which had taken hold of him as by the bizarre course of events itself. I had somehow, long ago, realized our strange encounters to constitute both a reality and something partaking simultaneously of the realm of symbol, sign, or portent. I could, in this fashion, understand the matter of the empty tomb if Annie lay entranced in mesmeric slumber. But there was more to it than that. There had to be. I had learned more about the phenomenon last night than I had known, from Ellison's remarks upon it. But even the doughty alchemist did not know all that much. There was no one I could really ask concerning the matter, unless—

I wondered. Prior to his departure, Ellison had introduced me to the large-eyed, raven-haired lady, Ligeia, a woman of such fascinating beauty as slowed the cadence of my thinking to at least half its normal pace. Yet, it was not entirely her appearance which, I realized after a minute or so, was doing this to me. It was some other element about her person which was producing an actual physical effect. Immediately I realized this, I stepped back a pace and took a deep breath. The sensation vanished. The lady smiled.

"Delighted to make your acquaintance," she'd stated as Ellison named me, her voice low, hypnotic, accented in the manner of a Russian immigrant I had once known, eyes staring into my own with an unusual intensity.

"This is the man of whom I was speaking earlier—"

"I know," she stated.

"—and he has agreed to manage the business to which I referred."

"I know," she repeated.

"So I would appreciate your placing our special resources at his service."

She nodded.

"Of course."

"However, he has had an extremely filled day," he went on, "and I feel that any farther excitement would not be in his best interest. So I suggest we postpone his introduction to your charge until tomorrow. He is already aware that Monsieur Valdemar is able to obtain us information from places beyond this version of reality."

"I understand," she said.

"I don't," I said, "but I'll take your word for it."

"I will obtain sailing information and relay it to Captain Guy before my departure," he said.

"Very good," I replied. "In which case—"

"—you may retire," he finished for me, "and I'll bid you farewell and good luck as well as good night."

He clasped my hand with a firm grip.

"All right," I said. "Good-bye and good night."

I nodded to Ligeia. "I'll see you tomorrow," I told her.

"I know," she said.

I headed back to the stateroom, where I cast myself face downwards across the big bed. I was asleep almost immediately, later going away to our kingdom by the sea. And now. . . .

Sufficient light streamed from the ports for me to shave by, drawing fresh water from a large tank at the alchemical end of my quarters, emptying my basin out the nearest port when I had done with it. When I had finished grooming myself I went in search of breakfast. In the mess I was told that I might be served in my stateroom and instructed in the system of signaling for service. Since I was already in the saloon, however, I elected to remain, while eggs and onions, toast and halibut were prepared for my refreshment. The night's shadowy farrago of dreams and bewilderments, puzzles and fears, was washed from my spirit by several cups of excellent coffee, the final of which I took with me on deck, to sip as I beheld the icy, sun-spotted waves, a few benign-looking clouds drifting like white islands in the placid blue overhead. The sun was still low in its corner of the heavens, and taking my bearings therefrom I sought in what I thought must be a shoreward direction for signs of the coast we had departed, but my gaze met land neither in that direction nor any other. A trail of gulls rode the winds behind us, dipping into and rising out of our wake. When the cook—a one-eyed Spaniard named Domingo—called something loudly (whether curses or snatches of song, I am uncertain) and dumped the morning's slops, they answered him and fell quickly to feasting in the churning waters. I moved forward then, seeking for some time in that direction after any sign of the great dark vessel *Evening Star*. But, it too, lay beyond the blue edges of my world.

I shivered and gulped more of the steaming coffee. I resolved to wear something warmer the next time I was above deck this early in the day. Turning to head below and return my cup to the galley on the way to Ligeia's cabin, I encountered a grinning Dirk Peters, who touched the bill of his cap in mock salute and growled, "'Marnin', Master Eddie."

I gave him a smile and a nod and returned, "Good morning, Mister Peters."

"'Dirk' will do," he responded. "Lovely day now, ain't it?"

"Indeed," I agreed.

"And how does it feel, bein' in charge?" he continued.

"Hard to say," I replied. "I haven't given any orders yet."

He shrugged.

"No need, so far as I understand," he said. "'Less some emergency comes along. Mr. Ellison should've taken care of all the orderin' for a time."

"That's how I understand it, too," I said.

"You much of a seaman?" he asked.

"I was abroad, as a child. I don't remember getting seasick, if that's what you mean."

"Good," he observed, as a dark shape fell from the rigging, to bound across the deck and come up beside him. He reached out to clasp the hirsute shoulder of his ape, Emerson. The beast responded in kind, and I could not help but note that they resembled each other more than slightly. I say this not to disparage the man who came to my aid in a time of need—for I agree that it is more pardonable to trespass against truth than beauty—but because the very ugliness of his physiognomy was, in some wise, a thing of far greater fascination than those paragons of handsomeness the artists favor. His lips were thin, his teeth, ever-visible, long and protruding. He might almost give the impression of amusement were one to pay him but a casual glance. On return regard, however, one might liken it more to the merriment of a demon. In fact, his face was twisted, as if convulsed with laughter, and of paler pigmentation in patches between some of these creases than others, leading me to wonder whether some areas of his face might not be formed entirely of scar tissue. It was a frightening face, especially when one realized that its transition from seeming jollity to ferociousness was entirely a matter of one's own deepening perception rather than of any action on the man's part—as if reaching after a jewel beheld in some shadowy recess, one realized it to be embedded in the head of a serpent. "Good."

"What can you tell me about Valdemar?" I asked him.

He reached up as if to scratch his head, passing his fingers beneath his fantastical crop of black shag, raising it in the process and revealing it to be a peculiar wig. Observing my fascinated gaze he grinned a genuine grin and said, "Cut it from the skin of a bear who'd meant me ill." Then, "Valdemar," he observed. "Never laid eyes on 'im. He keeps in his stateroom, next to yours."

While there was something of the sailor in Peters' speech and manner, there seemed even more of the frontier. So, "You from the West?" I asked him.

He nodded.

"My pappy was a *voyageur,* a fur trader," he said, "and my mammy was an Upsaroka Injun out of the Black Hills. I've tracked and hunted all over the West. I've walked through Colter's Hell and been down in a canyon so big you could drop Charleston in and lose it." He spat over the railing, striking a luckless gull with terrible accuracy. "I've been down in Mexico and up where the northern lights hang like curtains at the end of the day." He scratched under his wig again. "All b'fore I was twelve," he added.

While I was not unfamiliar with tellers of tall tales, the man's ruggedly bizarre appearance and casual manner of speaking had me believing him entirely. A liar cares whether people believe what he said, for he wishes to impress them. I did not believe Peters gave a damn what anybody thought.

"About Valdemar . . ." I suggested.

"Yes?"

"How long has he been aboard?"

"Don't rightly know, sir," he replied. "Longer than me. The men were told he's an invalid and likes to travel. But I kinda wonder how much enjoyment there can be, stayin' in one room like that."

"You think there's something involved we don't know about?" I asked.

He shrugged.

"¿*Quien sabé?*" Then, "The lady Ligeia, I s'pose," he finished.

"What do you mean?" I inquired.

"Somethin' strange about that lady, his nurse. 'Minds me of a Crow medicine chief I once met. Johnny-Walks-With-Two-Spirits. Spookiest fella I ever knew in his comins and goins. When he talked to you you could almost see the ghostlands at his back, an' hear funny sounds in the winds. She's like that, too. Dunno any other way to put it."

I shook my head.

"I was kind of sleepy when I met her," I said. "Didn't really talk at any length. Has a kind of striking appearance, as I recall."

He grunted.

"She pretty much keeps to herself, too," he said. "I suggest stayin' on her good side. Got a feelin' she could be a tough enemy."

"I'm all for harmony," I said. "In fact, I should be paying Valdemar my respects soon."

"I imagine the captain will be wanting to talk soon, too."

I studied him as I nodded agreement. He did not seem aware that Valdemar was Ellison's resident expert on the trail we were to follow, rather than a simple tourist. So it seemed prudent to depart the subject, though sooner or later I would have to discover exactly what he did and did not know. I mused aloud, "Wonder which I should do first?"

"Hell, you can see the cap'n anytime," he said.

"You've a point there," I agreed. "Who knows how long it might take to meet our mysterious traveler if things aren't well with him? Wonder when I should drop by?"

"You been hearin' the bells?" he asked.

"Yes. Don't know how they work, though."

"They mark the watch," he explained. "They ring 'em every half-hour, from one bell to eight. Then they start again. Eight-thirty was one bell, nine o'clock was two. Next'll be three bells, nine-thirty. Might want to go by at three or four bells. Give him a chance to wake up and freshen."

"Thanks," I said, extending my hand. He did not take it, but Emerson reached forward, seized it, squeezed it, and pumped it. Had he wished, I could tell, the beast could have crushed it like a handful of dry sticks.

Peters grinned a totally evil grin and nodded.

"Anything I can help you on, Eddie, just give me a holler."

Then he threw me another mock-salute, turned, and passed below. Emerson sprang upward, to vanish behind a sail.

Three or four bells. Okay. I went below, myself, to fetch another cup of coffee while I waited. By three bells I'd had enough. I returned to my stateroom, where I sought through my wardrobe once more. A white shirt and cravat might well be in order, I decided. By four bells I'd also turned up a suitable vest and jacket as well as a tin of bootblack, and I'd allowed my Army habits to take over.

I walked past the intervening stateroom and

knocked upon Ligeia's door. It opened immediately, and she met me with the faintest of smiles.

"I was expecting you," she said.

"I expect you were," I replied, finding a faint smile myself.

She had on a nondescript gray smock-like garment, and her fingers and wrists no longer wore the jewelry I half-remembered from the previous evening. Again, there was a peculiar feeling in her presence— as if lightning had just struck or was about to.

She neither invited me in nor joined me in the corridor. She simply studied me for several moments. Finally, "You are even more unusual than I first thought," she observed.

"Really?" I said. "In what respects?"

"Geography," she replied.

"I don't understand."

"You don't fit anyplace I know of," she said, "and I thought I knew everyplace. So you must be from someplace else."

"It would seem to follow," I replied, deciding not to pursue matters further as I could see a strange exercise in tautology upon the horizon. "And I will be happy to leave things there," I added, "if you will, too."

She furrowed her brows, narrowed her eyes.

"Where?" she inquired.

"Someplace else," I said.

Then her face relaxed and she smiled fully.

"You Americans are always joking," she said then. "You are joking with me, yes?"

"Yes," I said.

She leaned against the door jamb. Was there a slight sway to her hips as she did so?

"Is it that you wish to see Monsieur Valdemar

now . . . ?" she asked, as if inviting me to complete the sentence on a different note.

"I would," I replied.

"Very well," she said, gesturing toward the door to my left, which came between hers and my own. "Wait by that door."

With that, she withdrew into her stateroom and closed its door. I heard a bolt or bar fall or slide into place.

So I did as she'd ordered, walking to the next door and waiting there. Several minutes passed, and then abruptly, the door was opened for me. It stood perhaps a foot ajar, and I could detect nothing but blackness within.

"Come in," I heard her say.

"Uh— I can't see a thing," I said.

"That's all right," she replied. "Just do as I say."

Reflecting that Ellison had enjoined me to trust her, I took two steps on the oblique, sufficient to carry me past the door's edge into the dark interior. The door closed immediately, I heard the *snick* of a bolt, and I stood stock-still.

"Mightn't we have a little light?" I asked. "I don't know which way to move."

Immediately, I felt my hand taken.

"I will lead you," she said softly. "Monsieur Valdemar's condition is such that the light bothers him considerably."

"Even a small candle?" I asked.

"Even a small candle."

She led me back and to my right. After several paces, she squeezed my hand and placed her other hand upon my chest. "Halt," she said; then, when I did, "That's just fine. Stay there."

She released me, moved a few paces away. Shortly,

I heard a creaking sound as of a door being opened, from somewhere before me. There followed a total silence, and after several minutes of it I cleared my throat. She ignored this, so I finally asked, "Is everything all right?"

"Of course," she said. "Be patient. It takes a little time to establish rapport."

I could not tell what she was doing, though I detected the rustling of movement. Then I felt the peculiar tingling sensation which I immediately recalled from the previous evening. And I became aware of a faint line of light to my right. Of course, the connecting door between her suite and this one— it was not entirely closed. Then came the murmurs. She was speaking very softly.

"Let's not wake the poor fellow up now," I said. "Let him get his rest. I'll come back later."

"No," she answered. "He's doing just fine. It takes him a while to—pull himself together. That's all."

There followed a terrible moan.

". . . And I hate to put an invalid under such a strain," I added.

"Nonsense!" she replied. "It's good for him. Keeps up his interest in life."

Again, the moan.

I edged a trifle nearer, as my eyes were beginning to adjust to the darkness and I was hoping to discern something of interest beyond the movements of her arms over the dark object upon the bed. Again, I felt the vibratory sensation. Before I could remark upon it, however, the moan came again, followed by a distant "No! No! . . . Let me be. Please! I beseech you!"

"Are you sure . . . ?" I began.

"Of course," she responded. "He's always a little out of sorts when I rouse him. Just a matter of mood."

"Sounds the way I feel before I have my coffee," I said. "Perhaps we should send for some breakfast for him."

"Oh! Ooh!" he moaned. "I am dead!"

"No, he's not much for food or drink," she replied. "Come around now, Monsieur. There's a gentleman here I'd like you to meet."

"Please! Just—let me—go . . ." came a raspy, distant voice. "Let me die."

"The more time you waste arguing, Monsieur, the longer it takes," she stated.

"Very well," he said then. "What is it—that you want?"

"I wish to introduce Mr. Edgar Perry, who is now in charge of our expedition."

"Expedition . . ." he said softly.

" . . . In pursuit of Messers Goodfellow, Templeton, and Griswold, who have kidnapped the woman known as Annie."

"I see her," he said, "ablaze—like a crystal chandelier—before us. She is not of this world. They use her. They use her—to follow—another. Let me die."

"Von Kempelen," I said.

"Yes. But I know not—where they—are headed—because—it is not clear—where he is headed—yet. Let me die."

"We do not need that information now," I said, an extraordinary thought occurring to me and causing me to begin sidling to my right. "Tell me what you can of the connection between Edgar Allan Poe and myself."

"You are—somehow—the same—person," he said.

"How can that be?" I asked.

"Crossover," he said. "Poor Poe—will—never know. Never to find what is sought—through hollow lands—and hilly lands."

"Why not?"

"Let me rest!"

"Tell me!"

"I know not. Only Annie—knows! I am dead!"

One more step to the right, then I turned and kicked open the door. Daylight spilled through from Ligeia's own quarters, catching the lady in mid-gesture above an opened casket, within which lay a frightfully pale individual whose white whiskers stood in violent contrast to the blackness of his hair. His eyes were opened but the pupils rolled upward. His face was twisted, lips drawn back, teeth bared. His tongue, slightly protruding, appeared to be black.

"Good Lord!" I said. "The man is dead!"

"Yes and no," she observed. "He's an unusual case."

She gestured slowly and his eyes closed. She shut the lid.

"But then, we all have our problems," she added. "Would you care for some tea or hashish?"

"Have you got anything stronger?" I answered, as she took my arm.

"Certainement," she replied, and I cast a backward glance as we departed, surprised to note that the casket when closed possessed the shape and size of a large crate of wine-bottles, even to the point of bearing labels, producing the impression of a double-box of Chateau-Margaux, of the antelope brand, violet seal.

She steered me toward a comfortable-looking chair, saw me seated in it. Closing the connecting door, she repaired to the far end of her stateroom, where she opened a cabinet. Shortly thereafter, I heard the cool clinking sounds of glass upon glass and the splashing of liquids.

She returned after a few moments with a tall

tumbler of muddy, greenish liquid, bits of leaves and other matter floating on its surface.

"Looks like swamp water," I said, accepting it.

"Tastes like swamp water, too," I added, after a small sip.

"It is an herbal tonic," she explained. "Very relaxing."

I thought about it, then took another sip.

"Valdemar is—indeed—dead?" I said after a time.

"Yes," she replied, "but he tends to forget. Each time he remembers it becomes somewhat stressful."

"When, how did he die?"

She shrugged.

"Months, years, before we came aboard," she said. "Long before I found him."

I cast my gaze about her quarters, hung with bright tapestries, strewn with animal skins and oriental rugs. There were dark wood figurines I guessed to be African, decorated with copper wire and bright beads. A pair of Toledo blades hung upon one wall. There was a Turkish water pipe beside the huge, silk-curtained bed. The aroma of some exotic incense hung heavy in the air. It reminded me somewhat of a Gypsy caravan where I had once paid to have my palm read by a heavily rouged lady who, I felt, was somewhat overimaginative on my behalf. Yet there was something more to this ensemble than to that one. Peters had been right. I could almost see the ghostlands at her back.

"What is it that makes Valdemar special?" I asked.

"I gather he was part of an experiment in mesmerism," she explained, "on his deathbed. He is frozen at the exact point of transition between life and death. Because of this, he enjoys a unique perspective on events. It does require a particularly skilled mesmerist to deal with him, however, as he keeps trying to slip away into the darkness."

"And you are obviously a specialist in this regard." She nodded.

"Where I come from the phenomenon is somewhat controversial," I said.

"Here it is a fact of life."

"I believe I felt it somewhat—twice now—in your presence."

"That is quite possible," she said. "Finish your tonic and I'll show you what it's like."

I gulped what remained, set the glass aside.

"That stuff didn't do much for me," I observed.

"It's quite mild," she replied.

"I thought you said it was a potent brew."

"No, you asked for something strong. That will be the treatment." She raised her hands. They seemed to sparkle. Once again, I felt the warm pulse, the faint tingling. "The tonic is but a preliminary."

"What will the treatment do for me?"

"I am not absolutely certain," she said, "in your case. What would you like it to do?"

"I'd just like to escape from myself for a time."

She smiled, extended her hands, lowered them. It was like being suddenly splashed by a very warm wave. I leaned back in my chair and let the feeling run through me. She was on Ellison's payroll, and she knew I was important to him. She gestured again and I attempted to relax fully, letting the feeling wash through me. Nothing the Gypsy'd done had felt like this.

While her first several passes were exhilarating, I realized after a short while, that they were also somewhat numbing. There was a distancing effect between my body and my consciousness. Then I realized that

my thinking had grown sluggish. But it was coupled
with such euphoria that I did not resist the lethargy.

Her hands drifted slowly past me.

"I am going to cause you to relax very deeply,"
she said. "When you awaken you should feel entirely refreshed."

I was about to respond, but then it did not seem
worth the effort. Her hands passed me again and I
was hardly aware of my body any longer. Except for
my eyes. It seemed an awful lot of trouble, keeping
my eyes open. I let them close. I felt the shadows
of her hands go by once more. And then I was
departing—soaring, bright white, drifting, turning to
snow, falling. . . .

. . . Suddenly, my head felt funny, my stomach
worse. I raised my hands to massage my temples. I
opened my eyes. I lay in bed, propped by pillows. A
threadbare blanket covered me from the waist down.
As I lowered my hands they trembled slightly. I listened
to the sound of a catbird from somewhere beyond the
window. Looking about, I saw that I occupied a small
and rather shabby room. What was happening? I could
not recall how I had come to this place . . .

There was a note on the bedside table. I picked
it up. It was addressed to Poe. Even more puzzled,
I read it, hoping for some clue as to what was
happening:

Richmond, Sept. 29, 1835
    Dear Edgar,—Would that it were in my
power to unbosom myself to you, in language such as I could on the present occasion, wish myself master of. I cannot do
it—and therefore must be content to speak
to you in my plain way.

That you are sincere in all your promises, I firmly believe. But, Edgar, when you once again tread these streets, I have my fears that your resolves would fall through,—and that you would again sip the juice, even till it stole away your senses. Rely on your own strength, and you are gone! Look to your Maker for help, and you are safe!

How much I regretted parting with you, is unknown to anyone on this earth, except myself. I was attached to you—and am still,—and willingly would I say return, if I did not dread the hour of separation very shortly again.

If you could make yourself contented to take up your quarters in my family, or in any other private family where liquor is not used, I should think there were hopes of you.—But, if you go to a tavern, or to any other place where it is used at table, you are not safe. I speak from experience.

You have fine talents, Edgar,—and you ought to have them respected as well as yourself. Learn to respect yourself, and you will very soon find that you are respected. Separate yourself from the bottle, and bottle companions, forever!

Tell me if you can do so—and let me hear that it is your fixed purpose never to yield to temptation.

If you should come to Richmond again, and again should be an assistant in my office, it must be expressly understood by us that all engagements on my part would be dissolved, the moment you get drunk.

No man is safe who drinks before breakfast! No man can do so, and attend to business properly.

I have thought over the matter seriously about the Autograph article, and have come to the conclusion that it will be best to omit it in its present dress. I should not be at all surprised, were I to send it out, to hear that Cooper had sued me for a libel.

The form containing it has been ready for press three days—and I have been just as many days deciding the question.

I am your true Friend,
T. W. White

I let it fall. I couldn't remember when I'd felt this weak. Nevertheless, I struggled, I rose, I crossed the room to a small mirror and studied myself within it—my face yet not my face. Haggard, red-eyed. I rubbed my temples again. So poor Poe was drinking too much, and this is what it felt like.

How had I wound up in his body?

I recalled Ligeia's hands drifting past me, doing things with the stuff of life itself it seemed. I remembered Valdemar, Peters, Ellison. And my last encounter with Poe. Did he think Annie was dead? Could that be the cause of his present unhappy state?

If that were so, might it change things for the better with him if I were to leave him a message? I looked about for something to write it with.

"Eddie!" the voice of an older woman, from the

next room. I elected not to answer it. "Eddie! Are you up?"

There. On the small table by the window. A pen. An inkwell. I hurried to them. Paper.

Paper . . . ? The man was working for a magazine. He must have some paper. None in the drawer—

"Would you care for some tea, Eddie?"

Aha! In the box beneath the table.

I drew up the room's only chair, collapsed upon it. How to begin? I would have to refer to our shared experiences with Annie.

How many visions of a maiden that is, I wrote. And then the strength went out of me. I put down the pen. I could hardly keep my head up. At my back, I heard the door open. Curiosity bade me turn, but I was too weak to do it. I slumped.

"Eddie!" I heard her cry.

I was already losing myself again, floating, drifting away. Her voice grew tiny. My muscles went numb and the world turned gray. Then something stirred the currents of life inside me and shadows drifted across my eyes.

After a long while I sighed and looked upward. Ligeia's face was near, brows slightly knit in what might be an expression of concern as she scrutinized me.

"How do you feel?" she asked.

I shook my head and I patted my stomach. The feelings of hangover had vanished.

"Fine," I said, stretching. "What happened?"

"You don't remember?"

"I remember being in another place, in someone else's body."

"Whose?"

"Edgar Allan Poe's," I said.

"The one of whom you asked Monsieur Valdemar?"

I nodded.

"We go way back. And I'll bet he was here in my body while I was off in his."

It was her turn to nod.

"Yes," she said, "and he seemed either drugged, drunk, or mad. It was difficult to gain control, to send him back."

"Why did he come in the first place? Does this sort of switching happen often?"

"This was the first time I've ever seen or heard of it," she said. "That was a very strange man. It was almost as if I'd conjured some dark spirit."

I decided against asking what her experience was in the dark spirit area. I'd had enough excitement for one morning.

"He asked after an Annie," she continued, "and said something about his heartstrings being a lute. If he is not mad he must be a poet. But I wonder now—whether the thing that led to the transfer lies with him or with you."

I shrugged.

"Wait. Did not Monsieur Valdemar say you are somehow the same person?" she asked. "That would explain the metaphysics of it."

"Like all metaphysics, it explains nothing of any practical value," I said. "I am neither mad nor a poet. My heart is not a musical instrument. I'm just in the wrong world, I think, and so is poor Eddie Poe. I don't know how it came to pass, but the man we're following had something to do with it."

"Rufus Griswold?"

"I believe so. Yes, that's right. You know the man?"

"We met once, in Europe. Years ago. He is dangerous—in some highly specialized ways as well as the ordinary."

"I gather he's some kind of alchemist."

"More than that," she said. "A black magician of some persuasion I do not know."

"Ellison thinks he interfered in some fashion with a relationship between Poe and Annie and myself to produce the present state of affairs, giving him Annie as a guide, displacing us all from our respective worlds."

She spread her hands and met my eyes.

"I do not know," she said. "But I find the idea fascinating. Shall I see whether I can learn more about it?"

"Please."

I rose.

"However . . ." she said.

"Yes?"

"I'd like to question Monsieur Valdemar every morning, at about this time," she said. "The routine will be good for him."

"It will?"

"Even the dead need good work habits," she explained. "And I feel that, as head of this expedition, you should be present on these occasions."

"I guess I should," I agreed. "Too bad."

I headed for the door, halted when I reached it.

"Thanks for—everything," I said. "See you at lunch."

She shook her head.

"I take all my meals here," she told me. "But you're welcome to join me sometime."

"Sometime," I said, and I went out. The passageway about me was suddenly filled with white fire.

"*Comment?*" I heard Ligeia say, as at a great distance, right before her door fell shut.

"This way, Perry," a familiar voice called out. "Please."

It being the voice of the one lady I would walk through fire for, I moved ahead. But even the living can use a little peace and quiet, I reflected, momentarily envious of Valdemar.

IV

. . . Down the corridor of white fire, like a tunnel of flowing silver or a melting ice cave, rushing, I went. For Annie called, and it seemed she must be just a bend away. But I turned a corner, I climbed, I turned again, and the brightness flickered—almost pulsing— and she still seemed just as near, but no nearer. Again, I climbed.

"Annie!" I called out, at length. "Where are you?"

"Where I always am," she answered, her voice suddenly higher-pitched. "On the beach."

"I can't find you. I seem to be lost," I shouted.

Abruptly, the flames parted. For an instant, I was taken back to a long gone day. Nor did it seem unnatural that Annie as a small girl stood beside a pile of brushwood, a gleaming seashell in her hand, a line of troubled ocean visible beyond her right shoulder.

"Annie! What's happened?" I cried.

"It's Eddie," she said, "Edgar Allan. . . ."

"Poe," I said.

She frowned, then nodded. "Yes," she agreed. "Poe, too. And he's denying us. He is drawing away, and it hurts."

"I don't understand. What can I do?" I asked.

"Talk to him. Tell him we love him. Tell him we're real. Tell him—"

The flames closed again, hiding her from my sight.

"Annie!"

"I can't stay!" I heard her call out, weakly.

"How can I help *you*?" I cried.

I became aware of a pulsing in my hands, and then the ground began to sway and my shoulders were suddenly straining and the flames were flapping audibly.

"Annie!"

What I took to be the beginning of a response proved only the cry of a bird. But it might well have been a thunderclap for the drastic change it seemed to signal. Immediately, the flames became the flapping canvas of a sail, the throbbing thing in my hands a line leading to the nearby mast. My feet rested upon another line, the rolling of the vessel transmitted to me through it. My height above the deck made me uneasy and I gripped my line more tightly. I have always been bothered somewhat by high places, and a windy—possibly pre-storm—morning at this altitude troubled me considerably.

A clucking sound caused me to look to my left. Emerson swung toward me, anchored himself to the mast, extended his hand and took hold of my arm. Slowly, feeling the beast's strength and coming to trust his intention, I relaxed my grip upon the line and permitted myself to be led toward the mast and

down it, finally achieving the surer footing of a
wooden crosspiece, where I stood hugging the mast
till the worst of the vertigo departed. It had been
infinitely more frightening to find myself suddenly
in that position than had I made the effort to climb
carefully to it. I grunted my thanks to Emerson,
who must have realized that I felt safer now, for
he released me and moved off. Then I climbed
down slowly, troubled by the turns my childhood
visions seamed to be taking.

"Mr. Perry," came a familiar voice. "I am impressed
by your conscientiousness as head of this expedition.
Had I known you wished to inspect the vessel I'd
have been only too happy to provide you with a
guide—or have conducted your tour myself. I'd no
idea a landsman might possess such diligence in
nautical matters."

I clasped my hands behind my back to conceal
their shaking, and I nodded slowly.

"Why, thank you, Captain Guy," I replied "It was
hardly a tour of inspection—more a matter of satisfying my curiosity as to how things were secured
above."

He smiled.

"Most prudent. I trust you were satisfied by what
you saw?"

"Indeed. I was impressed."

"I was about to send you an invitation, sir, to take
your luncheon with me in my quarters at eight bells,
so we can get to know each other a bit better and
discuss this journey."

"Sounds like a good idea," I agreed. "Thank you.
I'll see you then."

I returned to my own cabin for a little cowering and
reflection. I sprawled on the big bunk, hands behind

my head, gazing abstractedly at the containers of colored liquid on the lab table at the end of the room, musing upon the fact that Valdemar lay just beyond that wall. I thought over the events of the past several days, also, when the tempo of my life had commenced its acceleration. Questions I had been too sleepy, startled, distracted, or confused to articulate began tumbling through my mind. What was the power of the enemy, and where did it reside, for them to have been able to move Poe, Annie, and myself from world to world the way they had? What was Ligeia's strength? And of main importance, to me, why were my experiences with Poe and Annie—which had been casual things spread out over a lifetime—suddenly changing in character, frequency, and intensity? Never having understood their mechanism from the beginning, I was at a loss to understand these new developments. This most recent one, which had left me hanging in the rigging, puzzled me most of all. We had always been of an age in our encounters. Could Time itself be subject to arcane manipulation? And if so, why was it suddenly happening to us?

Somewhere before the point at which it all seemed clear to me I fell asleep. When I woke I could not remember the answers. But it was the ship's bell that roused me. In that I was not certain how many times it had rung, I left my quarters to find out.

I encountered Dirk Peters near the companionway, smoking a cigar. Every now and then Emerson, who lurked in a shadow, would reach out, borrow the cheroot, puff upon it, and return it.

"Indeed, Mister Eddie, 'twas eight bells you heard," he said, "and if you're lookin' for the captain's cabin, it's over that way." He gestured with the smoldering weed, which Emerson promptly borrowed.

"That first door?" I asked.

"The second," he responded. "I hear as you come out of the riggin' without getting' into it proper."

"I guess that's half the story," I said, refusing to ask him whether he could hold converse with Emerson.

At this, he chuckled.

"Must run," I said. "Thanks."

A hairy hand waved a cigar at me.

Captain Guy welcomed me, saluting my health with a minuscule glass of wine. The kitchen mate who served us departed as soon as everything had been laid out and dispensed before us.

"Mister Perry," he said, refilling the glasses, "I have decided to give you a tour of the vessel immediately following our meal."

"Why, thank you, sir. You don't have to—"

"My pleasure entirely, I assure you. Mr. Ellison tells me that you will have no problem providing us with travel information as we go along."

"Yes," I agreed, as he began eating. When he glanced up at me suddenly, I added, "Hopefully, there will be no complications on that front."

"And you have made the acquaintance of the mysterious Monsieur Valdemar?"

"I have."

"The man is some sort of master calculator, is he not?"

"I am not certain," I answered. "The matter did not come up during our conversation."

"Oh," the captain observed. "I simply assumed he worked with abstruse formulas to keep track of the other vessel's progress."

I shook my head.

"No," I said, beginning to eat.

"Mister Ellison conferred with him for some time before his departure," he observed. "He informed me afterwards that our destination lay in southern Europe. He said further that you would provide us with more detailed information as it was required."

"I shall," I replied.

"Is there anything Monsieur Valdemar requires of us?"

"Not that I'm aware of."

"He has had no meals sent to his room."

"Special diet, I believe. Ligeia takes care of his needs."

"I see. Let me know if they want anything, will you?"

"Of course."

"A very interesting man. He must have a strange story to tell."

"I'm sure he does, though I'm yet to hear it."

We ate for a time in silence, then he asked, "Any idea at what point you might have further sailing instructions for me?"

"When will you need them?"

"Not for some time yet."

"Let me know when you do, and if I haven't already gotten them, I'll get them."

He smiled faintly then and turned the conversation to matters nautical and meteorological. Afterwards, he kept his word and I got the tour.

That night I watched a storm for a long while. It rumbled and spit fires on its way up from the south. I stood under a God's plenty of stars in a clear sky, there on the main deck. The storm came striding across the water like some bright giant insect. A cool breeze preceded it, and shortly the waves grew higher, their splashings against the hull more forceful. A little later and the ship was rocking, the breeze punctuated by gusts, the banging of the thunder much nearer at hand. The stars were drowned in a pool of spilled ink and the face of the deep was illuminated by countless flashes. I wondered whether it was storming on that other world, where poor Poe wrote or edited, his depressed alcohol metabolism in this place serving him ill in that. There came a blinding flash from directly overhead, followed immediately by a clap of thunder. Then a hard rain pelted the deck, and I scurried for the stair, half drenched before I reached it.

In the days that followed I maintained my resolve, visiting with Valdemar in the morning. Ligeia would open his wine-crate casket, and, secrecy no longer necessary in my case, a few tapers or an oil lamp would illuminate the scene, casting flickering shadows across the man's waxen features. The lady would exercise her art, performing mesmeric passes above him until he moaned, sighed, wailed, or barked, signaling the fact that we had his attention once again. Usually, on these occasions, I would feel the energies, also, as if water were somehow flowing through my body. Then we would exchange greetings:

"For the love of God, let me go! I am dead, do you hear? Have you no compassion? Release me!"

"What will the weather be like today?" I asked.

"Sunny. Winds out of the southwest. Thirty knots. Light midafternoon showers. Oh, oh, the agony!"

"A little rain never hurt anybody," Legeia observed. "Have you narrowed the range of Von Kempelen's flight yet?"

"France or Spain. I can say no more at this time.

I turn, I freeze, torn 'twixt the bournes of spirit and matter!"

"What became of the Kingdom of the Netherlands? You'd mentioned it the last time I asked."

"That probability has diminished. I say to you that I am dead!"

"I'm not feeling too well myself this morning. Are Griswold, Templeton, and Goodfellow aware that we pursue them?"

"Indeed they are. Oh! Oh! Oh!"

"Have they formed any plans yet which might bring us to distress?"

"I deem it likely, though I cannot tell you their thinking. They have taken no action yet which might cause you harm."

His lower jaw fell, revealing his long yellow teeth and his swollen and blackened tongue.

"Quick! Quick! Put me to sleep or waken me! Quick, I say! I say to you that I am dead!"

"Sleep well then," Ligeia said, passing her hands above him and closing the lid.

Other times, we discussed different matters:

"Good morning, Monsieur Valdemar," she said. "And how are you today?"

"Oh! The agony . . . !"

"I was wondering about this business of alternative worlds," I said. "I get the impression there are many, many such, each slightly—or, perhaps, greatly—different from the others."

"Nor are you incorrect. Spare me, I beg! Let me live! Or die! But no more of this twilight horror!"

"I was wondering, too, how the transportation of an individual from one such world to another might be effected."

"First, it requires locating extremely similar

individuals on disparate worlds who possess a—kind of resonance—with each other—"

"How could one possibly locate such people?"

"One would employ a special detector. Please . . ."

"Describe this detector."

"A person who is neither living nor dead—but partakes of both—may be directed to extend his awareness—in this fashion—"

"That sounds suspiciously like a description of yourself."

"It is."

"Are you trying to say that you were party to our world-switching?"

"No. I served only to locate the requisite individuals."

"You found Poe, Annie, and myself for Griswold and company?"

"I did."

"How?"

"It may not be described. Only experienced. Please . . ."

"Put him back to sleep, lady."

And then, again, on a gray, blustery day when the sea wore whitecaps and the decks did surprising things beneath our feet:

"Good morning, Monsieur Valdemar. How goes the world with you?"

"Pray unbind my spirit, lady, and consign these mortal remains to the deep."

"Mr. Perry has something he wants to ask you."

"I'll only be a minute, Valdemar, but something you said the other day has had me thinking. If the Griswold crew used you to locate us, what did they use to cause our transfer—physically—from one world to the other?"

"A person of considerable power was needed—one who could be used to create a kind of meta-place—a common ground—where the three of you might meet. . . ."

"Annie? You found us, and Annie was induced to perform the transfer?"

"Just so. If you would, dear sir—"

"I have no further questions at this time."

Ligeia waved her hands.

"Have a good day, Monsieur."

The ship pitched as she shut his lid, and it fell to with a crash.

"Would you care for some tea, or an herbal drink?" she inquired.

"I believe I would."

And the following day:

"A good morning to you, Monsieur Valdemar."

"If pity be not foreign to thy soul—"

"Good to hear you speaking so clearly. Edgar has something else he wants to ask you."

"Yes," I said. "I do not understand how Annie could have been induced to perform the exchanges to which you referred, a matter which worked to her own detriment."

"She was caused to do so by Dr. Templeton—a skilled mesmerist."

"I still do not understand. If her own ability in this area is so great, how could a lesser practitioner control her? And if he were actually stronger, what did they need her for?"

"His abilities are as a candle to the celestial orb when compared with hers. Yet he could influence her by reaching her at a vulnerable time—her childhood."

"How—could he do that?"

"Once she had been located the detector could be

employed to transmit Dr. Templeton's mesmeric energies to the desired point on her lifeline."

"*You* were used to focus his energies on her?"

"That is correct."

"Time itself is no barrier to your sentience?"

"Time is space—or spaces—among the worlds. And pasts are easier than futures."

I felt myself swaying, and this time it was not the vessel. I put out my hand to lean upon the bier, slipped, and struck his shoulder. It was as rigid as wood.

"There is nothing to be gained by striking a dead man," he observed.

"It was an accident," I said. "Sorry."

My mind was filled with images of happy children at play; and even as I framed the complicated question I could foresee his one-word reply:

"Are you telling me that Dr. Templeton, working through you, caused Annie to create conditions which influenced the lives of the three of us toward the point where this exchange became possible?"

"Yes."

"Three lives have been manipulated because of the greed of these men."

There was no reply, but I realized I had not actually asked a question.

"All to bring Annie here at this time to track the gold-maker and his secret?"

"For now," he replied, "she is such a tool."

"What do you mean 'for now'?"

"They need a lot of money soon. So Annie is—for the moment—a tool. Later—she will have other uses."

"What uses?"

"Her power is to be stripped—from her personality—to serve as an ingredient—in a Great Work."

"What then becomes of her personality?"

"It is—sacrificed."

"You cannot be serious."

"I cannot be otherwise," he replied. "Sir! I repeat! There is nothing to be gained in striking a dead man! Release me!"

"Go to hell!"

"This is a state of mind with which I am not unfamiliar."

I felt Ligeia's hand upon my arm.

"Come away," she said.

I realized by degrees that I had dragged the man halfway out of his casket and was shaking him. Ligeia's other hand passed down my spine and I felt a warm current sweep through me. I let Valdemar fall back into his box.

"Yes," I said. "Yes."

She turned him off and led me away.

Yet was I back again the following days, for his answers seemed always to breed fresh questions:

"Bonjour, Monsieur Valdemar."

"Lady, I speak to you as one racked in the House of Pain—"

"Then I'm sure you'll welcome a little distraction. Eddie has a few more questions for you."

"Yes," I said. "It did not occur to me to ask earlier, but how did your—uh—remains come into the possession of Mr. Ellison when they had been in the custody of Griswold for all of this business you've been describing?"

"Mr. Peters and Emerson managed to spirit me away one night recently."

"Does Griswold know that we have you?"

"Yes."

"And he made no effort to recover you?"

"He no longer needed me once he had Annie."

"She can do anything you can?"

"She lacks my unique perspective—but she can satisfy his special needs for astral intelligence."

"How did he ever find a person in your condition, to begin with?"

"In good health and normal spirits."

"I do not understand."

"You asked how he found me."

"Then what changed you?"

"He did."

"Oh. You mean . . ."

"He brought me to the point of death, then suspended me here."

"I'm sorry. I did not understand fully."

"Then release me. Let me die."

"I can't. We need you."

I drew back and looked away. Ligeia returned him to wherever he went between sessions and we blew out his candles.

"Coffee? Tea?"

"Yes."

It was three days before I approached him again. I watched storms come and go, I read some of Ellison's books and fiddled with his fascinating alchemical equipment. I even went to Captain Guy, had him open his armory and provide me with a saber. I commenced my old dismounted drills with the weapon then—at first, in my own room; then later, topside, at odd hours, when the deck was pretty much deserted. I liked working in the open air, I required the exercise, and, as my benefactor had pointed out, it seemed a skill worth resurrecting. And so I stamped and lunged, to Emerson's occasional applause from the rigging.

Still, these distractions were not sufficient to halt the speculative faculty for long; and Ligeia and I opened his casket once again. The tapers flickered, the mesmeric currents flowed. Shortly, a series of moans signaled our establishment of contact:

"Good morning, Monsieur Valdemar."

"Any chance of your letting me die today?" he inquired.

"Afraid not," I responded. "But I'll try to be brief. First, I've a general question. It wasn't clear to me from what you said the other day whether Annie had been forced to create the bond with Poe and myself."

"No," he replied. "I had merely to locate a person of her potential who already was party to such a relationship. Then Dr. Templeton caused her to create your kingdom by the sea."

"The odds, sir, on finding such a bizarre connection must be astronomical."

"It makes no difference—if one has an infinity of possibilities from which to choose."

It was not until that moment in my life that I began to appreciate the concept of infinity, a thing which was later to occupy considerable of my thinking. In the meantime, curiosity drove me but a step further:

"How can the human mind compass infinity?" I asked.

"The dead can view it from the vantage of eternity," he replied. "Speaking of which—"

"No. Not now," I said. "I will not discuss the joy of death with you."

"Eddie?" Ligeia said, accenting the second syllable as was her wont.

"Yes?" I answered.

"You have seen me about this business for some small while now, and I have observed you for just as long. You are not as sensitive to drink or to mesmeric influences as one who is native to this world. On the other hand, you have an enormous capacity for both."

"What are you trying to say?"

"It would be interesting to teach you the rudiments of the system—to see what comes to pass of it. We might start by having you return Monsieur Valdemar to his rest."

"I am not certain that I approve—" Valdemar began.

"Hush!" she said, taking hold of my hands. "What do you know of the subject?"

"I—"

Our first gesture silenced him, as I felt the current faintly.

"Well done," she said. "You really should keep at it."

I did, and though my efforts over the next few days met with some success they were accompanied by distracting side-effects. That is to say, whenever I would begin to employ animal magnetism as she directed there would come sharp rapping sounds from within the walls, from overhead or underfoot, furniture would be thrown about, and small objects would develop a tendency toward levitation or spontaneous shatterment.

"I'm going to have to give it up," I said on the third day. "It's simply too messy."

"It is appropriate for the place you came from," she replied. "But perhaps it is hazardous to continue these experiments aboard ship. The ocean is deep."

So I restrained my animal magnetism and we returned to our former operating procedures. The very next day Valdemar informed us that the field of probability had narrowed. Paris was to be our destination.

. . . And the circumstances of his death were as mysterious as events in one of his stories, nor did matters end at that point. He was buried in the Poe family lot in Baltimore's Presbyterian Cemetery. His grave was not marked by name but bore only the number 80 which the sexton had placed there in identification. Several years later, Edgar's cousin Neilson Poe ordered a tombstone for him. It was broken, however, by a freight train which jumped the track into the marble yard where it was being carved. Nobody tried again till it was too late for certainty. The 80 was lost, and time and the vicissitudes had their way with the Poe lot.

While nobody knows for certain just where the hell his body is, there is now a monument to Edgar Allan Poe; and generally, on the eve of his birthday, he is remembered. A bottle of bourbon may turn up at his tomb, along with a few flowers and an occasional stuffed raven. Baudelaire and a number of his countrymen thought him one hell of a fellow. Henry James disagreed, but he always was a bit of a spoilsport. Poe is one of those writers, as someone said, who holds a great special place in literature rather than a great general place.

It happened this year, too. But he doesn't touch a drop anymore.

V

There came a night when my sleep was troubled. I tossed fitfully, drowsing and rousing, and seem to recall at one point hearing the sounds of a November storm. My dreams were a rag-bag of ill-matched people and places, going nowhere. At some unmarked hour the storm faded. I found oblivion for a time and its taste was sweet. . . .

I found myself sitting up, listening, searching the shadows, waiting for awareness to catch up with my senses, uncertain as to what it was that had called me awake. It felt as if there were someone present, but moonlight streamed through a porthole and my eyes were entirely dark-adjusted. I saw no one.

"Who's there?" I asked, and I swung my feet over the side of the bunk, dropped to one knee and fetched out the saber from where I had stowed it beneath. No one responded.

Then I noted the glow upon the wall, near the apparatus table. Rising, I approached, halting when I realized it to be only the small, metal-framed mirror which hung there. The angle must be such that it was catching that intense moonlight.

Only, it retained a uniform luminosity as I crossed the room to inspect the armoire. Satisfying myself that no menaces lurked among the garments, I approached the mirror for a closer look.

It was not the moonlight, however, but an effect produced by its reflecting a foggy daytime beach, against which my own reflection was but a pale ghost. A young Annie, as first I had known her, stood before one of our sand castles. What I had heard now seemed to have been a call from her, for the ghostly echo of a plaintive "Edgar!" hung suddenly in memory's dim vault.

"Annie!" I said. "I'm here!"

But she paid me no heed. I continued to peer, but I could think of no way to make her aware of my presence. Then, through the fog which lay heavy upon the beach to her right, I saw a figure approaching, the form of a man moving slowly, unsteadily, toward her.

As I watched, she turned in that direction. Even before be came into view, I knew that it would be Poe. But I had not anticipated his appearance. He had on a thin, ill-fitting shirt and outsize trousers. He staggered and swayed, leaning heavily upon a Malacca cane. His face looked far older than my own now, muscles slack, eyes unfocussed, so that at first I thought him intoxicated. Closer scrutiny, however, changed my opinion. The man was obviously ill, his mien one of fever and delirium rather than inebriation. Annie rushed to meet him, but he moved as if unaware of her presence. When she caught hold of his hand he collapsed suddenly to his left knee, a wild sweep of his cane toppling several towers and piercing a wall of the castle. For an instant, he regarded their fall. Then his eyes met Annie's. She rushed to embrace him, but a moment later he was struggling to rise. Footing regained, he continued on his way, heading, it seemed, directly toward me. Annie followed, and though her mouth opened and closed several times, I could hear nothing that she uttered. He drew nearer, nearer. He seemed to be staring into my eyes. I felt his gaze. . . .

A moment later his body emerged from the wall, his face from the mirror, and he continued his advance without any sign of distraction from the transition. His gaze moved beyond me.

"Edgar!" I called. "Poe! Old friend! Hold up! Stop and rest. We want to help you."

He halted, he turned, he stared.

"Demon!" he said. "Doppelganger! Why have you haunted me down all these years?"

"I'm not a demon," I said. "I'm your friend—Perry. Annie and I want to help—"

He moaned, turned away and began walking again. I took a step toward him, just as he reached the patch of moonlight. It passed through him as if he were made of tinted glass. He raised his hand, staring at it, staring through it.

"Dead—and gone ghostly," he said. "I am already spirit."

"No," I responded. "I don't think so. I've an idea. Let me fetch Ligeia and—"

"Dead," he repeated, ignoring me. "But how can a spirit feel as I do? I am ill."

I took another step toward him.

"Let me try—" I began.

But he let his hand fall and went out like a snuffed candle.

"Poe!" I cried.

Nothing. I turned back to the mirror and it was dark now.

"Poe. . . ."

In the morning I wondered how much of the night's drama had been dream. Then I noticed my right hand still held the saber. I went and looked in the mirror and all I saw was my own curious expression. I wondered whether this was the mirror Ellison had used in some of his alchemical experiments; and, if so, whether such usage made it more readily available to whatever forces had been at play.

Later, during the day's regular session with Valdemar, I asked him how the bond 'twixt Annie, Poe, and I now stood.

"The same, the same as ever," he replied.

"Then I do not understand," I said. "Now the experiences are unlike any others I have known. Something must have happened."

"Yes," he answered. "But the bond remains the same. It is the character of the experience that has changed."

"So, what's causing it?"

"Annie is trapped in a cage of narcotics and mesmerism. They warp her perceptions, distort her sendings."

"How can I help her?"

"Too many probabilities come together in her presence," he said, "for me to see a single course of action as best."

"In effect, she is calling for help and there is no way we can help her?"

"Not at this time."

I turned away, grinding my teeth together, biting off an oath.

"Then there is nothing I should do?" I snapped.

"I cannot make a moral judgment on your behalf."

"Damn it! I just want to know how to help her!"

"Then you must protect yourself. You must be alive and unmaimed when the opportunity occurs to effect her deliverance."

"The opportunity *will* occur?"

"It is possible."

"Where and when will it be most possible?"

"I cannot say."

"Damn," I said. "Damn! Can't you tell me *anything* that might be useful to me?"

"Yes," he said, at length. "When things grow truly horrifying, not everything may be real."

"You've lost me," I said. "I do not understand."

"Even now," he responded, "Templeton and Griswold are seeking the means for turning Annie into a weapon."

"Annie? A weapon?"

"Yes. If she can move people from one world to another—she may be able—to do other things— to them—as well."

"Such as?"

"I do not know—yet. But whatever—may come of it—remember that you can tolerate—more poison or animal magnetism—than anyone—on this— planet. . . . Please! let me go."

I made the gesture myself, returning him to his doom.

After this pessimistic revelation I grew concerned

as to Valdemar's continuing value in this venture. If Annie's entranced condition canceled his second sight when it came to herself, what did I need him for? She was the only reason I'd agreed to head this odd odyssey.

I spoke of the situation with Peters during a card game that evening. We'd gotten in the habit of passing a little time in this fashion each night, during which I had confided my story as well as what ailed poor Valdemar.

As we talked, Emerson moved around the cabin considerably. At times, he came to rest somewhere behind my right shoulder. Sometimes, on those occasions, I would catch sight of peculiar gestures on his part. Generally, Peters would win that particular hand. Apart from the fact that each had rescued me from a dangerous situation, I could hardly accuse them of cheating because it felt stupid even to suggest that the ape possessed that sort of intelligence let alone the will to use it in such a fashion. Still, I took to placing my cards face down on the table before me whenever Emerson passed to the rear, and of discoursing at some length on my history or whatever was troubling me most. Peters did not seem unaware of my ploy and its precipitating action, but appeared vastly amused by the state of affairs and the unspoken assumptions each obtained, as well as genuinely interested in my story and my present dilemma.

That night when Emerson did his little dance at my back I put my cards aside and told Peter what Valdemar had said about Annie having become unpredictable.

"Ha!" he said. "So you take Kain-tuck windage."

"Beg pardon?"

"If the wind's blowin' from yer left, you aim a little to the left and let her carry yer shot over where you want her to go."

"Meaning?"

"Yer askin' the dead fella the wrong questions," he told me. "Ask 'bout other things likely t'involve the lady. Let the wind carry yer questions where you really want 'em."

Emerson wandered off about then, and when we ended our game—was it at about six bells?—we were fairly even in our winnings. On the other hand, I felt ahead for his advice, as the next morning I'd some fresh questions for Valdemar.

The tapers flickered, the currents flowed. . . .

"I hate to keep bothering you," I said, when Valdemar had finished with his moaning, "but can you tell me where the inventor Von Kempelen is right now?"

"Paris," he replied.

"Could you be more specific?"

"No," he said. "This information is blocked from my regard."

"Why? How?" I asked.

"Griswold has anticipated your line of inquiry," he answered. "Templeton has directed Annie to block my sight in this area."

"Already?" I said. "The man plans well ahead. I wonder whether there might be some more physical means of obtaining this information?"

"Mr. Ellison maintains a number of agents in Paris . . ."

"Yes, I've a list of them."

"They keep a watch over the Paris harbor and will recognize the *Eidolon* when it docks. The watcher will be in touch at that time."

"I am not sure we can make it past Le Havre," I said. "A ship this size may draw too much water to make it up the Seine as far as Paris. We may have to go by coach from Le—"

"It will make it," he said, "and when the agent gets in touch you must ask to be introduced to one particular agent—a Monsieur Dupin. This man will find Von Kempelen for you."

"And Griswold will come to Von Kempelen, and we can follow him back to Annie."

"Presumably. As I said, her presence clouds my view of outcomes."

"Close enough," I said, "for Kentucky windage. Thank you, sir," and I let him return to his rest.

Later, from within the hidden safe, I unearthed a list of Ellison's French agents. There was indeed a Dupin, a Cesar Auguste Dupin, entered there. His address was given as 33 Rue Dunot, Fauborg St. Germain, and beneath it was entered, "Completely reliable; first-class mind; poet, though, and other eccentricities."

Later, I checked with Captain Guy and he assured me that the *Eidolon* had made it to Paris before and would again. As I cut and parried my way through a saber drill I thought about Von Kempelen and his secret. I had to assume that Annie would locate him and Griswold reach him before I did. When I finally stood face to face with the man what would I say? Emerson came up beside me, aping my movements for a time. Would Griswold attempt to purchase Von Kempelen's secret? Or would he attempt coercion? Purchase, I guessed. Too much room for deception in detailing a complicated process—even if they made him perform it under scrutiny. No, I judged they would want the man's cooperation.

What do you offer a man who can make gold, anyway?

Tricky. The process might require expensive equipment, expensive ingredients for setup and operation. And even if this were not the case, Griswold might be able to offer him something else he wanted. As I toweled myself down following my exertions, I wondered concerning the efficacy of an appeal to the alchemist based on preserving the stability of the world gold market. For an ethical concept it seemed pretty abstract. I felt I might be better off trying to demonstrate Griswold's baseness. But even that. . . . Supposing Von Kempelen were somewhat base himself and not at all impressed by this argument?

As I drew on my shirt, I tried to imagine Seabright Ellison standing before me, considering the question. Without hesitation he smiled and reflected, "The secret dies with the man." I was not, however, about to kill anyone to preserve the price of gold. So what did that leave?

Back in my stateroom, I opened a hidden safe and considered the French letters of credit. It appeared I could put my hands on some very large sums of money should the need arise. While I did not like the possibility of Von Kempelen's turning the conflict between Griswold and my employer into a bidding situation, it might be simplest to try topping Griswold's offer. I resolved to try it, after doing my best to show the man up as a blackguard.

I strolled the deck feeling somewhat lighter of heart than earlier. At last I'd some information and something of a plan. The day was clear, brisk, bright, and dinner only a bell away.

Fair stood the wind for France. . . .

❖   ❖   ❖

The Seine flowed slowly, meandering in a generally southeast direction. And we ascended slowly, amid a great deal of other shipping. A small steam tug took us the last part of the way, under leaden November skies. The trees stood bare upon the banks. The water was gray. It was difficult to tell when the day began. I had stood upon the deck in darkness, watching the passing shadows, and the world brightened gradually about me but there was no real sunrise. There were bridges, windmills, passing carts. More and more buildings came into view—larger, closer together. . . .

"A few more hours, Master Eddie, and you can try out yer parlay voos," said Peters. I had not heard him come up beside me. I glanced about after his shadow but the simian was not in sight.

I shook my head.

"I'm afraid I lack the equipment in that area. You ever been here before?"

"A few times," he replied, "on errands for Mr. Ellison."

"You know the lingo?"

"Well, yes and no," he answered.

"What do you mean?"

"My pappy, like I said, was a *voyageur.* I picked up some when he was about—but the rest is *argot,* gutter French, from the folks I'd sometimes deal with. I can understand a bit, but I open my mouth around anyone respectable and he's gonna know there's somethin' untrustworthy about me."

"You mean he's going to *think* there's something untrustworthy."

"No, he's gonna *know* it."

"Oh."

He laughed then. So did I. But I wondered.

Later that morning, getting on toward noon, we reached the quay. The smells were a combination of spice and rot, and we heard the noise and witnessed the movements of the port before we had docked. I told Captain Guy that I would be taking Peters with me and heading into town as soon as we might disembark. He allowed that the formalities would not be overlong, suggesting, however, that we had time for a meal. So Peters and I headed for the saloon, taking a leisurely luncheon while the ship was herded to its anchorage and the port authorities dealt with.

Sometime after the gangways had fallen into place and the shouts of crewmen subsided, Captain Guy came to us.

"Edgar," he said. "Would you come with me, please? And bring Peters."

I was about to ask him what for when he caught my eye and brushed his lips with a fingertip. I nodded, got to my feet and followed him. Peters came along, and Emerson emerged from beneath a companionway and joined us.

Captain Guy conducted us to his cabin, where a small, slim lady of the dark-haired variety waited. She was attractive and tastefully, though not conspicuously, garbed. She rose from the captain's leather chair, smiling faintly, to acknowledge introductions.

"This is Miss Marie Roget," Captain Guy began, "one of Mr. Ellison's French agents. She was waiting for us upon our arrival."

I immediately wondered how Seabright could have gotten a message to her in advance of our arrival. But she explained, even before I asked, that an agent at Le Havre automatically passed word to Paris when one of Seabright's vessels was headed this way. Seeing that this was his personal yacht it was decided that someone had better be on hand to help deal with any problems.

Emerson seemed to have taken a fancy to her and she patted him several times as she spoke, as if he were a large dog. This seemed to please him in the extreme, and he cavorted about the cabin till Peters growled something at him which resulted in his immediate retirement beneath the table.

" . . . So, if there is anything I can help you with," she said, "just ask."

"All right," I said. "I will. We are following the inventor Von Kempelen. Or rather, we are following someone who is following Von Kempelen. I suppose it comes to the same thing—"

"The man has been seen in Paris," she interrupted. "He enjoys the reputation of being worth watching, here on the Continent. So we should be able to give you some assistance. Pray, continue."

I told her of Annie and of the Unholy Trinity and of the possibility of alchemical gold. I did not tell her anything of my own origin or of anything—such as Valdemar—not material to the problems at hand. "And so," I concluded, "we were about to go in search of Monsieur Dupin when you arrived."

She nodded.

"A good choice," she said. "I have worked with the man and can vouch for his brilliance and his integrity. And while I have not yet spoken with him on the matter, he may well know more about the Von Kempelen affair than I do. Shall I take you to him?"

"He is still at 33, Rue Dunot? I inquired.

"Indeed," she replied.

"How soon might we see him?"

"It is likely he would be there now. The

seriousness of the situation suggests we dispense with formalities."

"Then let us visit him immediately," I said.

"Very well," she answered. "If he does not have the information we seek he will obtain it quickly. The man's reasoning abilities are legendary."

We started for the door and Captain Guy pointed out that Emerson was immediately behind us, having removed himself from beneath the table and approached in total silence. It was decided that he might make a rather conspicuous companion, and so Peters ordered him to remain a guest of the captain's. Then with a shrug of his wig and a hitch of his trousers, he was out the door and we were on our way.

Down the gangway and onto the pier we proceeded, past dock laborers and crates of goods, making our way up to an avenue which led us past taverns, shops of cheap goods, and an occasional streetwalker.

"Finding a carriage hereabout is an uncertain matter," Marie announced. "We must go a bit farther. Then it will become easy."

I nodded, fascinated by the gracefulness of Peters' movements, though they were still governed by the rolling gait the sea had taught him. "I hope that I can persuade you," I told her, "to act as our interpreter full-time. Whatever extra cost this might involve, you're certainly welcome to it."

"I see no problem, Monsieur Perry," she replied.

"Make it 'Edgar,'" I said.

"'Edgar,'" she repeated, accenting the second syllable. "Very well. Turn here—Edgar."

We turned onto a side-street, down which a carriage was slowly jouncing. A ragman, soiled bag over his shoulder, was picking through some trash in a doorway. From far ahead, I heard voices raised in a tuneless work song, heavy on the beat. There were deep puddles in the street and the usual random heaps of horse manure, as pungent here as back home.

At the corner we turned left upon a broader thoroughfare. Here, considerable carriage and cart traffic hurried past, as well as horseback riders and pedestrians.

"Along this way we should find transportation," Marie remarked.

Five minutes later we were passing a flower seller's stall, a number of people gossiping or staring before the racks of dried arrangements. Just as we went by an elderly man stepped toward us from beyond the next stall—where cheap scarves were being sold—and the moment his eyes fixed upon mine, a bright glint of lunacy within them, I knew that all was not quite well. He was poorly dressed, save for an expensive ring on his left hand, and in that instant I realized it was not the hand of an old man. A quick step and he was at my side, right hand emerging from behind his hip, a flash of steel within it.

I moved forward as he struck, blocking the thrust with my forearm. I punched toward his midsection, and though he blocked it his breath was expelled and he jerked as if my blow had landed. It was several moments before I realized that Peters had delivered a kidney punch at that instant. By then the man had lurched past me and commenced running, his blade fallen at my feet. I turned as if to give pursuit but Marie's hand fell upon my arm.

"'E is but a common thug," she said. "I have seen

him about. There is no need to pursue. We will know his employer by this evening."

The man had already disappeared into a space between two buildings. I shrugged and kicked the knife. It slid about eight feet. Grinning, Peters gave it another kick and it bounced along, coming to rest six or so feet ahead of him. When next we came to it I kicked it, and so on until we found a carriage.

As we rode along she gave me a quick lesson on the town's disposition and taught me my first words of French. We rattled on for some time through the Fauborg St. Germain. The skies spat a few drops of rain upon and about us for perhaps two minutes then desisted. Occasional wraiths of fog hovered at the feet of hills and among trees.

At length we found ourselves traversing the Rue Dunot. The carriage slowed as we neared a grotesque and time-eaten mansion. Its crumbling eminence caused me to construct visions of the impoverished nobility when I saw its number to be the one we sought.

"*C'est le maison de Monsieur Dupin?*" I said proudly.

"La *maison*," she said.

"But that's the place all right?"

"Indeed."

She paid the driver and we descended. As the carriage rattled away we approached the doorstep, where Marie drew upon the bell-pull. Shortly thereafter the door was opened by an elegant young man—both in appearance and dress—who was obviously not a servant. He and Marie exchanged rapid-fire French for several minutes before he shifted his attention to Peters and myself.

"I am sorry," he said in an unusually rich tenor,

"but the information could not wait. You are looking for Von Kempelen." It was a statement, not a question. "Please come in."

He stepped aside and held the door for us. We entered, and he closed it behind us. "Come this way."

The place was musty and filled with shadows. The floor creaked beneath our feet. He led us down a corridor past dim rooms filled with ancient furniture. At length, we came to a study, somewhat better illuminated but as venerably furnished as the chambers we had passed. Within, a goblinesque voice shouted an amazing litany of obscenities as we entered.

"The same to you, mate!" Peters retorted, turning quickly to seek the source of the challenge.

"Grip, be still!" Dupin ordered. "Attend now! Repeat! The flames in Spain burn heretics amain!"

"Rawk!" said what I then saw to be a raven perched on a shelf above the door. It followed this with the sounds of champagne bottles being uncorked.

"Nevermore, Grip. Nevermore," Dupin persisted.

"Rawk," repeated the bird, followed by obscenities I had heard but seldom for all my years in the Army, save from the lips of an Arkansas mule driver who had complained earlier that day on the recurrence of a vicious rectal itch.

"Nevermore," said Dupin.

"Je m'en fiche," said the raven.

Our host swept past us, saw us seated in attractive and uncomfortable chairs of a gold and rose floral pattern, then offered us sherry.

"I write a bit of poetry," he confessed, "and it amuses me, teaching a few aphorisms to the bird. However, his previous owners were less than careful when it came to influences."

I refrained from inquiring concerning Grip's former residence.

"But he was an experienced speaker and a bargain, to boot," he finished. "Now, concerning Von Kempelen, his whereabouts are known to me. I make it a point to keep posted on the location of eminent visitors. Your problem as I understand it, however, entails more than simply finding the man."

"True," I replied. "The man is reputed to have developed a process whereby he can transmute baser metals to gold."

Dupin smiled.

"So I understand," he observed. "Many have made such claims, down the centuries."

"As I understand it, Von Kempelen is rather reticent concerning the process. Be that as it may, he is being followed by three men who wish to obtain the secret from him."

"By fair means or foul?"

"Fair, I'd judge. A process so complicated is not easily taken against a person's will. I believe they'd be willing to strike a genuine deal with him."

"What is the problem you seek to solve?" he asked.

I took a sip of the sherry.

"My problem is not the same as my employer's," I told him. "Seabright Ellison wishes to prevent such a deal because the appearance of large quantities of alchemical gold on the world market could damage his own position in that area, where he is strongly represented."

"Indeed," Dupin observed, "more than our employer might be injured by the injudicious release of great masses of precious metal. Look what the gold of Mexico and Peru did to Spain. Her present troubles—from the Inquisition through this hit or

miss war—may all owe something to the effects of
its superabundance on the economy of an earlier day.
How far is Mr. Ellison prepared to go in foiling this
transaction?"

"Pretty far," I said, recalling his hint that Griswold,
Templeton, and Goodfellow's relocation underground
would earn me a bonus.

"Might he be willing to outbid the others for the
secret?"

Thinking of the massive sums commanded by my
letters of credit, I nodded.

"I have been given considerable discretion in
this area," I said, "and the funds with which I might
attempt such a thing. What do you think?"

"I do know that Von Kempelen has met on
several occasions now with a trio of foreigners—most
likely American. So I would guess that they are talking business. On the other hand, I daresay he is suspicious of them—as he must be of anyone, under the
circumstances."

"I suppose so."

"There may be a way to capitalize on this . . ." he
mused. "But tell me, what did you mean when you said
that your problem is not the same as your employer's?"

"He wants to stop the deal because he's interested
in protecting his financial interests. My interest is in
the lady Griswold has kidnapped and still holds prisoner. She possesses psychic abilities and he used her
to track Von Kempelen here. He has other, darker
plans for her."

"Ah! There is a woman involved!" He leaned forward and squeezed my forearm. "I understand."

"Partly, I'd imagine," I replied. "But I would be
very surprised if even a Frenchman could unravel this
particular relationship too readily."

"You have roused my curiosity to the utmost," he said. "Pray, tell me of it."

So I did. Forgetting myself, I drank four of the tiny glasses of sherry as I spoke. In that I did not stagger off with delirium tremens, the performance may have helped to convince him I was telling the truth.

"Yes," he said, nodding, "it seems a relatively simple matter to one who is familiar with the German philosophers, particularly Leibnitz. The notion of a multiplicity of existences—"

"Dreck! Dreck!" cried Grip, flying down from his shelf and lighting upon Dupin's left shoulder. "Guvna! Scheiss! Mierda!"

"Hush, Grip!" Dupin ordered. "Alternate levels of reality do, as I was saying, become comprehensible when one considers the projective geometries of Desargues in light of Gauss's unfinished work on a calculus of probabilities—"

Marie Roget cleared her throat and rose to her feet.

"Excuse me," she said, "but I thought you had further instructions for me. If not, I must look into the matter of the assassination attempt on Mr. Perry."

"Yes, I was about to suggest some lines of inquiry."

She said something in French and Dupin rose to his feet. He glanced at Peters and myself, said, "Excuse me, gentlemen. I must see the lady to the door," and departed with her, speaking in French as they went.

"You understand what he was sayin', boss?" Peters asked. "'Bout them German philosophers and all?"

I shrugged.

"It seemed he was headed in a highly theoretical direction."

"Let's try changin' the subject on him when he comes back. That bird's got the right idea."

When Dupin returned several minutes later, Grip having transferred himself to his right shoulder, he cast his gaze from me to Peters and back again, then asked, "Where was I?"

"Concerning the matter of Von Kempelen . . ." I suggested.

"Oh yes," he said, "the creator of the so-called chess-playing automaton. A fraud, of course, as no machine can be made to play chess, it being a creative rather than a mechanical process."

"I suppose," I said.

"Furthermore, if one could build such a device," he went on, "it must inevitably win every game. The principle being discovered by which a machine can be made to play a game of chess, an extension of the same principle would enable it to win a game. A further extension would enable it to win all games—"

"Uh," I interjected, "it was his alchemical discoveries with which we were mainly concerned."

"Of course. Forgive me," he agreed. "A fascinating subject, alchemy. I—"

"How do you think we might get into his good graces to the point where he'd even be willing to acknowledge the existence of the process?"

"Hm. Several possibilities occur," he observed. "Generally, the simplest deception is the easiest to achieve and maintain. A moment. . . . I have it. You are two visiting Americans who happened to recognize him on the street. You present yourselves as such at his apartment, expressing a desire to meet the inventor of the chess-playing automaton. To gain access, you might even offer to bet him a large sum of money that one of you can beat the automaton. No need to worry on this account, for even if the game is begun it will never be completed."

"Why not?" I asked.

"You arrive at his apartment at eight o'clock this evening. Before then I will have spoken with Henry-Joseph Gisquet, our Prefect of Police, who owes me several favors. He will see that the neighborhood is unpoliced at that hour and he will provide me with several footpads who owe him favors. I will cause these men to break in at nine o'clock, as if intent on theft and violence. You and your companion will grapple with them and they will flee. This should serve to ingratiate you with Von Kempelen to the extent where he would welcome your company for purposes of protection. Continue your supposed fascination with his work and become friendly with him. After a day or so, introduce the subject. Impugn Griswold and Company if necessary, and offer to outbid them."

I glanced at Peters, who was nodding.

"Not bad," he said, "on short notice—and I've a feelin' we should be movin' fast."

"In the meantime," Dupin continued, "there is a Minister Dupin—odd coincidence, eh?—though the resemblance stops with the name; the man is a dreadful *poseur*—who may know whether Von Kempelen has actually made overtures to bail our government out of its latest crisis with buckets of gold. I may be able to learn what, if anything, the minister knows of the matter—which could cast illumination on your own prospects."

"We'd be very grateful for the effort."

He waved a hand, causing Grip to raise his wings and hiss.

"Save the gratitude for favors," he said. "I will have to prepare a bill for extraordinary services on this one.

"By the way, is there any possibility I might draw some of it on account today?" he added.

"Surely," I said. "I was planning to stop by one of the banking houses this afternoon, as I might be needing some extra cash myself. If you'll provide me with Von Kempelen's address—perhaps sketch me a map—and let me know how much you'll need, I'll be on my way."

He repaired to a small writing table where he scribbled and drew these items.

"If you're planning on returning to the *Eidolon* when you've finished in town," he said, "I'll be in touch with you there, to let you know that things are ready for this evening—and to pick up my advance."

"Excellent," I said, as he saw us to the door. "We'll be back aboard ship in a few hours. Thank you again."

"No problem," he replied. "By the way, might I have the loan of twenty francs till then?"

"Of course," I said, removing a note from one of the rolls of bills I had found in Ellison's safe and passing it to him.

"Pay you later," he said.

"Nevermore," said the raven, as the door closed behind us.

That evening, dressed warmly against a chilly wind, Peters and I set out to find Von Kempelen's place. In that Peters was unwilling to do without Emerson's skills in the event of an emergency, the ape followed us along the way. The people of the city were generally unaware of his passage over their rooftops in the darkness. The dogs of Paris did, however, take notice. Their barks and howls followed us from street to street.

Peters whistled as we walked along, at one point laughing maniacally when the dogs broke into a particularly wild cacophony, causing a woman who passed us just then to cross herself and hurry away.

At length, we found ourselves in the proper neighborhood, and there was indeed a light burning behind the top floor window which seemed to belong to the apartment we sought, a building bearing the legend Porte D'Eau.

"You think he'd do himself better'n a bloody garret," Peters muttered, "bein' worth a fortune an' all."

"He's trying to be inconspicuous," I said.

"He could do it at ground level," he growled.

Firing a quick phrase of his gutter French at the concierge who answered his pounding, Peters had us admitted by a frightened-looking man who stared out to where a ring of dogs had formed at our back in the street.

"*Porquoi les chiens aboient-ils?*" he asked.

"*Je suis loup-garou,*" Peters replied. "*Je veux Von Kempelen.*"

The man stared, then Peters laughed his crazy laugh again. Smiling weakly, the concierge got out of our way.

"*Trois?*" Peters asked.

"*Oui.*"

"*Merci,*" I said, not to be outdone, and we mounted the stair.

All the way up to the top we went, then knocked upon his door. There was no answer. We waited a few moments then tried again.

The third time I called out as I knocked, "Von

Kempelen! It's important, and I think you'd be interested. It would certainly be worth your while."

The door opened a crack and a large blue eye regarded us.

"*Ja?*" asked its owner.

"We're Americans," I said, "and I believe you are the creator of the famous chess-playing automaton."

"And so?" he said. "If I am, what then?"

I produced a wad of Yankee dollars—again, courtesy of Ellison's safe—and waved them at him.

"I'm a representative of the Baltimore Chess Club," I said. "I'd like to bet you a thousand dollars I can beat that machine of yours."

The door opened further, so that we beheld a short, stout man with sandy hair and whiskers, wide mouth, Roman nose, and large, protuberant eyes, of a sort I had once been told were associated with a peculiar glandular condition. Half of his face was lathered, and I saw that he held a straight razor in his hand.

"Gentlemen, I am sorry," he said, "but the machine is not properly set up at this time."

"Dear me," I responded. "It meant so much to the entire club that one of us get to try it. How long would it take to set it up? Do you think if I were to come up with more money—"

Suddenly, he opened the door wide, apparently having made some decision concerning us.

"Come in, come in," he said, and we did. He gestured toward a battered pair of chairs across the room. "Sit down. I am making some tea. You may join me, if you wish."

"Thanks," I said, moving that way as he lay the razor beside a basin on his dresser, picked up a towel and wiped the soap from his face, watching us the while in a cracked mirror as we passed behind him to the chairs. A pot of water was coming to a boil upon a small spirit-heater on a crate to our left. There were numerous crates stacked about the room, some of them opened and exhibiting odd pieces of chemical or alchemical equipment. Some of it had been unpacked and was set up upon a bench which ran the length of the far wall. Some pieces were installed beneath the bench.

Outside, the dogs continued their chorus.

Von Kempelen located three mismatched cups within one of the crates, wiped them out with the towel he had used upon his face and proceeded to prepare tea.

"It would take several days' preparation," he said, "to assemble the automaton and get it ready for a game—if I had nothing better to do. But I am expecting a request to engage in some delicate work soon, of a fairly complicated nature. I fear that I simply will not have the time to give you your match, as much as I would enjoy taking your money. Do you take sugar? Or perhaps a little cream?"

"Sugar," I said.

"Neat," said Peters.

He brought us two steaming cups, seated himself across from us with a third.

"I'm afraid I can't do any better than that," he finished.

"I understand," I said. "My fellow clubmen will be disappointed, also. But your business certainly takes precedence over hobbies." I glanced at the equipment on the bench. "You're basically a chemist, aren't you?"

Those impressive eyes studied my face carefully.

"I do many things," he said, "chemistry among them. Right now I am waiting to hear on a possible contract which will occupy me for some time, should it be approved. I may not discuss it, however."

"Didn't mean to pry," I said, tasting the tea. "Perhaps I'll get to try the chess player another day."

"Perhaps so," he agreed. "When did you arrive in town?"

"Just this morning," I said.

"Surely you didn't cross the ocean just to seek me out and engage in an unusual game?"

I laughed.

"No, I came into some money recently," I said, "and I'd always wanted to tour the Continent. When I learned earlier that you were in town I decided to look you up and add pleasure to pleasure, so to speak."

"How interesting," he said. "So few people are aware of my presence here."

Griswold or some French bureaucrat? I wondered. Where should I claim having heard he was in town? Blame the French government, I decided. There's ample precedent for that in all areas. But the decision was taken from me as the rear window was shattered.

A burly form finished kicking in the frame then stepped into the room from the pitched edge of the adjacent building. Damn! The timing was way off. I'd wanted at least to broach the subject before the attack occurred.

Another figure, leaner but appropriately villainous in appearance entered behind the burly man. I could see that there was yet another behind him. I was pleased that they seemed perfectly suited to their roles.

Von Kempelen dropped his cup and retreated across the room to stand before his workbench, arms raised in defense of his equipment. Peters and I rose to our feet, and the burly man gave us a puzzled look.

I growled as I moved forward, but I couldn't even mutter the appropriate reprimands, as I doubted any of them spoke English. I feinted with my left toward the big man's face. He blocked it with his right and drove his left into my midsection. It was at that moment that the thought occurred to me that these might not be the men I had contracted for come early, but rather the real thing keeping their own schedule.

I turned and twisted, hoping to avoid the rabbit punch I felt sure would come next. It didn't, however, for Peters reached out and caught the man's fist as it descended. I heard the big fellow laugh and saw him try to pull back the arm. His expression became one of surprise as it failed to move. Then Peters jerked the arm downward and the man bent forward. Moving forward, he caught hold of the man's left ear with his teeth and twisted his head to the side, tearing half of the appendage away. The man screamed as his cheek and neck were incarnadined. Then Peters caught hold of the arm with his other hand as well and broke it across his thigh. While he was doing this, one of the others struck at his head with a club. I was unable to move to his assistance or even to shout a warning.

The blow landed and Peters reeled but did not go down. He turned toward the man with the club and the second man leaped upon his back. In the meantime, the man with the broken arm and half an ear drew a knife from a belt sheath with his right hand and lurched toward the grapplers.

Unable to raise myself erect I bent forward, clasped my knees and rolled against the man's legs.

He uttered a French oath I added to my collection as he fell upon me. Dazed, I expected to be punctured at any moment, but the thrust did not arrive. I sucked several deep breaths and tried to rise, just as the screaming began.

When I straightened and turned I saw Emerson stuffing the body of one of the men up the chimney. Peters was twisting the other man's arms into a pretzel-like shape and the man I had knocked over was rising to his feet, knife in his hand, half of his face wet and red, his other arm hanging useless. I heard heavy footsteps on the stair and a cry of "Gendarmerie!" just as bones began snapping in the man Peters was twisting and the other lunged at me. Even as I blocked his thrust and struck him on the point of the chin a heavy blow fell upon the door. Something was obviously wrong in our supposed deal with the police. As another blow fell upon the door Emerson left off stuffing his man up the chimney, bounded across the room, seized the straight razor Von Kempelen had left atop his dresser, departed by way of the window, and vanished across the rooftops.

"Not a bad idea, that," Peters observed, casting his man aside. To Von Kempelen: "Thanks for the tea." Then he passed through the window and scrabbled away himself.

I cast a glance back at the inventor, who still guarded his work. Another blow fell upon the door.

"Uh, good night," I said "Good luck."

He narrowed those amazing eyes uncertainly, then, just as I departed, "Be careful," he called.

I heard his door burst open before he got to it. The tiles were damp and slippery, and I kept my gaze on the shadowy figures ahead. After a time,

the roof grew flat. There were shouts far to the rear.
I hurried.

Below us the dogs still complained.

For how long we fled, I am uncertain. At length,
I followed Peters through a window into a deserted
top-floor apartment. Whether he or Emerson had
located it—and whether by chance or some arcane
instinct—I never inquired, though it seems we mis-
placed Emerson at about that time. We lay doggo for
several minutes then, listening after sounds of pursuit. None followed, so we let ourselves out, took the
stairs to the ground without incident, and entered
upon the street.

We wandered for a time then, but the night
remained still. Even the dogs had grown silent.
Shortly, Peters found us a cafe where we rested over
a glass of wine, assessing our injuries—which seemed
minor—and repairing our appearance. Miraculously
it seemed, he had retained his bear-hide wig withal.

It seemed futile to speculate as to why the Prefect of Police had not done as he was supposed to—
or hadn't done as he wasn't, as the case might be.
We decided to wait a good while and then drift back
to the neighborhood we had vacated so abruptly, to
see whether we might be able to learn anything there.
In the meantime, Peters bit off a great chaw of
tobacco from a plug he had with him, amazing me
with his ability to spit out of the door—a good distance from where we sat—whenever it opened—
without touching the person entering or departing.
I, in my turn, drank four local tipplers under the
table, it taking slightly less than two normal glasses
of wine for me to do it. Our performances caused
considerable merriment among the other patrons

during the couple of hours we spent in the establishment.

A clock somewhere chimed the hour for the third time since our arrival, and so we settled our bill and departed. The night had grown considerably more chill during our interlude indoors, and we turned up our collars and jammed our hands into our pockets before heading back to the scene of our earlier confrontation.

The building was entirely dark. We passed it several times and no one seemed to be about in the vicinity. Finally, I went up and tried the door. The lock had been broken. It opened easily. I motioned to Peters and we entered.

Moving slowly, treading carefully, we mounted the stair. When we came to the landing outside Von Kempelen's door we halted and listened for a long while. A total silence prevailed. After a time, I reached forward through the darkness and investigated manually. This lock, too, was broken and the door frame splintered.

I pushed the door open and waited. There was no reaction.

I entered. There was moonlight through the broken window to the rear. By this illumination we could see that the place was entirely empty. Not a stick of furniture, not a test tube, spoon, or teacup remained. Even the bench itself had been removed.

Peters whistled softly. "Most pecooliar," he said. "What do you make of it?"

"Nothing," I said. "It could mean too many things. We must see Dupin first thing in the morning. He may have some answers."

Peters spit out the window.

"May not, too," he said.

We hiked back to the ship where a hairy form greeted us from the rigging.

"*Bonjour,* damn it!" said the raven, who had perched himself upon the arm of my chair and was studying me as I drank a cup of tea.

"*Bonjour* yourself, bird or devil," I said.

"He seems to like you," Dupin observed. "You actually got him to say 'nevermore' the other day."

"Rawk! Nevertheless!" Grip cried, spreading his wings and cocking his head.

"Concerning the matter of the letter," I prompted.

"Yes," he replied, smiling. "By means of a ruse involving a gold snuff box I was able to gain access to the minister's letter rack. It contained a number of delightfully incriminating items. But to the case in point, Von Kempelen had proposed selling his secret to the government, and there was indication in the form of a note in the minister's own hand, following the text, that the price was too high but that a robbery might be staged to obtain the man's notes. It was also suggested they act quickly, since others were interested and might come up with the price. This note was initialed by another minister and yesterday's date, the thirty-first, was written beside it."

"The government would do a thing like that?" I exclaimed.

He cocked an eyebrow at me and took a drink of tea.

"And the timely arrival of the police?" I said. "That was just a part of it? Your government now has Von Kempelen and his secret?"

"Not at all," he replied. "I was able to get word of this affair to Monsieur Gisquet, our Police

Prefect, who has long been on less than cordial terms with my namesake minister. Barely in time, as it turned out—and there was no time at all to get a message to you, though I understand you acquitted yourselves admirably. The body up the chimney remains a bizarre puzzle, however." Here, he raised his hand as I attempted to speak "No, I don't want to hear about it."

"Actually, I wasn't about to tell you," I said. "I was merely going to ask who, then, has Von Kempelen?"

"Actually nobody *has* him," he replied. "He and all his equipment are, at this moment, headed for the border. Gisquet's men packed his equipment and his personal belongings while an agent of the man explained the situation to Von Kempelen."

"All of this to spite a government official," I said. "Were you the agent?"

He smiled again. "I wouldn't tell you if I were."

"I know. I did not ask for informational purposes."

"We understand each other," he said.

He refilled our cups. I took a satisfying sip of the scalding brew.

"Which border?" I asked then.

"He is headed for Spain—Toledo," he said. "Though whether this is his actual destination or possibly a clever ruse to confuse pursuit, I could not say. Again, it was one of those matters I did not really wish to know. But as to the literal meaning of your question, I do not know whether he will be crossing the border at the independent Duchy of Aragon or that of Navarre on his way south."

"I understand," I said. "Thank you."

He cleared his throat.

"The reason I referred to it as 'possibly a clever

ruse' is because the man is playing a somewhat dangerous game. I should not spend too much sympathy on him should he meet with misfortune at some point along the way."

"What do you mean?"

"I said that that letter rack contained other incriminating items. . . ."

"Yes?"

"One of them even pertained to this affair. It was a summary of intelligence reports from agents in various capitals, indicating that Von Kempelen has made the same offer to a great number of people in different places—such as Italy, England, Spain, Navarre, Aragon, the Netherlands, even the Vatican."

"Goodness! All of them to the government, or rulers?"

"All of those I mentioned, yes. Among private individuals, a Rufus Griswold is on the list—as is Seabright Ellison."

"Really? This was not mentioned to me."

He shrugged.

"You may have passed the offer in transit. Whatever, it seems obvious from this that Von Kempelen is either incredibly naive or near-diabolical in his cleverness. To attempt to create a bidding situation among individuals and states such as these is to court abduction and torture or blackmail. Some of the individuals involved are totally ruthless and willfully treacherous. These are not the sort of men one seeks to play off against one another."

"And one such resides in Toledo?"

He nodded.

"Archbishop Fernandez. He'll wind up a Cardinal or an excommunicant—or a pile of ashes—one of these days."

"I keep forgetting the Inquisition is more than a page in history down that way."

"Is the Archbishop for it or agin it?" Peters asked. Dupin chuckled.

"He blows hot and cold on it," he explained. "Whichever'll help him to a red hat, I'd say. As the power shifts, so does he."

"You're sure Von Kempelen isn't really headed for Navarre or Aragon?" I asked. "You said they were involved."

Dupin shrugged and turned his hands palm up.

"I know only what he said—plus the fact that he sent a letter ahead to Toledo. Make of it what you would."

I sighed.

"Then it looks as if we're finished here," I said.

"In that case—" He withdrew an envelope from beneath his serviette. "—I would like to present my bill for extraordinary services at this time, since you are authorized to execute bank drafts and I may not see you again."

I accepted the envelope, opened it.

"There are two bills here," I observed.

"So there are," he responded.

I was just beginning to get a feeling for the monetary system, and I was taken totally aback by the extremely large amount of the second bill, for "unspecified services."

"This one," I said, shaking it, "to Madame Roget—I do not understand its significance."

"It is in the way of compensation to the lady," he said, "for the loss of her daughter. Marie Roget's body was found in the river, just a few hours ago."

"Oh," I said, and I asked for the use of his pen.

✧   ✧   ✧

Returning to the *Eidolon*, I decided it was time
to consult Monsieur Valdemar. Ligeia, however, had
gone ashore to make a few purchases. So I obtained
from Captain Guy a duplicate key to Valdemar's suite,
deciding to employ my own cumbersome mesmeric
abilities rather than wait. I invited Peters to join me,
but he begged off, pleading primitive superstition.
Actually, the reason I'd invited him was because my
own feelings on the matter were still not that far
removed from the same state and I'd wanted company. *Helas*! as they say in Paris.

I lit a few extra candles and raised the upper portion of the lid to the wine crate-cum-casket. Focussing my attention on the center of my body, I raised
the energy and let it flow to my hands. The candles
flickered. The armoire in the corner creaked. I made
the first pass and a series of rapping sounds occurred
within the wall to my left. I felt the energy extend,
pass into Valdemar. The chair in the corner of the
room lurched forward. There came the obligatory
moan, and seconds later his eyes opened.

Things did not stop there, however. Next, he sat up.

"Easy. Take it easy, Valdemar," I said.

"What have you done to me?" he asked.

"Just the usual," I replied, "to bring you within
reach of a few questions."

"Where is Ligeia?"

"I'm not certain, and I was in something of a hurry.
So I decided to go ahead on my own."

"Oh my! Oh my!" he announced. "I see now—what
has occurred."

"Tell me. Please."

"Her presence served to dampen somewhat—that
otherworldly energy of yours. Without her—it went
wild. I am animate once more—but still not living!"

He raised his hand slowly. One eye (the right) descended to regard it. The other remained blank.

"This is terrible," he observed, fixing me then with a baleful glare.

"I'll reverse the process in just a minute—as Ligeia taught me—if you'll answer a couple of questions. I haven't interfered with that ability, have I?"

"I still see as I saw," he said, bringing his hands slowly together.

"I think I should be heading for Toledo. Do you see anything in this regard?"

"I see us heading for Toledo, yes."

"That's all you see?"

"There is an intersection there with Annie. I can tell you nothing else."

"I'm inclined to take that as a good sign," I said.

He began rubbing his hands slowly. Then he raised them and felt his face.

"What can you tell me of Poe?" I asked.

"I do not understand the question. It is very general."

"Sorry. What is he doing right now?"

"'Now' is a meaningless term. Your worlds move on different time tracks."

"Projecting forward along his," I said, "from the time of our exchange, for the same period of time that I have spent here, what can you tell me concerning his situation in life and his state of mind?"

"I understand," he said, crossing his arms and feeling his shoulders. "He still does not realize what has occurred. He gives signs of doubting his own sanity. He would like to start a magazine of his own, but can find no one interested in funding it. He seems to be depressed."

"I would like to talk to Poe. Could you bring him here if I provided more mesmeric energy?"

"No. That is beyond me."

"Could you send me there?"

"No."

"What about Annie's kingdom by the sea? Could you arrange for us to meet there?"

"I don't think so, but let me— No."

"Could you just send him a message? I want to assure him that I am real, that Annie is real, that he is not mad."

"I might be able to, but I do not know what form it will take."

"Try."

He slumped suddenly and fell back, hands coming to rest upon his breast.

"It is done," he announced slowly.

"Was it successful?"

"Yes."

"Can you tell now what form it took?"

"No. Let me rest. . . ."

I reversed the pattern of my passes, withdrawing the energy I had extended. The rapping came again, in all of the walls as well as the ceiling. The chair slid toward me, then toppled to its side. Valdemar let out a particularly piteous moan, then his eyes closed and the casket slammed itself shut.

I extinguished the candles and went to make travel arrangements.

Edgar Allan Poe's sleep was troubled. He woke early and tried unsuccessfully to recollect what he had dreamt. Finally, he rose and dressed himself. The sky was just growing pale to the east, and he opened the front door and stepped outside to consider the dawning.

He beheld a miniature castle sparkling in the front yard. He moved toward it and it dissolved. There was only a heap of sand when he reached the spot it had occupied.

Some trick of the light perhaps. . . .

VI

She walked barefoot on the beach. It was a still, starless night. The sea itself glowed faintly, however, sufficient to provide what small illumination she required.

She walked in a circle, passing near the water and away from it. She could not remember why she did this, but she did remember that it was important. So she continued.

At one point a black cat hurried past her, at another a pit opened at the center of her circle. Flames leapt about it now, and a bright blade passed among them. She continued walking. Why was she doing this? It was important, that was why. Oh, yes.

A man lay prone beside the pit. Yes. He must be made to look into it. That's right. Easily done. Advance the flames. Yes. See him move?

She moved faster. And what does he behold? The horror. Of course. What he sees is—

She screamed and the sea rose up, reaching for the flames, the man, the pit—

She threw her hands wide and the fabric of space was torn. She stepped through the opening.

I opened my eyes to the steady jouncing of the coach, and the black cat stared back at me from the shadowy corner of the seat opposite. I watched it for perhaps ten seconds as my senses returned to me, and then I realized that I beheld Peters' wig which had slipped from his head as he dozed across the way.

I rubbed my eyes, sat up, and sought the water bottle. I drew the blanket upward from my lap to cover my chest as well. I took a drink, and then another.

We had been traveling in a series of hired coaches, pulled by relays of horses, for the better part of November. The Pyrenees had been awful and Navarre had been bleak. Just when I was beginning to obtain the rudiments of French I had to start all over again with Spanish. Peters again had the advantage of me, from times spent in Mexico, but as he explained, "It's all gutter Spanish, Eddie. No self-respecting *caballero* 'ud want to hear it in public— and believe me, they're all self-respecting.

"In public," he added.

Now I saw burnt fields, burnt houses, wooden crosses. The unmistakable ravages of war lay all about us. We had recently begun experiencing delays and other difficulties because of the conflict, but timely guidance from Valdemar and a good supply of gold coin kept us going. As a soldier, I was both fascinated and appalled. The Spanish had come up with a new word for the form of warfare by means of which they continued to resist the French—*guerrilla*. It involved hit and run skirmishing, ambushes, attacks behind the enemy lines. The Spaniards refused to stand and fight a pitched battle, and it was working against the French now as it had earlier in the century. It was costing the French too much. It was wearing them down.

I turned my gaze away from the depressing landscape. A little later the coach was suddenly jounced and our pace increased. I heard an annoyed "Rawk!" from among the overhead baggage and Grip fluttered down to pick at Peters' wig. The bird had apparently grown tired of Dupin's tutelage and fled from his house on the occasion of our last visit, appearing in the rigging of the *Eidolon* at quayside and greeting me with a cheerful *"Vingt francs pour la nuit, monsieur"* when I came topside following my interview with Valdemar.

Grip obviously wanted our attention because he did not approve of the driving. He always acted this way when Emerson seized the reins and drove the horses to a frenzied pace. The driver was loath to dispute matters with the simian, and what normally followed was that Ligeia was called upon to calm the horses mesmerically. Then Peters had to recover the reins from the ape and scold him a bit.

"Hey now, Grip! Give it back!" I heard him suddenly cry, and some sort of tussle ensued involving the hairpiece. This caused Ligeia to stir at my side and raise her head, taking a weight off my shoulder.

She yawned delicately and said, "Is he at it again?"

I nodded.

We were careening from side to side as well as bouncing when she stretched. Peters tickled the bird under his beak with one of his inhumanly thick fingers and composed his features into a frightful grimace which on anyone else would have been a slight smile.

"'At's a good Gripper," he said. "Let 'er go for Uncle Petey."

Grip saw fit to comply, and Peters immediately restored the wig to his pate, careless of the position it fell to occupy. Ligeia rose, leaning against the inside wall of the coach, parted the heavy drape on that side, hung out the window and gestured. Immediately, we began to slow.

"Might toss in a couple of heavy ones for Emerson," I muttered.

She winked back at me and leaned even farther. I caught hold of her about the waist. A half-minute later she signaled for me to help her return to her seat.

"My turn," Peters said, rising to his feet.

"Not necessary," she responded. "He has surrendered the reins to the driver."

"That ain't like him," Peters observed.

She shrugged.

"*L'ennui*, perhaps," she suggested.

"Oh, sure," Peters said, and he seated himself. After a time he began playing with Grip again. "Say 'Nevermore!'" he coaxed. "That's wot the gennleman in Paris wanted you to say. C'mon! Let's hear it!"

"Amontillado!" the sable creature screamed. And again: "Amontillado!" He finished with a burst of maniacal, almost-human laughter, followed by the sound of a cork being drawn from a bottle, this last was repeated many times in quick succession.

"I do believe that's a type of strong drink," Peters observed, squinting at me. "Ain't it?"

"Aye," I replied, my mind wandering ahead.

I wondered exactly what I was to do once we reached Toledo. Valdemar had given us no assurance that Von Kempelen was actually there—only that this was the right trail for me to follow to my ultimate goal of freeing Annie.

"Nevermore," Peters said softly.

"Amontillado," Grip insisted.

The day before we reached Toledo there came a rapping from overhead. In that Emerson lay curled at Peters' feet sleeping soundly (a frequent occurrence these days, with a little help from others), we assumed it was the driver signaling to us. Peters leaned out and hailed him on this account, but the man denied it.

The rapping came again, and Ligeia turned and studied me. "You have not been with the mesmerism making, have you?" she inquired.

"Me? No. Not in a long while," I responded.

"I feel something strange," she said then. Then she was calling out the window to the driver. We began to slow.

"What is it?" I asked.

"Most unusual," she said.

We came to a halt beneath a large tree. She ordered then that Valdemar's wine crate be unstrapped and lowered to the ground. Then she told the driver and his assistant to take a break, somewhere beyond the hill. Peters elected to join them. It was a strange sensation that overtook me then, because I heard the rapping again—from inside the crate.

"Open it," she instructed me.

I undid a final fastening and raised the upper portion of the lid. Both irises visible, Valdemar stared up at us.

"Worse and worse," he observed.

"What is it?" Ligeia asked.

"I come to you without being summoned. Could it be that the Life Force gains ascendancy?"

"I could not say," she answered. "Do you know why whatever brings you here has done so?"

His right hand moved, falling upon my own where I leaned on the edge of his casket. It took considerable effort of will for me not to draw away.

"You must part company with the others," he said, "before entering the city. If you do not, they will die in Toledo."

"What are we to do while he is within?" she asked.

"Turn and head east," he replied. "Query me again at sundown."

"I do not understand what I am supposed to do in Toledo," I stated.

"Neither do I," he said, his hand tightening on mine. "Something summons. You may answer it or not, as you choose. Your will is free."

"I must go," I said.

"I knew you would," he replied, and he slumped back, his hand sliding free of my own and falling back perfectly into place upon his breast.

Ligela motioned for me to close the casket, which I did. She took my arm and walked with me among a stand of saplings.

"I do not like this at all," she said. "It smacks of— interference. It may be a cosmic stroke of good fortune. It may be a trap. There is no way for me to tell in advance."

"What are we to do?"

"I wish to place you under control," she said, halting within the grove, "and to create a psychic bond."

"Remember what happened the last time you worked on me?"

"I have given it considerable thought since then," she told me. "This time you will not be evicted from your body."

"What will be the purpose of this—bond?"

"Hopefully, it will keep me apprised of your welfare," she explained.

"All right," I said.

I seated myself upon a gray log, my back against a boulder, at her direction. I remember the sweep of her hands past my eyes and a buzzing below my stomach. The plug of my mind was drawn and my thoughts drained away. . . .

How much later it was that I awoke I do not know. I felt very relaxed.

"Good," I heard her say. I opened my eyes, she smiled, extended her hands, and helped me to my feet.

"Did it work?" I asked as we walked back to the coach.

"I think so," she said. "We shall see."

The others were waiting when we got there, and we raised Valdemar and strapped him into place.

As we rode along, I wondered: Even if she became aware of some peril I faced, what would Ligeia be able to do about it, way off somewhere to the east? I studied Grip, who returned my gaze. He opened his beak several times, but said nothing.

Toledo stood on a hill, the Tagus river bent three-quarters of the way about it. It was situated some forty miles southwest of Madrid in an area not currently held by the French. Dark clouds hung above the city, and the ground was damp—as if we had just missed a storm. Our current coachman—older than most of the others—halted us outside the city walls, vowing he would only set foot or wheel within the place sometime between the freezing of hell and the Second Coming.

I took with me a goodly amount of gold, and a note Ligeia had written in Spanish indicating I wished to hire an interpreter. I had the name of a Padre Diaz Valdemar had assured us to be an honest and honorable man, and I had a rough map indicating the location of his church, Santo Tomé, and its rectory. Armed with these I bade my companions good-bye, tentatively planning to meet them in this same spot at this same time three days hence.

So I approached the fortress on the rock from its northern flank. I knew that the Romans, the Visigoths, and the Muslims had dwelled here. Ligeia had told me that its cathedral was a thing of exquisite beauty, dating back to the thirteenth century; and while I would have enjoyed viewing it under other conditions I heard Time's heavy tread, slightly faster than my own, somewhere in back of me.

I entered the city without being challenged. Apart from his non-physical insights, Valdemar was probably correct from a more practical point of view in suggesting that I separate from my escort of friends and allies outside the walls. Loyal and strong they might be, but they were also a somewhat odd assortment of people and creatures, and in time of war the political and religious arch-conservatives who ruled here were apt to be intolerant. As a wealthy American I could hope at least to be tolerated.

I did get a view of the cathedral, and of many little shops, and some fine residences, and some gilded coaches, and some dirty wagons, and some truly lovely horses, and some excellent examples of the damascened blades for which the city was famous. One of the most gorgeous was a dagger in the hand of the man who arrested me.

Four armed men of particularly uniform appearance approached me just as I succeeded in locating Santo Tomé. I had been wandering the streets for a couple of hours by then and was rather pleased to have located the church without assistance other than the map. In fact, I was still holding the thing in my hand when they came up to me and began saying graceful and incomprehensible things.

"No comprendo," I explained. *"Soy norteamericano."*

They said more things to each other, then one of them looked at my map, pointed to it, and pointed to the church.

"La iglesia?" he asked.

"Si," I replied. *"Santo Tomé. De donde es Padre Diaz?"*

They conferred again quickly, and when I heard Padre Diaz' name mentioned in close conjunction to another word I had committed to memory—that being "heretico"—I suspected I was in trouble. Nor was I incorrect. It was but moments later that I was given the opportunity to admire the gold and silver inlay of the dagger. There were several others in evidence, but the one belonging to Enrique—also referred to as "Jefe" by the others—was by far the most attractive.

"You—come—with—us," Jefe Enrique said to me.

"Soy norteamericano," I explained again.

"Si, norteamericano amigo de heretico," he said.

"No," I said. "I wanted help in finding an inventor named Von Kempelen. I was told that Father Diaz either spoke English or could find me an interpreter. See?"

I showed him the letter. He passed it to one of the others. The man glanced at it and handed it to the next man, who did the same. It occurred to me then that all four of them might be illiterate.

"*Por favor,*" I said. "*Interpreter, translator—para Ingles.*"

Jefe Enrique shrugged and gestured with his blade. "Come," he said.

Two of them flanked me, one walked behind, Jefe walked a bit ahead and to the right. I regretted not having learned the Spanish word for "misunderstanding" though I doubted it would really have done me much good. There was a certain air of dedication about them which did not seem to lend itself to debate.

And so I was taken to the local jail, my money and blade confiscated along with my letter and map. I was locked into a pitch-dark cell, presumably while it was considered whether I might be an accomplice of poor Padre Diaz. If they decided this to be the case, presumably I would be handed over to the Inquisition.

Extending my hands before me, I moved slowly, groping my way about the circuit of my confining walls, some of them stone and some rough iron. When I felt myself to be at the door once more I seated myself with my back to it and rested. I ate some bread and drank some water that I found there. I must have dozed then, for there seemed to be a break in my consciousness.

Upon awakening, I found myself sprawled prone, my right arm hanging downward. My cheek rested upon the floor of the prison, but my temple did not. A peculiar smell, as of decayed fungus, arose to my nostrils. I moved my arm about and came by degrees to realize that I had somehow come to rest at the very brink of a circular pit. I groped about until I located a loose piece of masonry which I managed to pry free. Letting it fall, I listened to its clinking against the edges of the chasm until at length it plunged into water. At that instant a door or panel was opened somewhere overhead and closed again. In the instant's illumination this afforded I was able to ascertain the good fortune which had permitted me to fall just as I had rather than a half-pace, say, farther ahead. It was a large circular pit, occupying the center of the cell. I withdrew immediately to the nearest wall, pressing myself firmly against it.

We seem to be entombed alive, Perry. It was almost as if Poe had spoken, as if he were seated beside me there in the dark, contemplating the abyss.

So it would seem, Poe. But it's only a jail. I've been in them before, I responded in thought.

Not like this one, Perry.

Embellishments, my dear Poe. Mere embellishments.

The pit calls to us.

Let it call. I'm not inclined to respond.

You're made of sterner stuff than myself, Perry.

Not so, Poe. We are the same—somehow. Circumstances have but provided—embellishments.

Perhaps it would be better to plunge into the thing and get it over with.

No thanks.

Everything ends in the abyss, anyhow.

No reason to rush things. Make it wait.

It does not know waiting. It is not sentient.

Then we are superior to it, for we are.

Sounds vaguely like something Pascal once said.

So it does.

Such philosophy from a man of action!

I'd a decent enough education, and I usually have a book about.

What's become of us?

We got switched.

I don't understand.

I don't know the precise mechanics of it, but we wound up in each other's world. It had to do with a misuse of Annie's power.

Silence. Three beats. Three more.

Then, *Or are we but a dream, Perry, in the mind of some demon? And is that demon myself?*

Against solipsism I have no arguments. Nobody ever succeeded as well as Hume in proving the unreality of the real. But as he himself said of Berkeley, such arguments admit of no answer and produce no conviction.

You are myself, my doppelganger, my dark other. We are opposing halves of the same spirit, to contradict so perfectly.

We're not that different, Poe. It's just the words that get in the way.

He chuckled.

More than ever I see this as unreal, he replied, *as a dialogue between the two spirits within me.*

What can I say?

Nothing, I suppose. Either that, or agree with me.

I will always maintain that it's better to have been than not to have been—even though it's only a feeling.

There came a clinking sound and a brief bit of light from the vicinity of the door, off to the left, just enough light to show that a tray bearing a piece of

bread and a small flask had been pushed into the cell
through a hinged opening at the door's bottom.

*I suppose it comes down to a choice between the
pit and the moldy bread,* Poe observed.

In that case, it's dinnertime.

I rose.

It's too bad you're not real, Perry, he reflected,
almost wistfully. *I could still like you.*

His presence being sort of metaphysical I did not
have to share, which was good. Shortly after I finished eating I was seized by an uncontrollable fit of
yawning. Fearful of being overtaken by slumber too
near the central fact of existence in this place, I lay
on my side with my back against the wall. I still felt
Poe's presence in some diffuse fashion about me.

When I awoke something was wrong. I'd no idea
how long I'd slept, but when I opened my eyes once
again there was illumination. A ghastly yellow and
red glow permitted me for the first time to see the
design of my prison. The place was differently shaped
than I'd thought on exploring it in the dark. It was
less square than I had deemed it to be and more in
the nature of a rectangle—the metal walls at its
farther ends, the stone ones at the nearer. Painted
upon these I could now discern pictures of fiends,
inverted crucifixions, dancing skeletons, people
being roasted and torn apart.

The floor was of stone, the great pit at its center—
which I could only discern with great difficulty. My
problem in this respect being my position as strapped
to some sort of framework. I lay upon my back atop
this structure, where I was held in place by what
seemed a single long strap. It was twisted about my
legs, my torso, my right arm and shoulder. My head
and my left arm were free and there was a plate of

food on the floor within reach. It was a somewhat spicy beef dish, and after the bread and water I had been given thus far it proved irresistible. I had the feeling I had been drugged the last couple of times I had eaten and drunk here. But what choice did I really have? I was hungry and thirsty. Sleep, for that matter—whatever its source—seemed a superior manner of passing the time in this place.

I groped then after the water bottle but could not locate it. It was then that I realized it to be the first real physical phase of my torment, for my thirst grew stronger by the moment.

Poe . . . ? I attempted, trying for my former mode of thought.

Perry, was there ever really an Annie? he seemed to say from somewhere.

Of course there was. There still is—

Demon! You lie!

No! Reach for her. Call to her.

Then he was gone, leaving me alone again with my thirst. I transferred my attention to the high ceiling, where I saw depicted Saturn devouring his children. In his one hand he held a pendulum, rather than the traditional scythe. After a moment, it seemed to me that this implement was quivering, performing minute movements. Then I was distracted, by a noise near to hand.

A rat—a beady-eyed little devil—had appeared on the rim of the pit, from which scratching sounds still emerged. He raised his nose and twitched it, whiskers moving in unison. Shortly, another, even larger specimen appeared at his rear. Still, the scratching continued and the first one vanished beneath my rack even as the second sniffed the air. Two more surmounted the rim of the pit as I watched. Then another. And another. By then the first one had located the plate which bore the remains of my most recent meal. I did not like having the beast so close to me—if for no other reason than some rumors of plague we had encountered on entering Spain—and I flipped my hand in its direction several times in an endeavor to frighten it. But it ignored this entirely and went on quite brazenly disposing of my scraps. A little later, however, the second one arrived and contested its right to the food. Soon they were locked together, biting at each other and uttering unsettling squeals as they tussled beside me. As their conflict continued two more mounted the plate and immediately had at each other.

I stopped waving my hand after a time, lest it be taken as a threat and attacked. By now the rodents were pouring out of the pit and swarming all about me, some of them even climbing my rack, running across me and using my body as a vantage from which to launch attacks upon their fellows below. I repressed my shudders as best I could, experiencing the while a deathly fear that if one were to take but a single bite of me the rest would suddenly consider me comestible and turn *en masse* to dining upon me. Fortunately, one of them slew another and they fell to contesting its remains. Several more rodenticides then occurred and the floor became a turbulent battleground and dining ground where gray and chittering forms swirled and rolled, rising and falling like some nightmare sea flecked with blood.

It was a long while before I tore my gaze from this, turning my head and looking upward once again. What I saw then caused my breath to catch within my throat. The pendulum no longer quivered but swept now from side to side covering a span of perhaps a yard. And it had descended. Its nether extremity glinted in the light in such a fashion as to indicate an extreme fineness of edge. The blade was perhaps a foot in length, slightly curved and dependant from a brass rod which emerged from Saturn's hand as he munched his offspring with the other and held several others beneath his feet. The entire contraption hissed and created a small breeze with each traversal of its course.

Now I was unable to remove my eyes from the thing. I counted ten passes before I saw it descend slightly. But another ten failed to see it lowered again. Several more, however, and it jerked downward again. I tried to visualize exactly where it would strike me should it continue inexorably on its course. It seemed targeted upon my heart. I wondered suddenly whether Ligeia knew what was happening to me. As with the spectral presence of Poe earlier, I tried communing with her.

Ligeia? Are you there? Can you hear me? Do you know where I am, and what is happening to me?

Nothing. Could it be that my focus upon the blade was too distracting of full concentration? Had the drugs dulled my mentality? Had she tried to exploit whatever bond she had created while I was unconscious, and given me up for dead?

Poe? Are you still about? I tried.

Horrors! he seemed to cry. *The abyss looks back at one!*

It was given you to fill as you would, I offered, expressing a sudden flash of insight. *You are an artist. Your imagination is the equal of its vacancy.*

Horrors! He repeated.

Where are you, Poe? Where are you?

His presence faded again. The pendulum jerked perceptibly downward, its arc lengthening slightly.

I forgot Poe then, and Ligeia. I even forgot the rats, so intently did my awareness seize upon the hissing edge which cleft the air above me. After a time—hours? days? I know not—I forgot even myself, becoming one with that glittering sweep of doom. I experienced a great calm, oceanic sensation during this period, an enormous sense of drifting peace.

At some point I lost consciousness.

Again, what space of time may have transpired, I do not know. I awoke to a dreadful, burning thirst. The rats went to and fro, squeaking of things below. Instantly, upon opening them, my eyes were caught again by the pendulum. It had descended considerably, its arc now traversing perhaps thirty feet, its singing, swishing note now an agonizing thing that cut the mind as it went, in anticipation of corporal contact.

It might be best to go unconscious again, I reflected, letting it write quietus with a single, cardiac stroke as I lay a-swooning. But now that I desired it, oblivion kept its distance. Alertness was all—alertness and anticipation.

Left, right . . . swish! From somewhere there came maniacal laughter, which I only gradually realized to be my own. I bit my lip until I tasted blood, and I closed my eyes. I opened them immediately, discovering it to be worse that way—not knowing where the blade was. But now my head seemed clearer and I forced myself to think.

I studied the pendulum rationally rather than permitting myself to be hypnotized by it. I counted my heartbeats between downward jogs of that blade.

Since I was at rest during this time my emotions remained relatively constant I assumed a uniformity to their progress. . . .

$$310 \ldots \text{jog.}$$
$$286 \ldots \text{jog.}$$
$$127 \ldots \text{jog.}$$
$$416 \ldots \text{jog.}$$

There was no pattern that I could detect. This was more interesting than any clock-like precision might have been. It told me that what I dealt with at the other end of the pendulum was a human operator rather than any mechanical device. I felt then my first small touch of hope. While the ironclad laws of mechanics might not be gainsaid there was a special order of predictability when it came to areas of existence ruled by human perversity.

I considered again the matter of my confinement. The strap which held me was in the nature of a surcingle—a single length of heavy material passed round and round me, many times. One slash through it—anywhere—by the destroying crescent and my entire wrapping would be loosened. A person capable of precision observation from a position such as mine—as well as a good head for calculation—might come up with an approximation of where its closest slash would fall before actual contact and whether to inhale or exhale. But I knew there was a human up there somewhere who delighted in inflicting pain. He was going to make this part last as long as he could.

It was no accident a surcingle held me either, I suddenly realized. Unless I did myself in by gasping at the wrong moment, the pendulum would sever my bond after the operator had had his fun. There would be time enough to roll from the rack to the floor. Such a roll could carry me right into the pit unless I were very careful. Somehow, I felt, what they really wanted was for me to choose the pit, to plunge into it of my own volition and perish below. All the rest was cake decoration.

So I kept my breathing slow and even and I waited.

Eight more passes of the pendulum and it was within inches of my breast. The next time by it had descended slightly. Four more, and it grazed my body as it went by. Now would come the toying with me, I guessed. It would remain at the same height or be raised slightly.

So I drew in a deep breath, gritted my teeth, and closed my eyes. There came a stinging sensation in my chest, and I flexed my arms, kicked with my legs, and rolled to the right. I was off of the rack then, falling. . . .

Dark bodies scurried, fleeing in all directions. The hissing sound ceased. I turned my head just in time to behold that damnable machine being drawn back upward into the ceiling. I massaged my aching limbs, attempting to remain alert to any new dangers.

It was only then that I realized the source of the hellish light which pervaded the place. It was leaking into the cell along the bottoms of the two metal walls—these being the one to my right (across the pit) and the one to my left. I could not make anything out through those slits, but even as I tried a suffocating odor entered my cell. It was in the nature of heated iron, and with it the ghastly pictures took on a certain fresh and wild character before their colors, in places, began to run. The walls jolted inward, taking on a richer hue of red than that

•

simple depiction of flame and blood. They began—
faintly, at first—to glow.

They moved again, they brightened again. I smelled
smoke and heard clanging and clashing sounds from
without. I rose to my feet, kicking off the remain-
der of the surcingle. I retreated a pace from the
advancing wall of heat. It would seem their greatest aim was still to force me to choose the pit.

The walls moved again. I retreated yet another
step. I moved along the pit's edge until I came to a
stone wall—the one which held the door. It seemed
the most logical place of retreat in the room.

And then, slowly, I turned. The pit had been calling to me, steadily, ever since I had discovered it.
Now I felt compelled at least to gaze into it, to
discover what it was that offered me such terror, such
spiritual destruction. I cast my vision downward. The
glare from the advancing walls shed further illumination now, and I forced myself to stare at the figures in the terrible tableau beneath my feet.

The short sidewhiskered man stood beside an
open coffin. He wore formal evening attire and also
had on black gloves and held in his hand a small
whip of the sort I had seen used in animal acts.
Somehow, I knew this man to be Rufus Griswold.
Before him—head hanging, hands tied—stood Poe.
Griswold gestured with the whip, indicating that Poe
should enter the coffin. Poe straightened and raised
his head, and then he became but an outline, a
blackness through which stars shone and comets
blazed; the wondrous majesty of the Milky Way
scaling the heights of infinity stood now before the
casket, and Griswold looked away and gnashed his
teeth.

Then the whip cracked and the figure was Poe

once again, and the walls advanced upon me but the greater part of horror lay below, where Griswold wished to destroy imagination, wonder, and the dark unknowns of the human spirit, placing them in a box, burying them in this pit forever.

The walls moved again. I was dripping with perspiration in the near-unbearable heat. The clanging continued, the smell of smoke was overpowering. I felt that I was about to pass out, and I pressed back against the stone wall.

"No!" I cried. "Don't do it, Poe! Damn you, Griswold!"

But neither seemed to hear me. I tottered upon the brink. From somewhere I heard voices. There came a crashing at the door beside me. A hairy hand seized hold of my shoulder. I fell swooning.

Any horror but this, I remember thinking.

When I awoke I lay in a cell. There was no pit in its center and its door stood ajar. Ligeia and Emerson were with me. Peters stood at the door.

"General Lasalle has taken the city?" I said, repeating what I thought I had just heard.

"That is correct," she answered.

"The bond you established. . . . It worked?"

She nodded.

"But everything that happened to me here—there's a dreamlike, drugged quality to it."

"Griswold has finally succeeded in using your Annie as a weapon against you," she told me. "He wanted her to destroy you, but she resisted Templeton's orders at the end."

"So our paths did cross here, in a way. In a place of illusions. What of Von Kempelen?"

"It was a ruse. Now that Annie is out of the picture,

Valdemar can see again. Von Kempelen actually fled
to the Duchy of Aragon."

"So we must backtrack."

"So it would seem."

I accompanied them out into the fallen city, heading north to where our coach would be waiting,
drinking water as I went.

Thus do I refute Berkeley.

She was the single artificer of the world in which
she sang. Builded of no mortal sand, and sea the
salt of her words, she passed through her kingdom,
itself become the self of her song. At his cave she
called forth the poet, unbound his hands, embraced
him.

"They would have me pluck my dark bird," she
said, "of the midnight flights."

Poe looked past her, at the turbulent sea. A cloud
covered the sun.

"Untrammeled be, and know I would not harm
you," she told him.

"Unreal," he said, and he turned away from her.

The space before him shattered like a wall of glass.

"Don't go," she said softly.

"Unreal."

He stepped through the crack in the kingdom, into
darkness.

VII

After the pneumonia had had its way with Elizabeth Poe and her head lay still upon the soiled pillow, long black hair framing her childish face, great, gray eyes finally closed, the tiny actress was dressed in her tawdry finery, the best of her paste jewels hung upon her.

They laid her to state in the milliner's attic, where the other members of Mr. Placide's company, along with Mrs. Phillips, Mrs. Allan, Mrs. Mackenzie, and their husbands—who had taken upon themselves the arrangements for the funeral—might come by and pay their respects.

Her resting place was to be close to the wall in St. John's Churchyard. There had been some protest from members of the vestry that an actress should be buried in consecrated ground, but Mr. Allan and Mr. Mackenzie, both members of the congregation, had prevailed. As it was, her grave was to remain unmarked for over a century.

And the gray-eyed boy who had been a pet of the company wondered. . . . How often had he seen his mother die and lie there like this, till it was time to come forward and take her bows? It was taking longer than usual this time. When would she come back to hold him?

It was a brisk December day in 1811. He was almost three years old. As Mrs. Allan's hired hack bore him away, along the cobbled streets of Richmond, he became aware at some point that his baby sister Rosalie was gone, also.

He was taken to the three-story Georgian brick house at the corner of Fourteenth Street and Tobacco Alley which was now to be his home. She did not come back for him. It was taking very long.

We came after considerable travel to the quiet duchy of Aragon. No signs of war here, as back in Spain proper. Some of Prospero's subjects spoke French, others Spanish, and still others English. The peace here was of a deathlike sort. If there had been foreign armies in this land recently, they had fled months ago. This domain was devastated not by war, but by disease. Traveling, we first heard rumors and then saw terrible evidence—funeral processions, chanting monks, deserted villages—of the presence of the Red Death, a variant of pneumonic plague.

We had entered a new year while working our way around a war zone. Valdemar, again, was invaluable in this respect. Another matter on which he'd advised us concerned Prince Prospero and his present situation. The prince had apparently removed himself from all human commerce only a few days before our arrival. Nor was it a simple sequestration. Rather, careless of what happened to the majority of his people, he had called to his side a thousand friends and companions. Determined to escape the Red Death, they—with a suitable staff of servants and a company or two of soldiers—had barricaded themselves inside one of his castellated abbeys where, well supplied with all manner of provisions, they expected to wait out the epidemic.

All of which would be pretty much academic, save that Prospero was apparently one of the men Von Kempelen had approached on the matter so near to everyone's heart. And Von Kempelen had elected to enter the refuge with the prince.

Because of the involvement of Annie, Valdemar could not be certain, but he felt it likely that Templeton, Goodfellow, and Griswold had also taken sanctuary with Prospero.

"Find me the place," I insisted.

"It is outside Tarragona," Valdemar explained, gesturing now. "To the northwest. A little village called Santa Creus."

And so we headed east.

The following week our coach rattled into Santa Creus. It was an eerie feeling, for the town was mainly deserted. We rolled about its streets for a time that afternoon, viewing at last what had to be the abbey, in the distance—an enormous building with soldiers on the walls and at every point which might possess a gate. I told our driver to head for it.

When our approach was noted several shots were fired in our direction, and orders to halt were shouted in Spanish, French, and English. We complied.

I stepped down from the coach. I took one step in the direction of the abbey.

"Halt!" a guard repeated.

"Certainly. I'd appreciate speaking English."

"What do you want, English?" one called back.

"I'm looking for some people I believe may have gone inside a few days ago."

"If that is the case there is no way to reach them," he said.

"It's very important." I flipped a gold coin into the air and caught it.

"We're billeted just inside the wall," he said. "Even we can't go any farther. The inner doors are welded shut."

"What about messages then? Is there no way to get a message inside?"

"No," he answered. "No way."

"All right," I said. "I understand. In that case, I'd like some information."

"Don't have any," he said. "You'd better be moving along."

"Wait! I'll pay you for it," I offered.

He laughed.

"Wouldn't touch your gold," he said. "Might be tainted with the Death."

I assumed my best parade ground voice then, "Soldier, was there a German named Von Kempelen? And four Americans—three men and a woman?"

He straightened visibly, his shoulders moving back.

"Sir, I do not know," he replied. "There were so many."

"Thank you, soldier. I take it nobody's doing business in town?"

"No, sir. And if I were you I'd not stop there. I'd head for the border and beat the horses till they fell. Then I'd start running."

"Thanks." I turned away. I entered the coach.

"What now?" Ligeia asked me.

"We ride away," I replied. "We stop as soon as we're out of sight of the place. Then we have a talk with Valdemar. Annie may or may not be inside, but it's not her I want to ask about."

We parked near a skeletal olive grove. The others helped get down the coffin, and then took a walk when I explained that Ligeia and I were about to open it— save for Grip, who stood upon my left shoulder and observed.

Valdemar's eyes came open immediately when I raised the lid, without any preliminary mesmerism. The daylight did not seem to be bothering him either. Ligeia gave me a strange look and passed her hands above him then. Even before she had finished, he spoke: "What place is this?" he asked. It was not at all like him to initiate conversation.

"This is Santa Creus, near Tarragona, in Aragon," she answered.

"What is there that is special about it?"

"The Red Death has apparently taken a massive toll here," she said.

"Ah!" he said. "Those lucky, lucky dead! How fine! How fortunate! Gladly would I trade caskets with any of them. To sleep! Perchance never to dream!"

I cleared my throat.

"I hate to keep bothering you with the mundane and earthly," I said, "but there's no one else I can ask."

"I understand your mortal predicament," he replied. "Ask."

"There is a huge abbey near here. We just visited the place," I explained. "There seems to be no way in. It is guarded. The doors are even welded shut.

But I believe that Von Kempelen is inside, and possibly Annie, Templeton, Goodfellow, and Griswold. It occurs to me that large ancient buildings often possessed secret entrances. Can you tell whether this is the case here? I want badly to get inside."

His eyes rolled back suddenly, showing only the whites once more. His hands fell into place across his breast. There was a long pause before he spoke, then, "There is a secret passage from the abbey to the city," came his sepulchral tones. "A tunnel. It has been out of use for so long that I cannot see where life may pass. It has been changed. Perhaps sealed. The town has changed above it."

Again, silence.

Finally, "Could you be more specific?" I inquired.

"No," he replied. "But Von Kempelen is within, and there is that ambiguous quality I have learned to associate with Annie. She may well be there, also."

"Could it also be as it was in Toledo? Confusion at the crossing of her path?"

"Yes."

"Still, I have no choice."

He said nothing.

"The tunnel is the only secret way in?" I asked.

"The only one that I see. Let me rest."

I executed the dismissing gesture myself, without thinking. His eyes closed and the lid slammed. At this, Grip did his champagne uncorking sound.

In a little while we were loaded again and on our way into town.

We parked in a mews near the plaza, and I hung my saber from my belt. The afternoon was running on toward evening. Peters and I thought to explore quickly, obtain a general notion of the place's layout

and perhaps gain an impression of the likeliest area
for the tunnel's terminus. Ligeia was to wait with the
coachman during our excursion.

And so we hiked about, Emerson flitting from
building to building and through an occasional tree-
top, pacing us. The town was very quiet. Storefronts
were boarded over. We saw no one, heard no voices.

"Does it bother you that the plague has passed this
way, and something of its essence may still linger?"
I asked Peters.

His grin remained constant.

"When yer time's up, yer time's up," he said. "An'
if it ain't, it ain't."

"I'm not quite that fatalistic about it," I said, "but
I've a feeling I'd have learned from Valdemar if this
were too risky a sojourn."

"More likely Ligeia'd've said something."

"What do you mean?"

"She's more'n a fancy hand-waver to put folks
asleep," he said. "Told you that back aboard ship."

"You mean she's a witch? A sorceress?"

"I 'spect," he replied softly.

We passed through an area where there had been
some burning, where blackened, half-fallen, windowless shells lay amid puddles and weeds. The odor of
stagnant water came to my nostrils, along with assorted
smells of decay. Emerson perforce descended to
ground level here and shambled beside us for a time.

At length we passed out of this section of town
and came into a rundown area crossed by rutted road-
ways. As we followed it Emerson vanished again. It
became obvious to us that all of these buildings had
been broken into. In consideration of the cost of
moving things—as well as the time of additional
exposure involved in transport—the merchants had

counted on the simple security of boards and nails for protecting their goods. Some inhabitants of this place had not fled, it would seem, and had engaged in a bit of looting.

Walking a bit farther we had almost passed a great decaying hulk of a building when we heard a sound of laughter from within. It was not the cheerful laughter of good fellowship, but rather a barking, fiendish sound. Still. . . . I exchanged glances with Peters and he nodded.

We approached the structure's front and Peters gave to the door such a kick that it flew inward and banged against the wall. I might have preferred stealth, but Peters—then, as always—seemed absolutely without fear. He appeared to possess an extreme confidence in his own physical ability to extract himself from any situation.

The laughter died immediately. Entering, we discovered the place to be an undertaker's establishment. Some excellent-seeming caskets were on display—all ebony and silver—and I regretted Valdemar's not being along to see them. Casting about quickly, however, we saw no sign of life. Then Peters pointed to an open trap door in the floor, in a corner to our right. I loosened my saber in its scabbard and we approached.

We looked down into a long range of wine-cellars whence the sound of a bursting bottle occasionally emerged. At the room's center was a table which held an enormous tub. Various flasks, bottles, and jugs were scattered about it. A human skeleton depended from a rafter above it, affixed there to a rig-bolt by means of a stout cord tied about one leg. The other leg jutted grotesquely, and occasional drafts and reactions of the rope caused it to jounce and twirl. There were a number of individuals seated about the table on casket trestles, and some of them seemed to be drinking from very white bowls which were strongly reminiscent of portions of skulls.

I could see the individual at the head of the table—a gaunt, near-emaciated man possessed of an enormously elongated skull, his skin jaundiced to an extreme yellow hue. He was staring back at me.

Across from this man sat two women—one enormously obese, in perfect complement to his leanness; the other petite, delicate, well-formed, pale, save for flaming cheeks, with a drooping nose which depended beyond her lower lip. I judged the latter lady tubular, and she was seized by a coughing spell just as the thought passed through my mind. A dour-looking, puffy old man sat to the left of the large lady, arms folded, one bandaged leg up upon the table.

There were two more men present, and though the angle of my view did not let me see them well, I could tell that one had enormous ears and bandaged jaws, and the other appeared to be somewhat paralyzed— reclined at an unusual angle, almost deathly still. Most of them wore garments fashioned of shrouds.

I saluted the man who regarded me.

"Good evening," I said.

The man banged the white, scepter-like implement he held upon the tabletop, causing the bottles and skull-bowls to jiggle. The proximity of one turning above him caused me to realize it a thigh bone.

"My friends, we have guests," he announced.

All heads turned in our direction, save for that of the paralyzed man. He just turned his eyes.

"You're welcome to come below and join us, good sir," the host invited.

Out of his line of sight, I signaled to Peters to remain in reserve.

"All right," I said, and I lowered myself onto the steep stair and descended it.

"And who might we have the honor of entertaining?" he asked.

"My name is Edgar Allan Perry," I replied.

"And I am King, these my pestly court. You are welcome to join us in our drinking and making merry in the face of imminent dissolution. Would you care for a skull of grog?"

"Not just now, thanks," I replied. "I am looking for a tunnel, one which runs to the abbey."

Their laughter returned.

"Why would you want to go there? The company is far far better here."

"I do not doubt your conviviality, but I am looking for an ancient tunnel. It may be somewhere hereabout."

"Nay, you'd best dig your own," said the man with the wrapped leg. "Start here. We'll fill it in after you."

The ladies tittered. The paralyzed man rolled his eyes. My host banged his bone and swilled a few drops of wine.

"Silence!" he roared. Then, using the bone as a cane, he levered himself to his feet. He lurched toward me and raised the bone, pointing it. Disconcerted, I saw that he held it as an expert swordsman might his blade. "You will be so good as to drain an entire skull of grog," he announced, locating one with his left hand and dipping it into their vat, "upon which you will be welcomed into our company and allowed to tunnel where you will. Otherwise you will be baptized in it by total immersion, till the cock crows."

He extended the dripping skull toward me and I drew my saber.

"An unkindly act," he observed, and he gestured to his opposite number. The fat lady began to sing.

Peters must simply have jumped into the opening. His feet struck the stair about halfway down and he leaped, catching hold of the skeleton upon which he swung. The singing ceased and shrieks arose. King Pest's minions must have been taken aback by one whose appearance was every bit as outre as their own and far, far more sinister. Peters let go and landed upon the table.

"Up the ladder, laddie!" he called. "'Tis time to drown all sorrows."

King Pest backed quickly away from me and turned toward Peters, pointing the bone. Peters moved forward and caught hold of the big vat. It must have been ponderous in the extreme, filled with liquid as it was. But he raised it, threw me a wink, and began to tip it. I swarmed up the stair as the gurgling began, mixed with screams.

A moment later I heard the rattle of the skeleton, a thud on a tread, and a chuckle. Peters emerged from the opening and kicked the trapdoor shut. A moment later he was raising a heavy coffin which he deposited upon it.

Emerson suddenly came into the shop, the light of a new-risen moon at his back, and commenced gesturing to Peters.

"I think we'd better be gettin' back," Peters said then to me. "We've done all the good we can here."

We followed our shaggy companion into the night.

Mews by moonlight: Lovely lady seated on a coffin, a few of our belongings piled nearby, nightbird perched atop them.

"Ligeia," I said, "what's become of the coach?"

"I heard the driver unloading it," she replied, "and when I got out to see what he was about he leaped back to his seat, snatched up the reins and rode off. He feared the Red Death."

"He took the time to say that?"

"He'd said it earlier, right after you left to explore. He said he thought you mad. He suggested the two of us depart."

"We passit a barrow back a ways, Eddie," Peters remarked. "P'raps I should fetch it."

"Good thought. Yes, do that," I answered.

Which is how we came to be wheeling a cart bearing our worldly and otherworldly possessions up and down the streets of Santa Creus when two men staggered across our path heading to the northeast, one of them clad in jester's motley.

I was about to hail them when I felt Peters' hand upon my arm.

"They're tipsy," he said.

"So?"

"Recall the ones in the cellar."

"These may well be part of some more normal group of survivors."

"Let's follow them then, rather than approach them."

"I'd prefer that, too," Ligeia said.

So we settled into a pace which kept us a decent distance behind the men, overhearing bits of their conversation on occasion. They reeled a bit as they went, though they sobered somewhat farther along and straightened their gait. I gathered that the one in jester's garb was named Fortunato. The other was called Montresor.

The latter looked back once or twice, but I could not tell whether he saw us following.

As other snatches of dialogue drifted our way I gathered they were talking, with considerable erudition, of wine. At least, their discussion seemed full of specialized knowledge.

They slowed as they neared a large, rambling, antique mansion, set among gloomy trees apart from other buildings. From their comments, I gathered it to be Montresor's house, despite his momentary difficulty in unlocking the door.

There came a knocking from inside Valdemar's box. Ligeia placed her hand upon its lid, possibly doing something mesmeric, as—after a time—she announced, "This is the place. We must get inside somehow, for the tunnel entrance is near."

So we kept going, right up to the front door. Shortly, I was knocking on it. Peters and I had to pound long and hard before Montresor answered. When he did he looked surprised, annoyed and vaguely alarmed in quick succession, and then simultaneously.

I suppose the general appearance of our group was not reassuring.

"Mr. Montresor?" I said, hoping hard that he knew some English.

He studied my face for several long seconds, then nodded.

"Yes. What is it?" he asked.

"It concerns the delivery of this case of Chateau-Margaux, of the antelope brand, violet seal," I explained.

His gaze shifted to the large case, where it was instantly taken prisoner. His wariness and annoyance faded. He licked his lips.

"I do not understand," he said. "I did not order this. Are you selling it? Is it a gift? Are you messengers?"

"You might say we are messengers," I told him. "Though in this city, at this time, ordinary messengers are hard to come by."

"True," he said, nodding. "And what sort might you be?"

"We are," I told him, "all that is left of a troupe of entertainers. We were sent for by Prince Prospero, but we were not able to reach the abbey before its gates were sealed. The soldiers refused to admit us, and they also refused to inquire of the prince himself whether he wanted us admitted.

"And so," I continued, "we have been reduced to trying to trade this crate of fine wine for food and a secure place to stay. It was originally intended for Prospero, but those who brought it here abandoned it and fled, for fear of the Red Death."

"Of course," he muttered, opening the door wider, still staring at the case. "Won't you bring it inside?"

At this, we all moved forward simultaneously. Eyes widening, he raised a hand. "No," he said. "The ape and the bird must remain outside."

"They can't be left unattended," I said.

"Then let the lady keep them company while you transport the crate," he suggested. "I cannot offer you assistance with it, as my servants are also fled.

"But a certain matter of great moment compels me to remain," he added, almost under his breath.

Fortunato suddenly lurched into view behind him, still wearing his jester's cap and bells. He took a swig from a small glass flask with a broken, jagged neck, then tried focussing his gaze in our direction.

"What's keeping you?" he asked. "I want to go at that pipe of Montal— Montin—"

"Amontillado!" Grip shrieked, and the man stumbled back, a look of terror suddenly upon his face.

"The Devil!" he cried, continuing to back away.

"No," I answered Montresor. "We don't bring it in unless all of us come with it."

"An ass! Luchesi's an ass! You know that, Montresor?" Fortunato suddenly exclaimed. "An ignoramus! Couldn't tell sherry from vinegar—"

The man in motley broke into a suspicious coughing fit.

"Nothing," he said quickly then, his English more heavily accented than Montresor's. "It is not the plague. I will not die of a cough."

"No," said Montresor, eyeing him thoughtfully. "I think we may safely say that you will not."

Montresor turned away from him then and stood back from the door. He gestured.

"Come in—all of you—then. This way. We must convey it below."

We entered and he secured the door. Peters and I followed him. Ligeia, Emerson, and Grip followed us. Fortunato stumped and staggered along even farther to the rear, alternately cursing, singing, and muttering about Luchesi's stupidity. Just your typical Friday night in a plague-ridden city.

Montresor led us down a curving stone stair to his vast cellar. Oddly, pitch-soaked torches and large candles blazed in numerous niches and holders. It seemed an unusual extravagance in such a sequestered portion of the house.

At last Peters and I reached the bottom and deposited the box, at Montresor's direction, in a subterranean passage which seemed to lead off into a species of catacomb. I was particularly anxious to go farther, for it seemed likely that the tunnel we sought must have its beginning somewhere nearby. There were skulls and other human bones visible in the nitre-encrusted walls, and the shadows flitted like dark fingers across them. Cobwebs hung like fishing nets at every irregularity, and the rustling sounds of retreating vermin brought to mind the ordeal in Toledo which still troubled my slumbers.

Montresor saw the direction of my gaze and smiled.

"This place was once the burial ground for the abbey," he said, with a gesture to the grisly remains. "That was back in the days before Prince Prospero's father had driven out the monks and taken the property for himself."

We transported the crate to a position near the wall which he had indicated, and there we set it down.

"There is some connection to this abbey, then?" I asked.

He did not reply, but—to my surprise—turned away. I had half-expected him to pry open the crate at once, to gloat over his acquisition. Instead, he took a few paces away from us, and I could see that his attention was on Fortunato. Fortunato had seated himself on a bony ledge, and I now noted that he was studying Ligeia's tall and slender figure, her curling raven hair, with an expression most simply described as lust.

Montresor muttered something about drink which the son of an actress might well recognize, "'Lechery, sir, it provokes, and unprovokes; it provokes the desire, but it takes away the performance . . . makes him stand to, and not stand to . . . and, giving him the lie, leaves him.'"

I did not applaud, however, as he did an about-face, as I was shifting my attention to Ligeia who was ignoring the drunken jester entirely.

Our host drew nearer, touched my arm lightly and steered me a few paces off to the side.

"Are you, my good fellow, still seeking entrance to the abbey?" he asked.

I bowed. That the gesture had in it more of mockery than of humility seemed only in character, no doubt.

"It is our profoundest wish, sir," I replied.

"Then let me show you. There is indeed a tunnel," he said. "It is sealed at the abbey end, walled up there in my father's time, or perhaps my grandfather's. The current prince himself does not know of this passage."

"Sealed!" I said. "Then how are we to get through?"

"It is simple enough," he explained. "I will give you tools—hammers, a prying bar. Stout fellows such as yourselves will have no difficulty getting through that thin wall at the far end of the passage. You will then find yourselves in the remotest corner of one of the abbey's storerooms. But—and this is important—you will seal up that wall again, as soon as you have broken out. And then you must hide your tools, put them down one of the many wells within the abbey's cellars. Otherwise the prince may discover the tunnel— know that someone has just come in, bringing possible contagion—and hunt you down, and—"

Montresor broke off here, and with a swift movement of his foot flattened and smeared a scurrying beetle on the stone floor. For a moment, we considered the result in thoughtful silence.

"The prince," he concluded, "fears one thing only. And that is the Red Death."

And so we agreed to Montresor's plan. The only problem was Valdemar. He would have to be left behind. I could hardly speak openly of this difficulty with my companions while Montresor was within ear-shot. But Ligeia perceived the difficulty at once. With a dramatic flourish of her cloak she turned to me suddenly.

"Edgar, I have given this more thought," she announced, a quaver to her words, a quiver to her lip. "I cannot accompany you. I fear to enter the stronghold of a prince whose cruelty is legendary. You must go on without me."

Was there once, or was there still, I suddenly wondered, some special tie between these two—Ligeia and Valdemar—which did not depend upon mesmerism? Odd thought. I was uncertain where it had come from or why it seemed possibly appropriate.

Montresor stared at her as if he were about to argue. But we were a formidable group, obviously strong and somewhat reckless. He elected to remain silent.

A snore reached us from Fortunato's direction. He had passed out, slumped on his stone ledge.

Peters eyed him, then advanced and took his cap and bells and tried them on. The sleeper stirred but did not wake as Peters stripped him of his motley jacket, too. Montresor watched but said nothing.

Peters and I took up the torch and tools. Then—Emerson following—we entered the dark tunnel. I had been surprised, in the alcove where we had obtained the tools, to catch a glimpse of a tub holding a quantity of freshly mixed mortar.

The passage was low, crooked, overgrown with spiderwebs. Plainly, it had not been used in many years.

We had not gone far before a bend in the passage took us out of sight of the two watching figures, Ligeia and Montresor, and the slumped form of

Fortunato in his white linen. A hundred paces and I knew Ligeia was on the stair, Grip upon her shoulder, on her way to a distant bedroom, leaving the others to their own devices. I could almost hear Grip repeating his wine-drinkers' joke.

He paced the decks of an ancient vessel, knees shaky, joints aching. Occasionally, he groped among his navigational instruments of tarnished brass and greening bronze. Mumbling to himself, he would go topside to take readings, polar mists drifting above the waters, ice floes sliding by. His ancient crew lurched about him and strange birds called from overhead. At times it seemed that someone attempted to address him in words mumbled and low, catching at his sleeve, pursuing him on his rounds. But always, when he turned, the figure would flit away, fade. The words never came quite clear. He would return to his cabin then, to rummage and reflect. . . .

Poe awoke in a cold sweat, hands trembling. There had been so many dreams, some of them utterly terrible—such as that of the pit and the pendulum—and while this lacked the horror of that one or the grotesqueries of the encounter with King Pest and his court, it bore an intolerable element of loss and abandonment. He massaged his damp temples.

. . . As if he had sailed beyond human ken, he reflected, past all normal commerce of thought and feeling. And yet must he go on, against the winds and the tides of change and becoming. Lost, lost.

VIII

We stand upon the brink of a precipice. We peer into the abyss—we grow sick and dizzy. Our first impulse is to shrink from the danger. Unaccountably we remain. By slow degrees our sickness and dizziness and horror become merged in a cloud of unnamable feeling. By gradations, still more imperceptible, this cloud assumes shape, as did the vapor from the bottle out of which arose the genius in the Arabian Nights. But out of this *our* cloud upon the precipice's edge, there grows into palpability, a shape, far more terrible than any genius or any demon of a tale, and yet it is but a thought, although a fearful one, and one which chills the very marrow of our bones with the fierceness of the delight of its horror. It is merely the idea

of what would be our sensations during the
sweeping precipitancy of a fall from such a
height. And this fall—this rushing
annihilation—for the very reason that it
involves that one most ghastly and loathsome of all the most ghastly and loathsome
images of death and suffering which have
ever presented themselves to our imagination—for this very cause do we now the most
vividly desire it. And because our reason
violently deters us from the brink, *therefore*
do we the most impetuously approach it.

> *The Imp of the Perverse*,
> Edgar Allan Poe

And so we followed the long, secret tunnel through
the catacombs, to its end against a blank stone wall.
We listened carefully, we listened long at this place,
but we could hear nothing. We looked for light at
the interstices between stones where the mortar had
crumbled away, but we could see none.

So we attacked the wall with hammers and bar.
The antique dust powdered our clothes, skin, and
hair, got in our eyes and mouths; but soon we had
made an opening large enough to admit a person into
the lowest level of Prospero's stronghold.

On the other side, Peters, Emerson, and I emerged
into a storeroom crowded with huge crates and bales
whose contents we wasted no time trying to guess.
Quickly, by the flickering torchlight, we piled back
stones we had removed, closing the wall at our point
of entry, leaving the tools just outside in the tunnel.
Of course we had no mortar, but in this dim corner
the chance of any inspection seemed remote. To make
that chance still smaller we managed to shift a large

crate to a place where it shadowed any sign of our labors.

"What now, Eddie?" Peters asked.

"I say we go topside and try to blend in." I considered his borrowed motley. "We're entertainers. You're dressed for the part. I'm not."

"You juggle? Know any acrobat tricks?"

I shook my head.

"Afraid not."

"Then I guess you're an animal trainer. Emerson, c'mere." The ape leapt down from a crate and came to him. "You be takin' yer orders from Eddie, we go upstairs. Unnerstan'?"

Emerson shambled over and stared at me. I extended my right hand.

"Shake," I said.

The simian reached forward, seized my hand and pumped it.

"I'd guess," I said, "there'll be a pretty big crowd to run things—servants, cooks, whores, soldiers, entertainers. If they've only been in here a few days they can't all know each other yet. A couple of new faces among the entertainers shouldn't be likely to startle anyone. I'll take Emerson up and see how we blend. Why don't you wait an hour or so, then come up and try the same thing."

"I'd judge it ter be fairly late. May not be that many about."

"On the other hand, Prospero's a reveler. He may keep going till he drops every night. We'll just have to see. Keep an eye out for a place to sleep, too."

"Right," he said.

And so we located the stair and I mounted it, Emerson at my side. We came to several choices of ways. I opted for ground level and centrality. This brought me in due course to a courtyard resembling nothing so much as an enormous gypsy encampment. It was lit by torches and campfires, roped off into sections filled with tents and lean-tos, through which the babble of tongues and the sounds of fiddles and guitars carried; people were dancing, drinking, eating, children were crying, dogs wandered, and two men were fighting at the far end. There were buildings on every side of the courtyard, interconnecting, though the most massive seemed the one to the north. It was the most completely lit, and as my wanderings bore me in that direction I became aware that a goodly amount of the noise I heard was actually coming from within it.

No one challenged me, and even Emerson was not unique as a performing animal. There were two trained bears and a troupe of clever dogs.

Several circuits of the courtyard and whatever curiosity we might have roused soon gave way to indifference. I learned that some of the servants, entertainers, and miscellaneous staff had taken up residence in the complex at the south end of the yard. But on inspection these quarters proved small, damp, windowless and poorly ventilated, in the main, and I could see why so many were camping outside. I later learned that these had originally been the monks' cells. While I could appreciate their spiritual fortitude I required something closer to the mainstream of life here.

A bit later I encountered Peters in his motley, proceeding as I had. He agreed with my feelings on lodgings. We spent that night in the stables, and no one seemed to mind or even notice. Further exploration of these quarters showed us an out-of-the-way corner behind the stables where Emerson could be chained in such a fashion that he could easily free himself in an emergency. Peters and I settled upon a small loft, a seeming repository for unused harness, as our own lodging. I had grown accustomed to stables during my time with the cavalry, and my continuing presence in this one seemed oddly bracing.

Peters and I dined on bread and soup at the entertainers' communal table. Emerson took to foraging in the small hours and seemed able to satisfy his needs in this fashion—I suspect with fruit and vegetable leftovers from Prospero's feasts.

And the days wore on. We spent the better part of a week exploring and creating a map of the place. As for the nobles and their consorts, the wealthy merchants and theirs, we saw a few in the distance but we did not see Von Kempelen. Nor did we see Annie. And while I felt as if I knew Griswold from my nightmare vision in the pit, I might have passed Templeton and Goodfellow without recognizing them. And January passed into February. I had been afraid to take any chances until we'd gained familiarity with our surroundings. Now we were near that point, and I was wondering as to our best course of action.

Events, however, preceded any action on my part. A few days later, Peters and I were returning to the stables from our breakfast, intending to practice an act we were working out—involving some miming on his part, some acrobatics by Emerson, and a bit of buffoonery by myself. We were hoping this would gain us access to an area of the abbey hitherto closed to us. As we approached, we heard a series of piteous shrieks and we hastened to learn its cause.

Its source seemed to lie at the center of a fairly large crowd in the area immediately before the stables. The shrieking continued as we pressed forward, but I could not see what was going on.

"Hoist me onto your shoulders, Eddie," Peters said.

I complied. I squatted, he leapt up, I grasped his ankles, I stood. He was heavy, but he was nimble. He was only at a height for a few seconds before he jumped down. He uttered an oath as he did so.

"What is it?" I asked.

"They're floggin' a lad," he said. "Just a boy. Back's all laid open. Usin' a cat."

He elbowed the man to his right.

"Hey, mate," he asked. "What'd he do?"

The man said something in Spanish.

"Stole some grain meant for the prince's horses," Peters translated. "Prospero ordered the floggin'. He and some of his men are up front, watchin'."

The shrieks stopped. We waited for the crowd to thin, as I wanted a look at Prospero. People began to drift off, and Peters inquired of another which one was the prince.

Prospero was pointed out to us—a tall, handsome man, standing among his ministers and courtiers, chuckling with them as the boy was untied. He said something then to the man who had administered the beating—what, I'll never know, as my gaze drifted past him.

She was standing in a doorway to the building off to my left, hand raised to her mouth, eyes wide with horror and quickly narrowing to dam tears. *Annie*. She turned away without having seen me and retreated within. In an instant I was after her.

This building—to the west—connected the monastic quarters to the castellated citadel where Prospero and his entourage had their residence and revels. There was a main corridor on every level, sided by rooms larger than the cells though lacking the magnificence of those to the north or even the spaciousness of those to the east.

I sought with my gaze in both directions when I reached the corridor. I caught sight of her fleeing form turning—northward, to my right—where I knew a stair to be located.

"Annie!" I called, but she was already out of sight.

I rushed after, and when I reached the stair I mounted it two steps at a time.

North again, this time to my left, not so far ahead now, still hurrying.

"Annie!"

She slowed, looked back, halted, studied me in the light from the clerestories as I approached. Her brow unknitted itself and then she was smiling.

"Eddie!"

She looked just as I remembered her from the visions—hair a light chestnut, ghost-gray eyes—and then she was in my arms and weeping.

"I'm sorry," she said, "so sorry. I didn't mean it."

After a time, I asked, "What are you talking about?"

"This. All of it," she explained, gesturing. "Poe's sufferings. Yours. Mine. I'm sorry."

I shook my head.

"I still don't understand what you're saying."

"All my life," she told me, "I've tried to bring the three of us together—in one solid, real world. Not just my kingdom, by the sea. That's why we're here. Templeton was able to take my efforts and twist them some way. I still don't know how—"

"I do," I said. "That way is closed to him now. On the other hand, he apparently could use you directly— with drugs and mesmerism—as he did in Toledo."

"Toledo?"

"The pit, the pendulum. Ligeia said he used you to warp my senses—possibly even reality itself. I still don't know how much of what happened in that prison was real, how much hallucination."

"The pit and the pendulum!" she exclaimed. "You really lived through it? I thought it just a nightmare I'd had. I—"

"It's all right. It's over. It's done with now. You were tricked."

I wondered as I held her: I had never considered that our uncanny tripartite relationship might be based on unnatural efforts on her part. In truth, I had always seen Poe and myself somewhat as rivals for her affection. It had been a long time now, though, since I had borne my poor double anything but a species of fondness; I thought of him rather as my brother, and felt a fierce wish to help him defend himself against our common enemies. But that Annie might be the source of everything—

"He is forgetting us, you know," Annie told me, drawing away, producing a handkerchief from her sleeve, drying her eyes. "Not me so much, not yet at least. But already he has more than half forgotten you. And he doubts the existence of any other world than the one he's being forced to live in. He doesn't realize that he is now condemned to live in the wrong world."

"I've already seen evidence of this," I said, "and I'm sorry for him. But there seems little I can do about it at present. Whereas now I've finally found you, I can get you out of this madhouse, take you someplace peaceful. Perhaps then we can work out a way to help him."

"Not that simple," she said. "Not that simple. But tell me, who is this Ligeia you mentioned?"

I felt my face grow warm.

"Why, she works for Seabright Ellison," I said, "the man who set me on this trail. She seems a powerful mesmerist, possibly something more. Why do you ask?"

"Ligeia was my mother's name," she replied, "and it's such an uncommon name that it startled me, hearing it."

"Was she tall, dark-haired, more than a little attractive?" I asked.

"I don't really know," she said. "I was raised an orphan, like you, like Poe. I'd been left with relatives while my parents traveled abroad. When the relatives died in an accident I was taken in and raised by friends of theirs. They moved about. My parents never came for me. My step-parents told me my mother's name, but they had no likeness of her that I might see."

"What was your father's name?"

"I'm not sure."

"Was it Valdemar?"

"I—I don't know. . . . It could be. Yes, it might."

I caught hold of her hand.

"Come on," I said. "We can sort these things out later. Let's get out of this place, this country, this world if we have to. I've a secret means of leaving the abbey."

She walked with me, down the stairs, back along the lower corridor, out into the courtyard, where I found Peters and introduced them. Peters was no longer alone. He had with him now a dainty, dark-eyed midget girl he had just met, another of the entertainers. He introduced her to us as Trippetta.

She was a dancer, and he explained that she was a Ree Indian from a village on the upper Missouri very near where he himself had been born, and possibly even distantly related.

I was loath to discuss our business before the diminutive lady no matter what her degree of consanguinity with my friend. Fortunately she was on her way to a rehearsal and bade us adieu moments later, though not before she and Peters had arranged to meet again later in the day.

"I don't know that you should have made that date," I said, after she had left. "I'm trying to persuade Annie to leave with us today."

We strolled through the courtyard as we spoke. The atmosphere was a bit more subdued than usual, and the sky had grown gray overhead.

"We cannot," Annie stated. "I hadn't a chance to explain earlier. But you see, it appears that Prince Prospero cannot match the offer Templeton and Goodfellow have made to Von Kempelen for his transmutation secret."

"You want to know something, Annie?" I said. "I don't really give a tinker's damn who finally amasses the most gold in the world. My only reason for making this journey was to get you out of here—and then to give Poe a hand, if we can. I am grateful to Seabright Ellison for his part in this, but he isn't going to starve to death if gold should suddenly be worth, say, half its present value. This morning's incident shows me just what a willful and capricious man Prospero is. I conclude that it is unsafe to be around him. And outside these walls the plague is doing its dance of death throughout the realm. The smartest thing we can do is to get out of this place right now and keep going till we're out of the kingdom."

She laid a hand on my arm.

"Perry, dear Perry," she said, "if only it were so easy. I care nothing about the gold either. Did you not know that gold is but the least part of alchemy? It is a game played for spiritual stakes as well. If Von Kempelen makes the deal with Templeton and Goodfellow, we will not be able to help Poe. Their involvement will result in his exile becoming permanent."

"I do not understand."

"It has to do with probabilities, and with key connections among individuals. Believe me, this is how it would turn out."

"You failed to mention Griswold," I said. "What of him?"

"He's gone back to America, I believe."

"What for?"

"I do not know."

We paced in silence for a time. Then, "Ligeia told me that Griswold may be something more than an alchemist or a mesmerist," I said. "She suggested he might be some sort of sorcerer."

"It's possible," she said. "Yes, that would explain many things. There is that about him which is unusual, and dark."

"Then I still say we should flee now," I said. "It does not seem to me that it matters so much whether Von Kempelen makes the deal with Templeton and Goodfellow here and now, as it does whether they actually get together with Griswold and perform whatever processes are involved. I say we flee now and foil them later, in America. Ellison could probably bankroll a private army for us back home, if that's what it takes."

She shook her head.

"We don't know why Griswold left," she said. "But there is no need that he be present for the process to occur. What if Templeton and Goodfellow come to terms with Von Kempelen here, and they decide actually to conduct the work here? If they succeed in transmuting any substantial amount of metal we will never see Poe again."

"They won't do it. Poe is still safe," I told her. "No one in his right mind would make gold while in the power of someone like Prospero. And don't tell me they'll do it in secret. Gold is heavy stuff. It would be ridiculous to manufacture it in a place like this, and then face all the perils of transporting it. Let them make their deal if they must. We'll stop them later."

"I am sorry," she said. "We cannot afford to take the chance. I would feel personally responsible if I left and it came about. If I stay I may well be able to stop it."

"If you're drugged? Mesmerized?"

"I'll be careful what I eat and drink. And I'm stronger than Templeton. They won't be able to use me again, as they did in the past."

"If you're no longer of use they may decide to dispose of you. These are ruthless men."

"No," she stated, "I'm certain they need me for something else. Later."

I recalled Ligeia's words about the sacrifice of her personality, and I shuddered. But there was nothing I could say on this count, since I didn't understand it and I'd no way to back it up with an explanation.

At that moment, I recalled killing a man. It was in the line of duty, under battle conditions. What difference does it really make whether you're wearing a uniform, or whether he is? Dead is dead. Why should the state have a monopoly on deciding who deserves it? It occurred to me that the simplest answer to our problem would be for me to kill Von Kempelen. Let the secret die with him. Annie would be safe, Poe would be safe, Ellison would be happy. I recalled the stout, popeyed man who had given us tea, who bade us good night and wished us good luck as we fled across the rooftop. He'd seemed decent enough and I could not bring myself to dislike him for the trouble he'd caused. Still, if letting him live meant that Annie would be destroyed, I guessed that I could steel myself to the task. I'd make it as painless as possible, of course. One quick saber thrust—

"Perry!"

Annie had halted and was staring at me, a look of dread upon her face.

"Please don't. Please don't do it," she said.

"What— What are you talking about?" I asked.

"I saw you with a bloody blade, standing above Von Kempelen," she said. "You must promise me that you will not kill him. Please! We must find another way."

I laughed.

"Please," she repeated.

"I just had a vision myself," I said, "of what it might be like living with someone like you. A man could never have an affair, or sneak off for a few pints with his friends."

She smiled.

"I only see things with a terrible urgency about them," she explained.

"Just what I said. Do you see my promise, too?"

She nodded.

"I'll have to find another way," I said.

"Thanks," she told me. "I'm sure you will."

We walked some more, and she took us into the

north building, giving us the general layout of the place, showing us where Templeton's, Goodfellow's, and Von Kempelen's rooms were located, showing us the great dining hall with its enormous ebony clock making a dull thunder where it stood against the western wall. Annie told me that its chiming was so loud and so peculiar a thing that if a musical entertainment were in progress when it marked the hour, the musicians must perforce halt in their playing until it had completed its task. We saw her to her own room then, and I arranged to meet her again in the afternoon.

Later, I suggested to Peters that we kidnap her, spirit her out of there that very night, for her own good. We could head back home then and hunt down Griswold.

"No, sir," he said. "She's another'n—like Ligeia. There's a ghostwind blowin' past 'er. She knows better'n you 'bout these things, an' I'll not be crossin' the likes of 'er."

"People like that aren't always right about everything, Peters."

"You've my last word on it, Eddie."

"All right," I said. "We'll wait and see what develops."

After that, I met with Annie every day and she was eventually able to point out Goodfellow—bluff, beefy, and smiling—and Templeton—tall, thin, possessed of eyes like pits under heavy brows. Peters and I went out of our way to avoid Von Kempelen, being uncertain where he stood in our regard. It was agreed among the three of us that we would interfere—physically, if necessary—should he attempt to create gold. The days fled quickly toward spring and he did nothing along these lines. Nor did he seem to have reached agreement of any sort with anyone, according to Annie. I wondered what kind of game he was playing, and how long he might tease someone like Prospero before he found himself in new quarters with a pit and pendulum of his own for company. I'd a feeling that something must break on this front before too long. Perhaps Templeton and Goodfellow might suffer accidents, leaving him with but the one customer and no way out. Or perhaps we were all waiting, for something—what?— that Griswold was checking into. I wondered whether Annie would object to my killing Griswold if I did it in a fair duel?

I wondered several times, in the days that followed, whether Peters might not have some secret command from Ellison, to follow Annie's orders rather than mine under certain circumstances. Though the issue never came up, I was curious whether he would actively oppose me should I attempt to take Annie away from that place against her will. I wouldn't try it, though. She was simply too persuasive and I too anxious to please her.

He seemed well on the way himself toward developing strong feelings toward the little dancer, Trippetta—another reason, I suppose, for him not to be too anxious to leave.

So we put more work into our act. We had rehearsed before simply to maintain the appearance of our announced roles. We had feared recognition, however, should we actually go onstage, since Von Kempelen knew us and there was always the possibility that Griswold or even Templeton had had some extra-physical means of summoning our likenesses for others to see. It did not seem worth taking chances. But the more we thought of it the more it seemed that masks or garish face-paint might not be out of order in a comic act.

Fortunately nothing like an organized schedule of performances existed. The prince or his steward called now and then, at any hour of the day or night, for one type of amusement or another. Also, many of the performers—musicians or jugglers usually—went freelancing among the crowd of guests, gathering scattered coins against the time when they should be free to leave the abbey and have a chance to spend them.

Peters was somewhat readier than I to take the stage, eager I suppose to do anything that would bring him into more frequent association with Trippetta. And so he actually accompanied a number of clowns and acrobats seeking to increase their number one evening, one of their members having suffered a broken leg during a particularly daring feat. I thought little of it, even on the following day when the troupe was sent for again. It was not until the prince began requesting solo performances of him that I grew concerned. As it turned out, I needn't have.

The motley costume concealed the inhumanly thick musculature of his arms and shoulders, and he displayed a talent I would never have expected for clowning. It was only a matter of days before he had become the prince's favorite jester.

Soon we were into March, and it became increasingly apparent—at least to me, in my garish garb, as I put Emerson through his paces—that Trippetta regarded Peters only as another of the freaks who appeared among the entertainers: amusing, but not to be taken seriously.

I'd even done a foolish and avuncular thing one day. Catching her aside following a performance, I

THE BLACK THRONE 185

did not exactly ask Trippetta her intentions toward
Peters in so many words; but I had wanted to find
where he stood in her regard, for having him smitten
and mooning about as he was might well interfere
with his ability to act and react quickly and with a
clear head should the necessity arise.

She gave me her pert smile and curtsied.

"Yes, Sir Giant?" she responded to my salutation.
"How may I serve?"

"Just a point of information, lovely miss," I
said. "You must be aware of my friend Peters'
attentions—"

"The jester? 'Twould be difficult not to, Sir Giant,
for he is always there, whenever I turn—grinning like
one demented, scraping, bowing, proffering a flower."

"He is very fond of you, Miss Trippetta. While your
affairs are none of my affair, so to speak, friendship
bids me exceed common civility and inquire as to
your feelings on his regard. That is to say—"

"Do I feel that the fool is making a fool of himself?" she finished. "Fairly put, and the answer is yes,
Sir Giant. I do not wish to hurt a countryman of his
stature, but Prince Prospero himself has smiled upon
me twice now and complimented my beauty. I have
considerably higher hopes than an alliance with one
who represents everything which caused me to flee
the American Wilderness. I am, Sir Giant, a lady; and
I feel my position in life may soon be elevated to
reflect my tastes and talents."

"Thank you, Miss Trippetta," I acknowledged. "It
is a refreshing thing to encounter in the midst of
courtly circumlocution."

"You are welcome, Sir Giant," she said, granting me
another curtsy. "And you might tell your friend that,
having seen many, I deem him an extraordinary fool."

"I shall convey the compliment." I turned on my heel then and departed.

Later, when I summarized our conversation for Peters, removing my premeditation to make it seem more spontaneous, he only grinned his broadest demon's grin and applauded it as an example of her wit. I realized then—perhaps had known all along— that talking was of no use, that he would break his heart over her one way or the other no matter what I said or how I said it.

I wished for Ligeia's counsel, or Valdemar's. But that would have to wait.

It was more than the place by which she walked to sing. Tonight she came to be alone, as more and more she did these troubled days. Barefoot, on the broad, brown expanse, she paced; and the sea boomed beside her and ebbed, the sky grown coppery mountains where cloud had been, echoes of that wave-clap out, out, out, returning sound for sea. Her contralto played against its lowering note as she turned and trod the emptied path of the whales, out through limp, damp weed, glass-slick stones of many colors, shells, skeletons, shipwrecks. It was among the bones of the sea, in a coral grove, that she found him— orange, red, green, and yellow still clinging to the dampness, like the distillation of all the rainbows arching centuries above. He looked away and dried his eyes when he felt that she was near. Turning again, he regarded her.

"Lady," he said, "I am sorry."

"And I," she replied, "for I meant this as a place of joy."

"You are—"

"Annie, of course," she answered.

"But you're all grown!"

"So I am. Come here."

He did, and she held him.

"You'll be my mother, then?" he asked.

"Of course," she told him. "Anyone, Eddie. Anyone you need."

Abruptly, he wept again.

"I'd a dream," he said, "that I was grown, too. It hurt so. . . ."

"I know."

"I think that I will not go back. I believe that I shall dwell here forever."

"If you wish. It is always your home, wherever you may be."

After an hour or a year he drew away from her and turned.

"Do you hear it?" he asked.

The echo of the retreating sea still hung in the air about them, and she only nodded in reply.

"It calls to me."

"I know."

"I should go to it."

"No. You need not."

"Then I wish to. The rest is pain."

She caught up his hand.

"I'm sorry," she said. "I never meant the world should use you as it has. I had a dream. For us. It has been broken. You were caught, in a place of pain. I love you, Eddie. You are too pure a spirit for what the world has offered you."

"It has given me vision, Annie."

She looked away.

"Was it worth the price?" she asked.

He bowed and kissed her hand.

"Of course," he replied.

They listened to the echo of the melancholy, long, withdrawing roar. Then, "I must go now," he said.

"Bide a while."

"Then sing to me."

She sang, and singing made; the sea became the self that was her song. The tiger-shadows fell like bars about them.

"Thank you," he said, at length. "I love you, too, Annie. Always did, always will. I have to follow it now, though."

"No. You don't."

"Yes. I do. I know you can hold me, for this is your kingdom." His gaze fell upon their hands. "Please don't."

She studied the gray-eyed child's face, the light of forty years upon it, as if looking up from a coffin. Then she opened her hand.

"*Bon voyage,* Eddie."

"*Au revoir,*" he said; and, turning, he headed into the east, where the sea had gone and its voice thudded, warbled, then rose in pitch.

She turned the other way and walked back to the shore. The copper mountains turned to coal. The sky filled up and the lights came on. She sat on a cliff beneath their blaze and listened as the blood-warm tide came in.

IX

"Of all melancholy topics, what, according to the *universal* understanding of mankind, is the *most* melancholy?" Death was the obvious reply. "And when," I said, "is this most melancholy of topics most poetical?". . . the answer, here also, is obvious—"When it most closely allies itself to *Beauty*: the death, then, of a beautiful woman is, unquestionably, the most poetical topic in the world—and equally is it beyond doubt that the lips best suited for such topic are those of a bereaved lover."

The Philosophy of Composition,
Edgar A. Poe

It was into April's days, warm sunlight in that patch of blue we comics call the sky. The nights came balmy—guitar-noted, flamenco-stamped, fire-flocked, with constant sounds of revelry to the north. More sedate the pleasures of the courtyard. Honest fatigue had come to rule here. Prince Prospero had grown heavier and more florid of face, and he had developed a slight limp. It has been suggested that he now numbered oriental drugs among his pleasures— smoking the opium of Bengal which leads to horrid nightmares, I am told.

I was not present when it happened. I had been taking one of my nightly walks with Annie—which, despite the circumstances, I shall always mark as among the happiest times of my life; such a light in the midst of peril and despair must, I daresay, gleam more brightly by reason of contrast.

A servant to one of the minister's wives rushed up to Annie as we paced a candle-lit gallery, admiring the exquisite artistry of ancient tapestries hung there and lamenting their state of repair. She clutched at Annie's sleeve and hissed a tearful account of events she had witnessed but minutes before.

I felt a coldness in my breast when I overheard her say, "Poor little thing. . . ." When she had departed, I glanced at my dear lady and she nodded. "Trippetta," she said. "The prince was with his seven chief ministers trying new wines and an African drug said to grant the pleasures of god-like madness for a brief time. They sent for her to entertain them."

There was a long silence.

Then, "They forced her to drink wine," she continued. "It does not take much to affect one so small. And then they made her dance upon a table. She could not control her balance. She fell from it and broke her neck."

I couldn't think of a single thing to say. I might

be deemed a bloodthirsty wretch for my sudden desire to rid the world of this man, also. But I knew, of a devilish certainty, that no action on my part would be necessary.

A little later I was in the right place—or the wrong place, as the case might be—when her diminutive body was carried by on a board for interment in a local crypt used for those who died during our sequestration. I heard Annie gasp as the tiny form with the twisted neck went by.

I feared for my life when it came to telling Peters of it. But it had to be done. I held Annie tightly for a long while before I bade her good night.

I had been right to fear so. Peters' eyes unfocussed and his face darkened as I spoke. He drove his fist through a nearby wall, and he cursed long and loudly. I backed away, uncertain how long it would take for him to come to his senses, uncertain whether he would turn on me.

About a minute, I'd judge. Maybe a little more. Then he stopped making holes in the wall and turned to me, eyes focussing again. I braced myself.

"Ah, Eddie," he said then. "She was such a little thing and meanin' no one harm. I'll see that man dead an' in hell a piece at a time for this."

I reached toward him, thought better of touching him in this mood, withdrew and said, "It won't do her or anybody else any good if you rush off and get yourself made into a pincushion by the prince's archers."

He'd picked up a piece of brick by then and was squeezing it. I heard a grating sound. He opened his hand and gravel poured from it.

"You hear me?" I said. "I don't care how strong you are. An arrow through your heart and it stops beating."

"Ah, yer right, lad. Yer right," he said. "I'll do 'im proper, never fear. And I'll send milady a nest o' Dukes for servants in the spirit land. Never fear I'd spend my life cheaply. Yer right."

He began to wander southward and I made to follow.

"No. No, Eddie," he said, prodding his wig back into place. "Let me go off alone now, as it should be."

I believe he spent the night in one of the monk's cells. I walked through the south wing several times later, and I'd swear I heard the sounds of a tomtom, and perhaps some chanting.

As I understand what transpired thereafter, he dissembled craftily, playing the jester once more. I was told that he later mentioned to his masters the Eight Chained Ourang-Outangs, a diversion which provided excellent sport by terrifying the ladies (not to mention the men) by creating the impression that the beasts had gotten away from their keepers.

This was to be done, he'd explained, by garbing eight men to resemble the simians and equipping them in chains connecting them in pairs. At a signal, they would rush into the hall uttering savage cries. He suggested the effect to be exquisite in the way of producing fright.

I gather that Prospero was quite taken with the idea, to the extent of ordering Peters to provide costuming for such an entertainment that very evening, for himself and his seven ministers to enact these roles.

Now, I was to be present in the great hall myself that night, with Emerson, to provide an acrobatic entertainment and some mummery.

This, he felt, was excellent timing, filling the

audience's eyes and minds with images and notions of hairy, man-like beasts. In fact, he suggested I preface the performance with an observation that we had eight others of Emerson's sort but that they were untrained, far too vicious to be loosed in public and, so, kept chained.

I suggested he make me party to whatever he was planning but he refused, only going so far as to suggest I find a way to get my saber into the hall beforehand and conceal it there, "Just in case," as he put it.

I did not like the sound of this, but, as he refused to elaborate, I contrived to enter the hall while it was deserted that morning and hung the weapon in the hall amid a display of ancient shields and armor, near to where I'd be performing, covering it with a shield so that only the hilt protruded.

That evening, I arrived ahead of time, Emerson in tow, hoping to discover just what Peters had in mind, to assist if I might, foil if I must, avoid if necessary. But the only change in decor that I could discover was that the massive chandelier had been removed (at Peters' suggestion), its drippings in an unusually warm April to have been impossible to prevent upon the rich garb of the guests, to be replaced by a flambeau, emitting sweet odor, in the right hand of each of the Caryatids which stood against the wall—some 50 or 60, I'd say.

During my act, at some sign from Peters, the prince and his seven ministers absented themselves for their costuming—which, I later learned, consisted of their donning tight-fitting stockinet shirts and drawers. They were daubed with tar which was then covered with a coating of flax. They were then tied together with chains (by Peters) and formed into a circle, their chains crossing at its center. Peters had intended their entrance to occur at midnight, but the men's eagerness to astound and affright prompted them to shamble into the great hall ahead of schedule. My prefatory remarks had been made, however, and the resulting shrieks and tumult arose as anticipated.

The excitement was immense, the prince and his cohorts amusing themselves prodigiously with each fresh swooning or outcry. As anticipated, there had been a general rush for the doors; but Prospero had ordered them locked immediately on his entrance, and Peters had picked up the keys in the absence of pockets to the prince's costume.

At some time during this activity Peters vanished, to be replaced by yet another hairy form. Emerson had left me, though by now no one was paying any heed to what had been our act. He cavorted with the fake apes, and I noted after a time that the chain from which the chandelier normally depended, and which had been drawn up on its removal, was lowered slowly till its hooked end hovered near the floor.

I sought about for Annie who had been present in a simple scarlet Harlequin mask, accompanied by three fully costumed individuals who could only have been Templeton, Griswold, and Von Kempelen. All of them appeared already to have departed, however.

The chains which bound the ape-mummers moved about at the center of the circle they formed. All of them did not quite coincide in their crossings, though. Emerson took hold of the hook, and to it he affixed a chain, a second chain, a third chain. Though he caught hold of the fourth one on several occasions he could not draw it near enough to the hook to suspend it therefrom. There simply was not sufficient slack.

Finally, the three snagged chains were drawn taut. Their wearers felt the tension, began glancing back to the thing which seemed to have restricted their movement. At this, the hook began to rise. I looked upward, then down again in another direction to the place where the other end of the chain was wrapped about a drum, off in a shadowy corner where a diminutive figure in motley turned a crank.

Six of the ministers were hoisted into the air.

Prince Prospero and the minister to whom he was attached remained grounded. A shadow flashed by me. I moved to my shield.

Peters had rushed to the wall where he wrenched a flambeau from the hands of its Caryatid. He moved to a central position, to the place where now hung the six of the ministers who had watched Trippetta dance to her death.

He applied his torch to each in turn. The tar proved very flammable. Each burst into flame.

Shouts of fear rose on every hand, but these were submerged by the cries and moans of the living candles which turned and writhed overhead. The chains clinked and rasped; shadows darted like crazed spirits about the hall. And a hellish sound penetrated everywhere. It was several moments before I realized it to be Peters' mirthless laughter.

Turning, the prince took in the situation quickly. Reaching inside his costume, he withdrew a pistol. He raised it, then took aim in Peters' direction. A hairy form interposed itself, rushed toward him. He fired.

Emerson fell.

There followed total panic. I had my saber in my

hand. The six ministers twisted, screamed and blazed overhead. Peters bellowed, locked the winch he'd operated and rose. He attempted to move forward then, but his way was blocked by a rush of bodies.

Then commenced the striking of midnight upon the great, dark clock.

Before the final echoes of the last chime faded the entire assembly had grown still. I was not certain what had occurred. It was as if some psychic wind had blown through the hall, touching upon everyone present, disarming us of sound and movement.

Save for one. I first became aware of the figure because it was the only thing moving, from out a dark corner which might well have concealed a passage; second, the grotesque costume it had on held every gaze from the moment of beholding. In all respects it was the form of one long dead, most likely from the very cause this crowd was here assembled to avoid—the Red Death.

Its gait was ungainly, lurching, its skin both pale as a toadstool and bright as blood as it passed from shadow to glare and back again, reflective of the blazing spectacle overhead; progress stumping, terrible, within a cloud of charnel-house smells which only then reached my nostrils; guise maggoty, moldy; manner single-minded; mien horrific. It came on, perfect embodiment of the group's nemesis.

But even more than the great horror this presence evoked was the revelation, to me, that this was not a matter of mask, makeup, or costuming. I knew this man, having seen him at our tunnel's farther end, where Peters had stripped him of his motley, his cap and bells. For this was Fortunato—plaguey, drunken associate of Montresor, dead, dead, dead, yet some how animate, moving down the aisle which opened before him, lurching subject of every stare as he reached to embrace Prospero, who shrieked at the contact and fell to the floor, retreating feet tangled in his chains, dragging his final minister with him.

The spell was broken. The noise and tumult returned. Daggers appeared in shaking hands. I brandished my blade and called to Peters. I snatched a torch, and when he looked my way I gestured in the direction where I thought the hidden passage lay. Casting a final look at his handiwork and a lingering one at his whilom companion, dead Emerson, Peters beat his way through the crowd and followed me into the passage.

These recent days be bloody stuff,
And also recent dreams.
I seem to hear a phthisic cough
By life's eternal streams.
Death lurks and laughs his ass off.
At least that's how it seems.

Untitled verse,
Edgar Allan Perry

X

Edgar Allan Poe is dead. He died in
Baltimore the day before yesterday. This
announcement will startle many, but few
will be grieved by it. The poet was well known
personally or by reputation, in all this country;
he had readers in England, and in several of
the states of Continental Europe; but he had
few or no friends; and the regrets for his death
will be suggested principally by the consideration that in him literary art lost one of its most
brilliant, but erratic, stars.

New York *Daily Tribune*
"Ludwig" (Rufus Griswold)

The passage we followed contained a stair which
led down to another passageway, running beneath the
courtyard. As we rushed through it, Peters moved in

a daze of grief and exhaustion. I said nothing at first, simply moving and keeping him in motion till we emerged in the tunnel behind the storeroom where we had originally entered, its way almost totally blocked by a partial collapse of one wall. We finally sidled through via a narrow and very dusty adit.

I was able, at that point, to persuade Peters to discard his jester's costume. After that, we picked up the tools we had left behind on our entering, earlier in the year.

At the town end of the tunnel we discovered that Montresor had walled us in, which of course meant that he had also done it to Fortunato—a deed as grisly as any described in the tales of that master of the macabre, E. T. A. Hoffman, whose stories had filled many a slow hour for me at isolated army posts. Had we dropped our tools down a well as Montresor had suggested we would have been trapped.

Peters swung his hammer with terrific force. Rather than helping him, I simply stayed out of his way. In a matter of minutes he had knocked a hole through the wall large enough for us to pass through.

Mounting quickly from the cellar we sought about the house. While there was no sign of Montresor, Ligeia responded to my hailing, emerging from an upstairs room, Grip perched upon her shoulder.

"Perry, damn it! Damn it, Perry!" the bird greeted me.

"Are you all right, Ligeia?" I asked.

"I am."

"Valdemar?"

"As always."

"Where's Montresor?"

"Gone away," she answered.

"I've a feeling we should do the same."

"Yes, I've packed a few things."

"I'll fetch your bag."

"It's already downstairs."

"You knew we were coming?"

"I sent Fortunato for you."

"Why?"

"The time was right."

"How will we travel?"

"There is a coach," she said, "beside the stables, out back."

"Then I think we should hitch up a team and head for the border," I said.

"No," she replied, "for Barcelona, and the sea. The *Eidolon* should be waiting."

"How did that come about?"

"Annie put it into Captain Guy's mind to sail there, quite some time ago."

"How do you know that?"

"I was about to do it myself one day when I realized it had already been done."

"Really," I said. "Is she your—"

"There are no horses left alive in the stables," she continued. "Help me fetch that tapestry down from the wall."

I looked in the direction of her gesture. The tapestry in question involved a man stabbing another man, somewhat to the rear, while an enormous and unusually colored horse stood statue-like in the foreground. I moved a small table near to the wall, mounted it and succeeded in removing the tapestry. As I was rolling it, I inquired, "Any special reason we need this thing?"

"Yes," she replied.

Peters and I wrestled Valdemar's crate out to the yard, transporting the tapestry along with it. While we were loading Valdemar, I heard the neighing of a horse.

Coming around the side of the coach then was Ligeia, leading a colossal charger. She gave the beast a series of mesmeric passes as they approached.

"Help me hitch him up, Eddie," she said.

My old cavalry instincts surfaced, and I gentled the animal a bit, working him by degrees into a place between the traces. I felt sorry for the brute no matter how strong he might be, taking the place of four regular horses. Of course, we'd be riding without Emerson or our old coachman, and most of our baggage was gone.

Walking about the coach I beheld the tapestry spread upon the cobbles of the courtyard. While the one man was still engaged in stabbing the other, the great horse was missing from the foreground. I didn't even want to think about the meaning of this. I heard a laugh, however, and when I turned I saw Ligeia, hair blowing in the wind, white teeth bared; and for a moment only it seemed that a strange pale light hovered about her, but it retreated into her eyes.

"You, Eddie, shall be coachman," she said.

"I don't even know the way to Barcelona."

She pointed.

"That way," she said. "I'll give you more directions, as you need them."

I opened the door for her and handed her up inside. As I mounted to the driver's board Peters came climbing and settled himself beside me.

"If it's all the same, I'll ride up here with you," he said.

"Good. You can give me a hand with the driving."

I released the brake, shook the reins lightly and the horse began to move. We were going at a smart pace when we left the courtyard. When we struck the road it increased. Shortly, we were moving at an amazing pace. Yet the horse barely seemed to be exerting itself. It was one of the strangest things I'd ever seen. We kept going faster and faster. Soon we were racing along at the fastest pace I'd ever traveled. The countryside was becoming a blur about us.

I drove for several hours, then switched with Peters. The beast which drew us showed no signs of tiring; it still barely seemed even to be running. I drew my cloak tightly about myself and leaned back. The night-smells of spring were all about us. Only the stars stood still. Ligeia shouted another direction, and Peters took us leftward on a fork.

As I dozed, it seemed that it was Poe rather than Peters who sat beside me. But no matter how I addressed him, he refused to answer. Finally, he leapt down onto the horse's back, cut him free of the traces and left me there atop a stranded coach. But that couldn't be right. . . . I could still feel our movement.

And then it was Annie who sat beside me. I felt her hand upon my arm.

"Perry," she said. "Eddie."

"Annie. . . . It seemed as if Poe were seated there—just a little while ago. But he ignored me. Then he went away."

"I know. He moves farther and farther off. I cannot hold him to us."

"What of yourself, dear lady? I saw you at the party which turned into a dance of death. But you, Von Kempelen, and Griswold's cronies vanished at some point."

"I could feel the nearness of the doom. The others trust my warnings by now. We fled."

"I wish you had come to me."

"I know. So do I. But we've been through this before. I must not let them seal his exile."

"What of yourself otherwise? Are you all right?"

"I'm fine physically. No plague, no injuries."

"Where are you now?"

"Aboard a boat, heading downstream to the sea. Looking at a flame in a lamp, seeing you. A ship awaits us at the mouth of the stream. It has lain at anchor there for some time, against this emergency."

"What's her name?"

"The *Grampus*. We shall have boarded her, weighed anchor, and raised sail before you reach your own vessel at Barcelona."

"Where are you headed? I must follow, you know."

"London, to pick up some equipment."

"What sort of equipment?"

"Something Von Kempelen wants."

"For the experiment?"

"Yes."

"And after you've got it?"

"Back to America."

"Where?"

"I'm not certain yet. Somewhere up north, I believe."

"Where in London are you headed?"

"I haven't an address. But. . . ."

"What?"

"I've a feeling we shall not meet there. Something else looms before you. I see its cloud. That's all."

"A man can only try."

"You've striven harder than most."

"I love you, Annie. Even though it was born of the artifice of a lonely little girl looking for playmates."

"My brushwood boy. . ." she said, and I felt her

hand touch my hair. "I could not have found you had the need and the capacity not been in you, also."

We sat in silence for a time, and then I felt her presence weaken.

"I'm getting tired, Eddie."

"I know. I wish the Red Death had been a little more enterprising when it came to your companions."

"Templeton protected them," she said, "as you and your companion were protected by the remarkable lady who released the force which drives your coach."

I wanted her to stay with me forever, but I bade her good night. Then the real dreams came on—burning bodies hanging from a chandelier, people screaming, a bleeding ape, a walking corpse. . . .

"Damn it Eddie damn it Eddie damn it Eddie."

I opened my eyes. Grip was perched on my shoulder, calling my attention to a luscious show of pinks and oranges which had begun in the east.

"I'll take over now, Peters," I said. "You rest."

He passed me the reins and nodded. Grip moved over to his shoulder.

"Damn it Peters damn it Peters damn it Peters. . . ."

We passed many neglected farms, their fields blooming with a spring growth of weeds. We paused at one point and gathered food from the cellar and store house of a farm whose owners had either died of the plague or fled the country. Our nameless steed seemed barely winded, and when I placed my hand upon him he did not feel heated. The only change I noted in him from his first appearance back at Montresor's home was a certain odd, rumpled quality to his hair and mane, as of a garment losing its hem, in the first stages of unravelment.

We rode on, Ligeia directing us to a road that

followed a river downstream. It took us through a region of dark tarns and bleak woodlands. Once more—possibly twice—during this phase of our journey I thought that I felt Poe's presence. But it was gone quickly, without communication.

That afternoon we came to a hill—overlooking Barcelona, so Ligeia informed me. I had come to enjoy our unnatural speed, to the point where I wished there were time simply to ride that magnificent beast for pleasure. He was looking more and more tattered, however—large chunks of his hair blowing away with almost every pace, every breeze.

Grip came flying back from what appeared to be a harbor area.

"Damn it Guy damn it Guy damn it Guy," he announced brightly.

I heaved a heavy sigh.

"I think he's spotted the *Eidolon*," I said loudly.

"Follow him," Ligeia directed, and I did.

We made our way down into the town. The streets were largely deserted, though I could hear sounds of activity at either hand, and I could see people through the windows of shops and residences. There were a few on the streets, also, hurrying, and they tended to converse over a distance. I'd a feeling the worst of it could have passed here, leaving no one in a hurry to resume face-to-face sociability.

We turned a corner and much of our horse's tail was whipped away by a sudden gust of wind. Only a single strand remained where it had depended. When we were nearly to the bottom of the long slope we had been descending, one of his ears vanished, along with much of his mane. Turning upon a well-tended road which followed the waterfront, I was amazed to see that the animal's hindquarters appeared to be narrowing visibly with every few steps that he took. Looking downward, I was puzzled to see that he was treading upon what appeared to be a long strand of his own hair, a thing which seemed to emerge continuously from his own person. Looking back, I saw that it extended behind us back to the most recent corner we had turned.

I was about to petition Ligeia for advice, when a barrel came rolling down a hilly sidestreet, escaped from a pair of men who were loading a cart up that way.

For the first time, our steed was distracted. As if aware of his diminished condition, he turned his frayed head in the direction of the oncoming barrel. For the first (and last) time, also, he uttered a strange sound—a half-neighed bellow, which sounded as if it rolled and echoed its way to us from a great distance, off peaks and down mountain passes. Suddenly then, he was galloping. Whatever force it was that had moved him at supernatural velocities earlier, it came over him once again. Ships, piers, waterfront buildings became a blur. And the horse before me began to dissolve. Soon he was the size of a Shetland pony, though much more irregular in outline. Yet his strength held, despite the diminishment in stature; and we rushed through the harbor at a terrible pace. Soon it was as if a large dog drew our coach, a small one, an unwinding shadow. Then, realizing its plight, the shrunken creature reared, emitting a small, trumpet-like note. The coach passed over it. I looked back and all that I saw was a piece of string lying in the street. I drew hard upon the brake, but it did not slow us. Peters reached over then and pushed my hand away. He drew back upon the lever meant to restrain a wheel. Feet braced against the board, he pulled. His shirtsleeve was torn by his expanding biceps and a smell of smoke rose from below. But we began to slow.

It was fortunate that traffic was very light. We halted near to a stack of crates, piers to our left, gray gulls swooping and calling. Peters released his grip by degrees, raised his arm slowly then and pointed.

"There be the *Eidolon,* Eddie. The beasty did a good job o' gettin' us where we was goin'."

As we were climbing to the ground, I overheard Ligeia mutter, *"Pax vobiscum,* Metzengerstein."

Later, as Peters and I were unloading Valdemar and a few other items, and crewmen were coming in our direction from the ship to assist in their transport, I happened to glance skyward. My gaze was taken by a cloud formed in the distinct colossal figure of a horse, of an unnatural color.

I told Captain Guy to set sail immediately for England, and that I would brief him as soon as we were underway as to the exact state of our affairs. The three of us ate a quick light meal while we were casting off, and I quaffed a brandy afterwards which caused everyone who passed to stare as if waiting for me to fall over. Then I headed back to my cabin where I washed the dust of the road from me. Afterward, I made the mistake of stretching out on the bed for a moment.

I was awakened by a terrible pitching and rolling of the vessel. I finally stirred myself, drew on my garments and went topside briefly. I watched the storm and the flow of shipped waves but a few moments. Then I returned below and managed to locate Peters. I had slept for over twelve hours, he told me, though the storm had begun but recently.

Bad weather dogged us out of the Mediterranean, and when we attempted a northward course to England a fresh storm descended upon us, of greater ferocity than anything encountered earlier. Since no headway could be made we simply prepared to ride it out. We were blown far out to sea, however, and it was three days before the storm let up. When it did, considerable pumping and repair was in order.

Whatever evil genius might rule this section of the sea, it seemed to have taken a particular dislike to ourselves. For no sooner had the *Eidolon* been restored to full serviceability than another storm broke upon us, driving us farther south. And this was the worst, by far, of them all, to that point. It bore us without letup into the Tropic of Cancer, equator-wards.

"This storm . . ." Ligeia said to me on the morning of the seventh day.

"Yes?" I said.

"It seems to be ending now."

I reached out to knock on a wooden railing. "Thank God!" I added. "Sailors really do have it worse than soldiers. I'm ready to believe it now."

"Don't. Not yet," she said.

"What do you mean?"

"I'm not sure this storm was natural."

"Oh?"

"Just at the end here, just for a moment, I thought I felt her fatigue, allowing a slight slippage of control where personality might show through."

"Go slow," I said. "I'm not at my best."

"I believe they have Annie drugged again," she stated, "and that she was the motive force behind this storm. But a week—even with drugs and mesmerism—was about as much as she could manage. After all, they don't want to hurt her permanently. She has greater uses than simply brushing us out of the way."

"Are you sure of this?" I asked.

"No, I'm not," she replied. "Even under the influence her mind is a subtle thing."

There was a lull with a clearing that afternoon. The crew actually cheered on seeing a blue sky for the first time in what seemed ages. More pumping and patching were undertaken. Fortunately, the masts had remained intact.

In a way, I guess, it was good that a lot of work was going on, as the sails had not been run up again when the next storm broke, when they simply would have had to come down again.

And so we rode for a day, and Ligeia assured me that it was a natural storm and not one of Annie's doings. It delivered us to another and yet another took over after that. We were below the equator now, somewhere in the Tropic of Capricorn and still being driven south. Ligeia still felt this was simply a piece of seasonal bad fortune.

Finally, it broke, and the skies stayed clear that day, that night, and on into the next day. All refurbishings were effected, a propitious breeze came upon us. We ran up sail and turned our nose north. The crew cheered again. The demons had departed. The hour was ours and it was golden. People sang and whistled at their tasks. Hernandez was instructed to produce an extra-fine dinner, which he did.

The good wind held, and the sky was clear as the sun went down. What more could we ask that night when we crawled into bed, more content perhaps than in an age of days?

The next tempest struck like an angel with a fiery

sword, and this by far was the worst of them all. I
was up, dressed and out on the deck in a trice, for
it might well be that every hand were needed, to
struggle yet another time against the weather's perversity. This time, several crew members were lost
overboard, as well as sail and rigging. Even one mast
splintered and went by the board, leaving the *Eidolon*
half-crippled, though still in no immediate danger of
sinking or capsizing. It was fortunate we had been
able to complete our latest round of repairs before
this one broke.

For many days it persisted. We could no more guess
at our position on the sea. But this time there was a
different feeling to it. On several occasions I experienced the same sense of communication and division
as I had back on the coach during our flight: It was
as if Poe were somehow near again—somehow.

And then Ligeia told me, "She walks the night like
some dark goddess of old. This is Annie's storm.
Directed at us."

"Not of her own volition surely!"

"She is not their creature out of choice," she replied.
"They have succeeded in gaining control of her again."

"Is there nothing you can do? Or Valdemar?"

"Valdemar still suffers his psychic blindness wherever Annie is concerned. As for myself, I have been
holding her back as best I could for some time now.
I think we should be on the bottom by now, except
for the few small victories I have achieved. She has
grown incredibly strong."

"Is there nothing that can be done?"

She shook her head.

"We must wait for her to tire again. I cannot
attack her directly, but only defend against the
attacks she sends. Once she tires, we must head for

the nearest shore. Otherwise she'll swamp us, sooner or later."

And so it went, Ligeia shielding us as best she could. The following day I was in the rigging trying to cut loose some tangled lines and shrouds which threatened to take down another mast. Oddly, the altitude bothered me less during the storm than it had on a fine, clear day.

I doubt I could have heard a shout from below, against the awesome scream of the wind. For some reason I glanced downward, however, and I saw a pair of crewmen needlessly exposing themselves to the elements, holding tightly to a stanchion, one of them pointing to starboard. I shifted my gaze in that direction to find myself completely confounded by the vision presented there.

A ghostly vessel came on, plowing through the heavy seas like some sailing juggernaut. St. Elmo's fire danced upon its spars, pale green luminescence against the blackness of cloud, lightning flashes granting its deck occasional fleeting shadows. The craft gave the impression of enormous age, and was built in a style of centuries ago. But it was larger than any ship so designed had a right to be. Most frightening of all was the fact that it bore full sail, in the very teeth of the storm.

Again, I had the momentary impression that Poe was somehow near. And then it seemed that Annie was, also. She was fighting with Templeton, struggling against whatever drug or artifice he had administered. I knew this because I heard her call my name, sounding as if she had just come out of a deep slumber. This occurred as the thought crossed my mind that I might hail the approaching vessel. But there was no time.

Annie screamed just as the two ships collided, and it seemed to me that I was hurled bodily into the stranger's rigging by the impact.

At first, I had no doubt that the crash was physical. But later I was to conclude that my transition from one ship to the other had been something of an entirely different nature.

> That the universe might *endure* . . . it was required . . . that the stars should be gathered into visibility from invisible nebulosity— proceed from nebulosity to consolidation— and so grow gray in giving birth to unspeakably numerous and complex variations of vitalic development . . . *during the period* in which all things were effecting their return into Unity with a velocity accumulating in the inverse proportion of the squares of the distances at which lay the inevitable End.
>
> *Eureka,*
> Edgar Allan Poe

XI

To the few who have loved me and whom
I love—to those who feel rather than to
those who think—to the dreamers and
those who put their faith in dreams as in
the only realities—I offer this Book of
Truths, not in its character of Truth-Teller,
but for the Beauty that abounds in its Truth;
constituting it true. To these I present the
composition as an Art-Product alone:—
let us say a romance; or, if I be not urging
too lofty a claim, as a Poem.

Eureka
Edgar Allan Poe

Clinging to the ancient lines, one foot upon a spar, I watched as the two vessels separated. I found that I still clutched the knife I had been using, and I resheathed it against future need. If only there were one more roll bringing our rigging near again I felt that I might spring back to my former perch. Alas, the strange vessel's momentum carried it far beyond the *Eidolon* before it rolled again. Odd as it seemed, looking back and looking down, I saw that neither gave evidence of having suffered damage in the collision; and the *Eidolon* was still afloat when she vanished from sight.

Slowly, I worked my way down from the rigging, those great sails bellied and booming about me like Titanic instruments of music, my course directed toward the swinging lanterns far below.

The first thing I realized when I set foot upon the deck was that things seemed more stable here below. From above, I'd seemed to see a lot of pitching and rolling; but at this level, the sensations were somehow minimized, possibly because of the greater ballast of something on this scale. Also, the sounds of the storm seemed somehow muffled here below.

I fully expected some crewman to rush up to me momentarily, inquiring after my well-being, and offer succor of any sort needed. But it was as if I were not present. They went about their business of shifting several cases from stern to stem and lashing them into new positions without directing any attention my way. For a moment, I thought it rudeness. But only for a moment. I moved to stand immediately before a man who carried a coiled line over his shoulder. As he came on, weak-kneed and wheezing, his gaze seemed to pass right through me. He veered slightly and passed about me as if I were some fixture. I moved to another, engaged in a bit of caulking about what looked a loose board inside the port gunwale. I fluttered my hand before his eyes but he paid it no heed. Puzzled, I regarded a number of the others in turn. They were uniformly age-worn, decrepit, thin of hair, shaky.

I drew away then from the men and moved nearer the side, as if the demon wind might offer some explanation should I pay them sufficient heed. They screamed, they buffeted, but the ship plowed on. No explanation, however, was forthcoming. What did come forth, some time later (ah, Time!—how twisted and dreamlike it seemed here!—burning in the green fires which clung like fungoid growths), was an ancient man I took immediately to be the vessel's captain. His knees tottered with his load of years, his entire frame quivering with the burden. Yet he bore with him various instruments, and he chose a spot well forward, produced a curious telescope of venerable appearance and put it to his eye while the lightnings danced before him and screens of rain were shaken from out the tormented sky. Nodding then as if satisfied, he recased the instrument and opened another. He proceeded to regard compass and sextant, as if there were actually something for him to fix upon. Then, muttering to himself in some language I could not understand, in a low and broken tone, he recased these instruments, also, after recording some observations in a log he bore, then turned and headed back toward the companionway from which he had come.

I made haste to follow him, strangely attracted by this weak yet, paradoxically, powerful individual. I entered his cabin behind him, stood near its door and regarded the place as he moved around in it. The floor was thickly strewn with navigation charts, iron-clasped folios and moldering instruments of science. The captain seized one of the charts, spread it upon a table and pored over it. His head bowed down upon his hands then, he stared.

I cleared my throat. There came no reaction.

"Uh— Sir?" I said.

Nothing.

It could simply be that he was hard of hearing, but I knew somehow that this was not the real reason. I made my way forward carefully, repeating my queried salutation and attempting to place my hand upon his shoulder. A bit of the green fire seemed to bloom between us as I did, and my hand slid off as if I had trailed it in a waterfall. The old man did not even look up. I continued to stare at him, not knowing what to do.

Abruptly then, he rose to his feet. In stature, he was nearly my own height—that is, about five feet eight inches. He was of a well-knit and compact frame and body. His ancient eyes were gray. I was suddenly stricken with feelings of awe, reverence and wonder as I regarded him, his manner a wild mixture of childlike peevishness and godlike dignity. Following him, I saw him take up a paper which I took to be a commission, and though I peered intently over his shoulder I could not make out the name upon it, though it appeared to be a short one. It did seem to bear the seal and signature of some monarch, however. . . .

"Yes," I heard what seemed Annie's voice say. "Yes. . . ."

The captain glanced suddenly in the direction from which the words seemed to come, and I did the same. There was no one there. Our gazes swinging away then, they met for a brief electrical moment and we stared into each other. Then he shook his head and turned away.

"Good riddance," he growled.

I heard something like a muffled sob from what had seemed the direction of Annie's invisible presence.

"The banishment is almost complete," I heard or felt her say.

The old man looked up, his features softening. His pale lips moved soundlessly as he stared in that direction. It looked as if they formed the name "Annie."

"I must leave you, Perry," I heard her say.

"No!" I responded.

"I must, for now," she said sadly. "If I am to keep a doorway open to Poe."

"Don't leave me. There's never been anyone else who really mattered."

"I have to. I've no choice. You are a good man, Perry, a strong man. You can deal with this world or any other. Poe can't. But what will our world be like without him in it? I must stay near him if I can. Forgive me."

And then she was gone.

Tears blinding my eyes I tore out of that accursed cabin. I wandered. It didn't matter where I went. There was no need for concealment in a place where I was effectively nonexistent.

Timeless and haggard I went, snatching pieces of moldy bread and draughts of tepid tea from the galleys. I paced the boards of that ancient stranger, its elder crew tottering about the business of its mysterious voyage. They took not the least notice of my presence, and the green fires of St. Elmo flickered at the edges of everything important.

Again, after what might have been days, did I feel myself addressed.

"Eddie."

"Annie? You've come back?"

"No. You are so far away, Eddie. I can scarce reach you."

"Ligeia?"

"Yes. Better. That's better. You must return to us."

"How? I've no idea where I am or why. I've just lost the most important thing in my life."

"You must try. Try, Eddie. The decision is more important than the means."

"I don't even know how to try."

"Find a way."

I stalked the decks, I cursed the ship, its captain, the crew, the weather. A chaos of foamless water boiled in the blackness about us, though through it occasionally passed floes and mountains of ice. At one time, to either hand, rose immense ramparts of cold whiteness, towering into the darkness like the walls of the universe. Onward, we rushed always onward.

Neither prayers nor curses seemed to avail me. I believe that I was mad for a time, from the loss of Annie, trapped in an environment which did little to improve one's state of mind.

The winds blew cold, out of the blackness, among the icy pillars. I watched the captain come and go, about the business of his observations, but I never approached him again. I noticed by degrees, over what might have been a long span of time, that our speed seemed to be increasing. We still carried a full load of sail and the wind had come to roar with an even greater fury.

The first time the vessel was lifted bodily out of the sea I was frightened, though it was a long while before it happened again. But there came a time when this was occurring at regular intervals. I saw the old man, knowing him now, somehow, as some version of Poe, once more, in the distance. This time, he was not taking measurements or doing calculations, but merely watching as the ice mounts raced round and round about us, his expression one of pain, loss, and beatitude—whether in succession or simultaneously, I do not know (such the consumption of Time in this place, like a green flame . . .)—and even as I apprehended our circumstance—that we must be spinning, plunging into the mouth of a whirlpool— I felt again for him that kinship I had known in days of old, and I wanted to go to him, take him in my arms, rescue him, bear him away from this place. Only I knew that I could not; and even if I could, I knew that he would not desire it.

And so I looked inward upon our dizzy whirling about the borders of our gigantic amphitheater of ice, and I saw that our circles were growing smaller, amid a roaring, a bellowing, a thundering. Suddenly, I knew what Poe was feeling, in icy eminence with an eye so close to Death's that he beheld Life with full clarity. I saw as he saw and knew that I could ride as he rode into the final globe of globes, clear-minded, pure, to perfect unity—

Saw, but did not wish it. Once we had almost been the same man. He was an artist, and I almost his creation. I mourned him in that instant of his exaltation. Now I remembered Ligeia's words, "Find a way" and I turned from him.

The world had been opened, was totally devouring. What could a man do?

I tried.

A dark unfathom'd tide
Of interminable pride—

A mystery, and a dream,
Should my early life seem:
I say that dream was fraught
With a wild, and waking thought
Of beings that have been,
Which my spirit hath not seen,
Had I let them pass me by,
With a dreaming eye!
Let none of earth inherit
That vision of my spirit;
Those thoughts I would control,
As a spell upon his soul:
For that bright hope at last
And that light time have past,
And my worldly rest hath gone
With a sigh as it passed on:
I care not tho' it perish
With a thought I then did cherish.

Imitation
Edgar Allan Poe

XII

The tall, dark-haired woman regarded the shorter gray-eyed one there upon the sand streaked orange and sable. A wall of mist passed landward. The sea was a sheet of reflected flame. A sand castle the size of a Georgian townhouse stood half-in, half-out of the fog, a tiny crack flowing up its face.

"So this is your kingdom by the sea," the taller woman said.

The other bit her lip till she tasted blood, nodding.

"Cleverly assembled, my dear. Like all the best designs there is a classic simplicity to it."

Thunder rolled somewhere inshore. A dark cloud drifted into view overhead, its shadow falling upon the bright waters.

"I did not know you could enter here," the younger woman said softly.

"Believe me, it was not easy."

"Do not harm this place."

"Not if you will help me, rather than fight me."

"What do you want?"

"We must bring him back."

Two more clouds came into view, followed by more thunder.

"Which one?"

"The only one we can still save. Or they will both be gone."

The younger woman began to weep, as the rain fell.

"I want them both."

"I am sorry, child, but it will not work that way."

"They call for me again. It is too late."

She stepped backward and the ground opened. She fell into the crevice, but her descent was abruptly halted.

The other extended a hand.

"Now, you must help me now. They've both gone so far away."

"Very well," the younger replied, lowering her hands from her face and reaching forward. "Very well."

The sky grew black and the ocean swirled. They walked upon it.

I came to full consciousness atop a piece of floating wreckage. My memories ceased somewhere before reaching that place. I was cold and the waters dark, though for the first time in what seemed an age the sky was clear, blue. . . .

I moved, drawing a cold left foot out of the water. I shifted my numb arms about, feeling the circulation come into them again, painfully. I gradually became aware that the back of my neck was sunburned. I scooped a little water with my left hand and splashed it onto it.

If Annie's powers verged upon supernatural manipulations, Poe's upon unnaturally acute perceptions, where might mine—the third member of our trio—lie? It would seem to follow, if we were somehow the same, that I— Of course. Each of them was, in a different respect, otherworldly. But I was a child of this world, the Earth; mine was the religion of life—survival. I was the necessary component for the grounding of fantasies, ideals. I placed my palms flat upon the shifting wood beneath me and I pushed, raising myself. I had, as Ligeia suggested, found the way, again; and I knew that I must turn my head to the left and open my eyes. As I did so, I felt as if some bright presence were departing my company.

I saw a sail, and I struggled to remove my shirt, to wave it.

It was the *Eidolon* which finally drew alongside, lowered a boat, recovered me. Save for Ligeia, they had given up on me along with the other crewmen who had been washed overboard nearly two weeks ago, back in May. They had been forced considerably farther south since that time, and they had only changed course and come in this direction today because Ligeia had convinced Peters that the two of them must persuade Captain Guy to do so.

As I was taken aboard the boat I saw that the pieces of wreckage upon which I had floated bore the nameplate of a ship, covered until that moment by my body. I reached after, but it drifted away before I could make contact. I was able to read it, however. It said *Discovery*.

I was carried to my stateroom, where I was brought

water, broth, bread and brandy. I had Peters find me clean garments in one of the sea chests and help me out of mine and into them. Captain Guy was present and insisted I get some sleep, and I told him I had been unconscious long enough, that I wanted to hear what had transpired during my absence. I also told him that I could not sleep until my thirst was slaked. He sent for more water and broth.

Ligeia returned at about that time, also. She had been next door talking with Valdemar. She studied my eyes, checked various pulses and departed.

"What might that signify?" Captain Guy inquired.

"That I'm about to be brought some swamp-water with peculiar things floating in it," I answered.

A little later this prophecy on my part proved correct. As I sipped it, the captain nodded.

"I'm grateful you've sufficient wits about you to talk now rather than later," he said. "I've seen men pulled from the sea after only a day or two in much worse shape than you seem to be in."

"I guess I was lucky all the way around." I said, taking another sip. The stuff was actually beginning to taste good. Maybe my taste buds had been damaged.

"We are reduced to a crew of six men," he continued, "not counting Peters here, who is acting as First Mate. I have all the weapons, of course, and the men are afraid of Peters. But they have been more than a little unhappy over our run of bad luck since we left Spain."

"Can't say as I blame them," I said.

"During your absence," he went on, "a number of the rooms were burst open and inundated during one of the storms we encountered."

"I think I know what you're going to say," I told him.

He nodded.

"Monsieur Valdemar's coffin was washed out into the corridor and its lid torn open. The men know we have this strange dead man with us, and they think he's the Jonah."

It was my turn to nod.

"They'd have cast him overboard had not Peters intervened," the captain said. "So there is this matter between us."

"Will they calm down, d'you think?" I asked.

He shrugged.

"If nothing else happens," he said. "Unfortunately, it well may."

I sighed.

"Please explain."

"We are farther south now than even explorers' vessels have previously penetrated. These are unknown waters. God knows what we might encounter."

"And if it's bad, they'll mutiny?"

"There's a good chance of it," he said. "Your saber's beneath the bed. It was somewhat nicked. Peters put a new edge on it for you."

I nodded to the smaller man.

"Thanks, mate."

He winked at me, and his eye had all the seeming of a demon's that was dreaming.

"'Snuthin', mate."

"Well, I guess we just have to wait and see," I told the captain. "What is our heading now?"

"Due south," he replied.

"Why haven't we turned around and tried to get out of here?" I asked.

He chuckled.

"We're caught in a current," he said. "We can bear to the southwest or bear to the southeast, but that is about it. We're crippled, too, remember, in the sail we can lift. We've no choice at this time but to go south."

"I've a question then," I said. "Why isn't it colder? I caught sight of a few floes while I was being fetched aboard, but the air lacks the frigidity I associate with the notion of the polar climes. This seems almost like a mild winter back home."

"I can find no reference in any of my navigational volumes on this paradoxical warming effect," he replied. "If we make it through this I've a hunch we'll be the authorities on the matter."

"Tell 'im 'bout them black bears, cap'n," Peters remarked.

"Oh, yes," Captain Guy acknowledged. "Recently we've spotted a number of them—great black fellows with red eyes and teeth."

"Red teeth?"

"Aye, them, too. You ever hear of such a creature?"

"I have not," I replied. "Have we encountered any land masses hereabout?"

"A few islands," he said. "Nothing striking about them."

"Is that everything?" I inquired.

Peters and the captain glanced at each other, which meant, of course, that there was more. Captain Guy nodded.

"Seems as we're movin' faster and faster," Peters said then. "Pickin' up speed ever' day."

I had a sudden vision from my now faded dream-like excursion aboard the *Discovery*.

"Meaning that the current is moving faster, and faster," I stated.

"Exactly," the captain acknowledged. "Which means we must seriously consider a theory propounded by a Colonel Symmes of Ohio, to the effect that the Earth is hollow, and that the currents of the seas pour through a vortex at the South Pole to emerge from an opening at the North Pole, thence to recirculate. . . ."

And my vision continued. Round and round like a colossal drain from which the plug had been pulled. . . . Was this in some fashion premonitory of our present plight as well as indicative of whatever it revealed on its own.

I raised my hands, massaged my eyeballs with their heels.

"I seem to recall reading a magazine piece on this notion, some time ago," I told him. "By a fellow named Reynolds, I believe."

"Yes," Captain Guy said. "I saw it, too. While the welfare of this vessel and that of everyone aboard her is my responsibility, Mr. Ellison has requested that I discuss matters of great moment with you. In other words, sir, what is your opinion as to the best course of action we should take?"

"Lord!" I said. "It's a guessing game!"

"Then give me your guess," he insisted.

"Very well," I replied. "Whether the Earth be truly hollow or whether something else be the cause of our precipitate rush, I believe we're likely to go smash when we get there. So I feel we should start veering off immediately, as a delaying action." I groped in the pocket of the trousers I had discarded, found a Spanish coin, tossed it. "Heads," I announced. "Let's go east."

Captain Guy smiled bleakly.

"As good a way to choose as any, I suppose," he acknowledged. "Very well—"

There came a tapping, as of someone gently

rapping on the distant wall. It resembled the effect I often produced when attempting mesmerism. Ligeia was on her feet immediately.

"Excuse me," she said, and she was gone out the door.

"What might that be about?" the captain asked.

I glanced at Peters, who nodded.

"I take it you know *all* about Monsieur Valdemar now?" I said.

"Concerning his extra-normal abilities? Yes. Ligeia explained the situation to me, once the—cat was out of the bag, so to speak."

His face suddenly brightened. He half-rose from his chair.

"Of course!" he said, and I nodded.

Moments later, Ligeia returned.

"Bear full to the southwest at six bells tomorrow morn," she stated.

"Certainly," the captain said.

"Indeed," I noted.

They gave me another brandy, and then I went to sleep.

We continued to see a good deal of ice on our new course, but the weather had grown even more clement. I did catch sight of one of the great black bears but even more interesting—the following day—was a glimpse of a canoe filled with black-skinned, ebony-toothed folk. We shot past them, however.

And another day came and went.

Then Ligeia emerged from Valdemar's cabin, catching me on the companionway as I was returning to my stateroom from a stroll about the deck.

"Soon," she announced.

"Soon what?"

She gestured Indian-style with her chin, back up the stair. Turning, I reascended, and she followed me. She took me aft then and indicated the north-northwest.

"It will come from that direction," she said. "Watch for it, will you?"

"What? What will come?" I asked.

"I forget your word for it," she said, and she turned and was gone.

So I jammed my hands into my pockets, leaned against the rail and watched. Nothing happened for a long while. I found myself almost hypnotized by the bright flashes on the rushing water.

"Damn it Perry!"

"'Ey, Eddie! Whatcher up to?"

Peters had come up soundlessly behind me, Grip perched upon his shoulder.

"Nothing much," I said. "Just watching for it in the sky, to the north-northwest."

"Watchin' fer what?"

"Ah— Well, she didn't exactly say."

"Really," he said, turning his head in that direction. "Somethin' sort of like a big fool's cap, upside-down, with a basket hangin' under it?"

"What?"

I turned and stared. I squinted. I shaded my eyes. I saw nothing.

"You speak hypothetically, of course," I said, after a few moments.

"Dunno what that means, Eddie. But yer know I don't talk fancy."

"You don't really see something like that up there, do you?"

"Now why ud I make up somethin' that stupid, Eddie. 'Course it's there."

I kept looking. The best I could make out was a tiny speck against the blue—either a distant bird or a trick my eyes were playing.

"There's a black band goes 'round it, with somethin' like a silver buckle on it, too."

"You actually see the thing?"

"Sure. She's there, Eddie."

I began to recall stories about the remarkable vision of the Indians of the Plains.

"You say it, you see it," I said. "What else is there?"

He continued to stare.

"Looks to be a man in the basket," he finally announced.

I continued gazing in that direction myself. The speck had grown larger.

"Bear shit," Grip commented, as we passed an ice floe where one of the scarlet-fanged brutes was relieving itself.

"'At's a good Gripper," said Peters, rummaging in his pocket for a cracker and passing it to him. "Quick learner."

"Yo," said the raven.

It grew larger still, though it was several minutes more before it became distinguishable to me as possessing the shape Peters had attributed to it.

"'At dead man sure knows his business," Peters observed.

"Got to give him that," I agreed.

And the thing came on and on, and I recalled articles I'd read about balloons, remembering the basket beneath the gasbag to be called a gondola. Nearer still, and I saw that this one did indeed possess a human inhabitant. The device was obviously headed right toward us, and it was descending. I began to grow concerned that it might upset or rupture itself amid such masts and sails as we still possessed. I heard a hissing sound as it drew nigh. Then it drifted past us and settled gently into a mild sea off our starboard bow.

Peters and I had a boat over the side in record time and lines to him and his balloon in less than a minute after we hit the water. The man spoke some English and some French, poorly, explaining that he was one Hans Pfall, of Rotterdam, at which Peters allowed that he himself spoke "gutter Dutch" having done some errands for Mr. Ellison in the Kingdom of the Netherlands and it might be faster if he tried interpreting for him, if all parties were willing to make allowances.

All parties were, and the man explained that he had been airborne since leaving Rotterdam several weeks ago. He claimed to have been borne away from Europe by high altitude winds of terrific velocity.

Captain Guy, Ligeia, and the crew were on the deck, and the balloon still being partially inflated and its owner madly anxious that it should not be lost, the captain gave orders to deflate the huge gasbag slowly and carefully, and to see that it was hoisted with extreme caution onto the deck—along with the gondola, which contained some mysterious equipment.

Once on deck, at the vigilant direction of its pilot, the bag was dried, folded, and eventually stowed away belowdecks, along with the huge wicker basket and other gear.

We all had some doubts concerning Mr. Pfall's fantastic story. Still, the fellow must have come some impressive distance across the ocean.

Our voyage continued, almost helplessly, ever farther and farther south. Days went by, and the occasional small islands, the drifting ice, even the water we observed were increasingly strange.

We bumped gently into a drifting floe, and from the part that overhung our decks briefly we broke off chunks for drinking water. Melted in a pot, this fresh water displayed an amazing *stratification*. At first we were afraid to taste it because of this. It was layered and possessed of every conceivable shade of purple. We allowed it to settle thoroughly within a white basin. It formed a series of distinct veins therein, and we discovered that upon passing the blade of a knife downward through them the water closed over it immediately, and on withdrawing it all trace of the knife's passage was instantly obliterated. If, however, the blade was passed between two veins a perfect separation occurred and did not immediately repair itself.

Peters laughed, cupped a handful and swallowed it, while we were discussing its visual characteristics. He announced it to be a "good, cold swig." In that nothing untoward occurred with him several others of us tasted it and were so gratified. Peters then explained that it had "smelled" all right, water-sniffing being a thing he'd learned in childhood, on the Plains.

Meanwhile, the current bearing us along grew stronger and stronger, until we were completely helpless in its grip.

Two days later we awoke to what I first took to be a snowfall, but a visit topside showed it to be a fall of volcanic ash that was graying our deck. We had come into the vicinity of the legendary Mt. Yaanek, bursting with gray cabbage-leaf clouds, lightnings tunneling among them, an occasional show of a bright heart beating at its center. Its distant grumbles came like thunder. The skies were ashen and sober as we went by.

I had avoided visiting Valdemar for some time, perhaps he somehow served to remind me of the night of the Red Death at Prospero's abbey. However, it appeared obvious to me that we must rapidly be nearing the Symmes' Hole, and since I did not know what to do next it seemed that a little unearthly advice might be in order. The temperature had grown milder, the ocean almost hot, and all traces of ice and snow had vanished. All these things considered, I'd a feeling it was probably time to act.

Ligeia seemed still to be asleep, but since I possessed a duplicate key to Valdemar's cabin I simply let myself in, bringing a lighted oil lamp.

I made the necessary passes, and again the noisy disturbances began, his casket itself being levitated briefly. At this, Valdemar sat up and reached forward, opening the lower half of his crate as well. Not stopping at that, he swung his legs up and out, rising, and then lowering himself, so that he sat perched at the edge like some cadaverous scarecrow.

"Oh, Eddie!" he said. "Again? You bathe me in even more life than last time, child of the Earth!"

"Sorry," I said. "It's something of an emergency, though. I believe we're nearing the South Polar Symmes' Hole."

"Nor are you incorrect!" he agreed. "What a glorious way to go! I misjudged you. Thank you for bringing me around to witness our final passing. It is about the only thing I might regard with something resembling pleasure."

"Uh— Sorry to disappoint you," I said, "but I'm looking for a way to escape it."

"No!" He rose and tottered. "I refuse to help you elude such a fine and honorable death!"

"I hate to pull rank," I said, "but I've the power to compel you in this."

I began the preliminaries to the administration of even more mesmeric energy.

"Stop! You could not be so heartless!"

He tottered toward me, arms extended before him.

"You will tell me what you know in this," I said, "or I will animate you even further."

"Ask me anything else," he replied. "The secrets of the ages are open books to me. What would you care to have? Sophocles' missing dramas? The proof for Fermat's Last Theorem? The precise archaeological location of Troy? The—"

"You're stalling," I said. "Why— I see. We're that close, are we?"

His arms fell.

"Yes, we are," he said.

"But we've still a chance to make it, haven't we? It's going to be close—so close that minutes could actually make a difference, one way or another."

"You're smarter than I gave you credit for, Perry."

"I don't want your flattery, just some facts. The balloon must be the only way out. How long does it take to inflate?

"Approximately two hours," he answered.

"How long till we plunge into the Hole?"

"Perhaps three hours."

"How many people can it carry?"

"Four."

"That will never do. There are twelve of us."

"It will do," he replied, showing all of his teeth.

"I do not understand."

"Shall I explain?"

"I'm sure you'd like to. I'm also sure there isn't time. Good-bye."

I turned and rushed for the door.

"Eddie! Wait!"

I halted at the strange note of urgency I had never heard in his speech before.

"What?" I asked.

"Go armed."

"Why?"

"I've nothing against you personally. Just get your saber and wear it."

"All right," I said. "Thanks."

And I was out the door and running.

I came out of my quarters buckling the thing into place when I heard the cries from above, and a clash of metal on metal. Rather than heading for the cargo area where the balloon was stowed I climbed the companionway, to see what was doing.

As my head and shoulders came out of the companionway, a crewman who had apparently been guarding it thrust a staff at me. I fell back, drew my blade and cut at it, knocking it aside. He raised it again and I executed a simple chest cut, feeling it shear through ribs. He screamed. I surveyed the situation clearly then.

Captain Guy, Peters, and Hans Pfall were all aft, trapped upon the poop deck by the crewmen, who'd apparently decided the time was right for their mutiny. I noticed a stack of supplies beside one of the boats, a splash of red on the deck nearby. Captain Guy had blood on his shirtfront, also, and he leaned against the railing as if partly stunned. I suspected he had caught the crew in the act of abandoning ship, and the mutiny had commenced at that point.

Peters held a belaying pin in either hand. Pfall held
a saber similar to my own. The five remaining crewmen looked back at the one I had just cut down. My
presence at their rear seemed to influence their
decision to attack forward. Uttering a cry, they rushed
the three men.

Peters threw one of his clubs at the foremost, who
had attacked the captain, knife in hand. It struck the
man on the head, and he fell. Another was rushing
toward Peters himself, saber upraised. In the meantime, Pfall had raised his blade into a guard position
and was staring wide-eyed at his attacker, a burly
fellow with a stiletto in one hand and a club in the
other.

I shouted a hopefully distracting cry as I mounted
the final stairs and headed in their direction, bran-
dishing my blade. For the first time, as I did this,
I became aware of a low, thundering sound, like a
buried storm, coming from somewhere far forward
of our vessel. It was more than a persistent note, for
it also constituted a physically felt vibration which
one detected down to the roots of one's teeth. To my
horror, I understood its nature. I shouted again, and
the rearmost man turned to face me. He was a tall,
lean, wall-eyed individual who brandished a spiked
club quite capable of snapping my blade if the nails
with which he'd studded it connected properly.

I saw Peters avoid the swordsman's cut, stepping
inside to parry with his club against his attacker's
wrist. Then he drove his massive right fist forward
and upward. It was lost to sight of me then, blocked
by his assailant's body. But suddenly the man was
raised above the deck, bending double while lofted,
blood spewing from his mouth. To my other hand,
I saw Pfall fall back, blood upon his shoulder.

Then I had no attention for anyone's problems but my own, and I halted as my attacker's club was swung at me like a bat. I dropped my guard and retreated rather than risk my steel against such a juggernaut. He swung again, cross-body, and I retreated again, studying the way he moved, looking for an opening.

I heard Hans Pfall scream—a heavily accented outcry—and his blade rattled to the deck.

A flight of birds crossed over us from out of the northwest, crying *E-teke-lili!* as they passed.

My attacker raised his club over his right shoulder, and with both hands swung it in a diagonal cut past my chest. He laughed as I retreated again, and cried out. "You come to somethin', you gotta stop! No more runnin'! I get you then!" and I could only nod politely and smile, for I had noted that his recovery from a downward stroke was noticeably slower than from one which moved in a horizontal plane.

I heard Captain Guy's new attacker—to whom Peters had turned his attention on dispatching his own man—commence screaming, as Peters had caught his wrist, jerked him forward and torn his ear off with his teeth. While this was happening, the man Peters had knocked down with his thrown club began rising.

"*E-teke— E-teke—* Shit!" cried Grip, swooping by and defecating on Peters' attacker.

In the meantime, the *Eidolon* jumped, as if we had actually been lifted bodily from the waves—and I could not but be reminded of my strange experiences while aboard the ghostly *Discovery*—and when the *Eidolon* came down, our speed seemed to have increased. I half-expected green fire to dance along my blade.

Suddenly, it did. Had my thought summoned it? Did I possess some strange connection in this place even stronger than memory—with things I had touched in the past?

The tall crewman's eyes widened as the baleful gleam walked my weapon's edge. Yet he drew back his club over his left shoulder, and he swung it again. Again, I retreated. But not as before. Recalling an expensive lesson from a fancy-legged French fencing master who had once passed through town, I retreated but a single step with my left foot, drew back my right in an enormous hurry, brought my saber up, out, around and over, transforming it then into a point-weapon as I executed a stop-thrust which tore into the man's upper arm before he could recover from his missed swing. Immediately, I withdrew the point and executed a second thrust, to my assailant's throat. He took it properly.

I looked up then to see Peters throwing his unearred opponent against the one who had just risen. The man whose chest he had smashed lay sprawled, leaking blood through his ears and nose as well as his mouth. I glanced back, a precaution. The man whose chest I had cut open still lay beside the companionway. He was not breathing.

Three of the six, then, were down, two were attacking Peters, and the final one was just withdrawing his stiletto from a point somewhere below Hans Pfall's left ribcage. He turned his attention now to Peters, who had crouched and extended both his hands toward the two men he had dealt with before who now faced him again. Smiling, the burly man moved to assist them, swinging his club almost jauntily in his left hand, knife in his right, low and near to his hip. As he passed the still form of Captain Guy I heard a pistol's sharp report. The club slipped from his fingers and he dropped to one knee, left hand moving to clutch somewhere at his midsection.

Above the eternal growl of the Symmes' Hole I heard the man say, "I thought you was dead!" Then he dropped to his other knee and I could see past him to where Captain Guy still lay, back propped against a bollard, a derringer in his right hand, a small smile upon his lips.

"You were wrong," the captain said.

I advanced upon the two who faced Peters, one of whom had snatched up the saber dropped by the earliest attacker. As he heard my approach, this one turned to face me. He bent from the waist and extended the weapon out to his side, point angling back in toward me, his other hand fluttering forward— an obvious and cumbersome attempt to transfer knife-fighting technique to the larger weapon. I strode forward almost contemptuously then. This was no problem for a trained fencer.

My heel struck a patch of bird feces and I slipped. Thus is arrogance occasionally brought down by the lowly. My attacker was on me in an instant, trying to lay the edge of his weapon across my windpipe and lean upon it. We both, of course, tried kneeing the other in the groin, and both successfully turned a thigh against it. In that my right arm had gone high and then out to the side during my fall and that my opponent now had a knee upon its biceps, I released the blade. I couldn't swing it from that position, and it was just an added burden of weight. I brought the hand over quickly, getting it beneath his blade, where it joined the other in holding the weapon back. Unfortunately, it was the edge that I was blocking. Fortunately, it was not too sharp. Unfortunately, it was sharp enough. . . .

I felt it cut into my hands and he grinned as the blood began to run and drip upon my shirtfront; and he breathed on me, which nearly proved my undoing. His teeth were in very bad condition.

I still heard the sounds of struggling from Peters' quarter. The ship skipped again, and the *forte* of the blade ground heavily against my left palm. The Symmes' thunder came like some thousands of Niagaras now, and from the awkward angle at which I lay I saw that far off to my left and high up in the sky a great tower of mist and fog had grown up, drifting, looming, inclining toward us like an enormous shrouded human figure, white as bone, snow, or the skin of a cadaver. . . .

I spat full in my assailant's face—ungentlemanly, unsanitary, and not a thing I'd learned from the French master; but rather a trick told me by a young British officer called Flash with whom I'd gone drinking one night, described by him as so unnerving it had almost cost him his life in a duel. It had remained in my mind as a particularly egregious breach of etiquette ever since. Fortunately, I am neither an officer nor a gentleman, and it worked beautifully. He drew back sufficiently for me to grit my teeth and push, which gave me just enough of an opening to form my right hand painfully into a fist and drive it forward against the source of his bad breath. He did not rock back as far as I hoped, his weight still holding me pinned, but a leaning corpse-white figure other than the misty apparition in the sky caught hold of his neck then and twisted, raising him from me. The man's body swung toward Valdemar as he was drawn to his feet. His right elbow went back like a piston, and the point of his blade against Valdemar's abdomen; then he drove it forward, running my rescuer through. Valdemar twisted his neck and I heard it crack. Then he released him and looked downward.

"Oh! The irony of it!" he observed. "To send others to that shore I may not tread!"

He withdrew the weapon from his middle and let it fall, also.

"Thanks," I said. "We'll do right by you one of these days. Really."

There came a short, barking laugh from my right and I looked that way just in time to see Peters rising from the deck, ruddy blade in his right hand, a scalp in his left.

"Counting a little *coup*," I observed.

"It's been a *coup-coup* day, Eddie," he replied, and we both turned toward the captain and Pfall.

Both men were still living but in very bad shape. We gave what aid we could. None of the mutineers had survived. Pfall grunted something in that guttural language of his.

"He says to get the balloon up here pronto, an' he'll tell us how ter set 'er up." Peters translated.

"Right," I answered. "Let's go."

Our rush took us past Ligeia, who stood in the companionway, smiling. For a moment I'd have sworn I saw a drop of blood at the corner of her mouth, but her tongue flicked and the illusion vanished, leaving only the smile.

We dragged the thing topside and unfolded it, not knowing how much time remained.

Pfall directed us in its inflation. Peters had to lean close to him for every instruction, for his voice had weakened and the Symmes' sounds increased yet again in volume. Valdemar and Ligeia labored with us, also; and when Pfall breathed his last after giving us some final information, Valdemar cursed bitterly that yet another man went unwilling to the place he most desired.

Captain Guy gestured to me and I went to him, there being nothing more to do just then but wait for the gasbag to achieve proper inflation.

"Eddie," he said weakly, "I've a favor to ask."

"Anything, sir," I replied.

"Take me forward, that I might see this thing that's about to swallow the *Eidolon*."

Peters and I fetched up a comfortable chair from my stateroom and placed him in it. We strapped him there for security's sake and carried him forward then.

"It's bigger than that canyon out in the West," Peters announced, when we beheld the great dark thunderhole beneath its shifting tower of mist.

"Find a way to secure the chair here, men," Captain Guy directed, and we fetched more lines and did that for him. In the meantime, he'd produced his pipe and filled its bowl and fetched his tinderbox from somewhere within his bloody jacket.

"Let me give you a hand with that," I suggested.

"I can manage."

"You really propose to remain here?"

"Haven't that much time left," he replied, taking his first puff, "and I wouldn't miss this for anything. How many masters get to follow their vessel to the end in a fashion such as this?" He took another puff. "Leave me now. You've work to do and I want to enjoy the view."

I squeezed his shoulder gently, leaving a bloody palmprint.

"God be with you, Captain," I said. "You did right by us. Thanks."

Peters said something, too, but I couldn't make out

the words. When we turned to head back astern I realized how far we were inclined. Glancing forward again, I knew that we were seeing deeper into the Hole than we had before. We hurried.

Ligeia and Valdemar were already in the basket, the balloon tugging at its lines we had dogged to ring-bolts in the deck.

"Cast off," the lady said, and I cut the lines and we shot skyward.

In a matter of moments we beheld the battered *Eidolon* quivering upon the brink of Symmes' abyss, pathetic human invention about to launch itself against eternity. For a moment, I thought of Poe.

Valdemar uttered a strange hissing noise, then observed, "To think that *I* should be a survivor."

> There are many moments when, even to the sober eye of Reason, the world of our sad Humanity may assume the semblance of a Hell—but the imagination of man is no Carathis, to explore with impunity its every cavern. Alas! the grim legion of sepulchral terrors cannot be regarded as altogether fanciful—but, like the demons in whose company Afrasiab made his voyage down the Oxus, they must sleep, or they will devour us—they must be suffered to slumber, or we perish.
>
> From *The Premature Burial*,
> Edgar Allan Poe

XIII

Science! true daughter of Old Time thou art!
Who alterest all things with thy peering eyes.
Why preyest thou thus upon the poet's heart,
Vulture, whose wings are dull realities?
How should he love thee? or how deem thee wise?
Who wouldst not leave him in his wandering
To seek for treasure in the jewelled skies,
Albeit he soared with an undaunted wing?
Hast thou not dragged Diana from her car?
And driven the Hamadryad from the wood
To seek a shelter in some happier star?
Hast thou not torn the Naiad from her flood,
The Elfin from the green grass, and from me
The summer dream beneath the tamarind tree?

Sonnet—To Science,
Edgar Allan Poe

We continued to rise at a rapid rate, the thunder from the Earth's polar aperture finally beginning to diminish. Ligeia insisted on cleaning my lacerated palms thoroughly, then dressing them with heavy bandages. Fortunately, she had been able to provision our gondola considerably while Peters and I were occupied with our late captain.

Our wish was to return to Europe, or at least to some other civilized land. But we soon discovered that we had very little control over our course. At least, we were being borne northward by steady winds. We found that we could control our altitude to a great degree, by throwing over ballast or releasing gas, thus managing to maintain a sequence of favorable winds. But it was hard to tell directions.

Valdemar curled up on the floor, Ligeia covered him with a tarpaulin, and he became a general-purpose piece of furniture. Ligeia would sit and meditate upon him for hours at a time. Peters used him as a pillow; I, an ottoman.

There can be too much of excitement, too much of sensation. Our first day airborne was an affectless thing. We were psychically drained from all that we had experienced of late, from all that we continued to experience. As my feelings had been for a time following my ordeal at the hands of the Inquisition, as well as that maddening other-worldly journey aboard the *Discovery,* or the morning after Prince Prospero's party on the night of the Red Death, so now I knew the distancing of fatigue within a consciousness too stimulated for slumber and a consequent sense of the unreality of my present surroundings—akin, I suppose, to that of a late-night reader's, of some fantastical romance, with the difference that I could not escape by closing the book. (While this comparison may not be unique, little has been made of that reader's own prisonerhood within my life—so to speak—and the special solace for us both that the glory of language with its bright procession of tellings preceded the spurious consolations of philosophy by an age, as demonstrated in the fact that none misses sleep for philosophy.) And my mind in this state is wont to divagate, eyes go unfocussed, body wisdoms rise to swamp all thinking.

The second and the third day were of the same order, though reality came scratching at the door more and more often, and we ate and we talked again and Grip granted us an occasional obscenity from basket rim or cable.

We maintained our swift, high-altitude northering for the better part of a week. I tried to discover whether it might be June, July, or August and neither Peters nor Ligeia was certain. And it seemed mean to rouse Valdemar on such a small matter.

So we sailed on, landing only once the following week on a tropical isle in a valley of many-colored grasses. We took this chance only because the one thing we were low on was water, and this colorful spot with its River of Silence come out of some hill by a route obscure and lonely, also bore numerous pot-holes and fissures, whence volcanic gases rose. After we had drunk our fill and loaded every container we possessed to its limit we were able to reinflate the balloon at one of these openings.

So we ascended again, rising till we picked up another strong wind of what seemed a northerly persuasion. Soon our course took us above a heavy cloud cover. And this went on, and on, and on.

We discussed descending to take our bearings but argued ourselves out of it, in that we were unlikely to sight any really familiar landmarks, and we might—in the matter of descending through what could prove massive foggy banks—encounter some mountainous prominence to our detriment.

We even lost track of the days after a time. For so long as our supplies lasted, though, we were determined to continue rather than risk falling short of our hemisphere, our temperate zone.

It was not until the gasbag began to leak and the decision was taken from us that we finally entered the clouds, drifting through them with the distinct feeling that all motion had been suspended—as if we had been imbedded in cotton. The only indication I had as to how long we had been in transit now was that my hands were well-along in their healing.

When we finally emerged from the clouds it was above a green landscape that was not a jungle. Beyond that, we had not the least idea where we were.

We kept on, hoping for some sight of civilization, having stabilized again at a lower altitude. A night passed in this fashion.

Dawn came into the upper atmosphere, though the Earth was still in darkness when we descended upon it. The sounds and smells and—after a small while—the sights were all hearteningly familiar. A brief reconnoiter along a rural roadway showed me a sign at a crossroad saying RICHMOND 10 MI.

We deflated our balloon the rest of the way and concealed it in a wood. Valdemar being slow and unsteady on his feet, we were unable to travel very well. So, leaving Ligeia with him in the wood, Peters and I set out in search of some sort of vehicle in which we might transport him.

After having hiked a mile or two we heard the sounds of voices. Changing our course slightly in that direction we came shortly to a metal gateway which stood slightly open. A portly man who stood within bade us enter. He shook our hands as we did so, introducing himself as Mr. Maillard. He was a fine-looking gentleman of the old school, well-dressed, well-mannered, dignified. At his back, however, strolled a number of peculiarly garbed individuals—that is to say, they were accoutered in the costumes of many periods and many lands—including a woman who paused periodically to flap her arms and announce "Cock-a-doodle-doo!" in a surprisingly deep voice.

"We'd like to rent or borrow a cart, a wagon, a wheelbarrow, a coach," I said. "Might that be possible, sir?"

"I believe so," Maillard replied, "though I'm not the one you should talk to in this regard. Come with me to the main building and we'll find someone in the office to help you."

We followed him in the direction of a large old mansion house, and on the way were accosted by a man walking on all fours who rubbed up against our legs and purred. After he had departed in pursuit of a rabbit, I said, "Sir, we are not from this area, and while I have my suspicious I must inquire as to the nature of this—institution."

He smiled.

"As you have guessed," he reported, "it is an asylum for the insane. Dr. Tarr and Professor Fether established it here some years ago after leaving France, where they had developed radical experimental treatments for patients of this sort."

We mounted to the old house and entered there. Mr. Maillard left us in a large, once-elegant living room, now somewhat shabby, saying he would locate someone concerning the cart and send him to us. Peters and I collapsed onto the slightly worn furniture.

"Hard to believe we're back, Eddie," he said. "Be sure an' find out what month it is 'fore we leave."

"The month, sir, is September," said a small man largely submerged in a dark chair in a dark corner, off to our right.

"Beg pardon," I said. "We didn't notice you there."

He chuckled.

"It has its advantages," he observed. He rose then and bowed, a silver-haired and goateed individual, bright blue eyes enlarged through heavy spectacles. "Dr. Augustus Bedloe, at your service."

"Ah, you are a member of the staff."

"No. As a matter of fact, I am a patient here."

"I'm sorry. . . ."

"No need. I am not demented, if that is what you fear."

"I—do not understand."

"Might I inquire as to your professions?"

"I am Edgar Perry, U. S. Army, retired," I stated, extending my hand. "My friend is Dirk Peters, First Mate of the *Eidolon*."

He clasped our hands and shook them.

"Merely attempting to ascertain whether you were in any fashion associated with the courts or law enforcement establishments. I am pleased that you are not."

"Always glad to please." I glanced at Peters, who shrugged.

"I am actually one of the only two sane persons in this institution," Dr. Bedloe announced.

"Of course," I agreed.

"I am serious, sir, and I speak only for your own benefit—to warn you."

"How did this state of affairs come about?"

"The inmates took over three days ago," he explained, "confining Tarr and Fether to a padded room. Mr. Maillard, a dangerous maniac, was their leader."

I studied his face. He sounded so convincing.

"And why should you believe me?" he said. "Well, consider: Why should the gate be unlocked and the inmates wandering the grounds?"

"That did sort of bother me, Eddie," Peters said uneasily. "Tell me, Dr. Bedloe, whatcha doin' here if yer sane?"

"The alternative was to be hanged for murder a few years ago," he answered. "It was preferable to fake lunacy and live. That was why I inquired concerning any affiliations on your part with the legal business."

"Oh," Peters said, and I agreed.

"I am harmless," the man assured us. "But a patient suffered a fatal heart attack on coming out of a trance I had put him into, and his ignorant relatives held me culpable."

"Trance? You are a mesmerist?" I inquired.

"Indeed, sir, and once accounted a fairly good one."

"I find myself at odds," I said, "with a man using that art in a far more nefarious fashion than yourself."

"May I inquire as to his identity?"

"A certain Dr. Templeton," I replied.

"I am not unacquainted with the man," he told me, "and I do not doubt what you say in the least."

"You actually knew him?"

"Yes, and I know, too, that he has not changed his ways. Even now, he and his cohorts—a certain Good-fellow and Griswold, I believe—are up in New York at the Domain of Arnheim, cooperating with the millionaire Seabright Ellison in the manufacture of alchemical gold, to the formula of some German inventor they've hired."

"What?" I was on my feet, moving toward him, reaching to clasp his lapels. "How could you possibly know such things?" I cried. "You said yourself that you've been here for years."

"Please, sir! I'm an old man. I only wish you well, which is why I've warned you about this place. Do as you choose with what I've told you, but do not harm me."

"Just tell me how you came to know their current doings?"

"It is the affair of the other sane patient I spoke of," he told me. "Mr. Ellison had hired him as a personal secretary and he had been employed at Arnheim for some months. Actually, he was a journalist who wished to write a piece exposing Ellison's illegal affairs, which cover several continents."

"If the man was discovered, why wasn't he killed?"

"He was too well-connected, with others knowing what he was about. So Dr. Templeton had him committed elsewhere as insane."

"They simply took Templeton's word for it?"

"No. The man, Sanford Martin, was entirely insane at the time of his commitment. It is not that difficult for one skilled in our art to induce this state temporarily. Later, since the condition would pass, they had him transferred to this institution and registered under a different name. He told me of the goings-on at Arnheim."

I clutched at his sleeve.

"Sir, did he at any time mention the presence of a lady called Annie?"

"He did," Dr. Bedloe replied, "as a lady possessed

of very unusual ability, who is working as Von Kempelen's assistant."

I turned away. I sank into a chair and buried my face in my hands.

"To have come so far," I said at last. "To be so late. . . ."

I felt Peters' arm about my shoulder.

"Now, Eddie, yer dunno yer late. As I'd heard Mr. Ellison say in the past, these experiments takes some time."

"I could arrange for you to speak with Sanford Martin, if you wish to verify what I've told you," Dr. Bedloe said.

"That won't be necessary, sir," I told him. "You couldn't very well have made up something like that, something that fits so closely with the facts as I know them."

"Eddie, yer won't make good time travelin' with Valdemar," Peters told me, "and Ligeia won't leave him."

"I know."

There came a babble of voices from the rear of the building, seeming headed in our direction.

"I repeat my suggestion that you depart quickly," Dr. Bedloe said, "and seek your cart somewhere else."

"Do you want to come with us?"

He shook his head.

"Can't," he replied. "And in here I do some good. I've cured a number, to date."

We got to our feet. We shook his hand again.

"Good luck, boys," he told us.

"We'd better run, Eddie," Peters said, as the sounds of angry cries drew nigh.

We ran.

✦   ✦   ✦

Once we were off the grounds and into the woods I opened my money belt, extracted gold coins and shared them with Peters, enabling him to obtain transportation for himself and the others. And a new casket for Valdemar. I had suggested that he remain in their company, as protector, while they were on the road north. This was not complete altruism on my part, as I still wondered at the strength of whatever loyalty he might have had for Seabright Ellison. I had never learned its nature or how it had come about. I had the feeling, however, that he, too, was happy about remaining down here while I headed up there, to settle matters.

I embraced the sinister dwarf, with an affection I have felt for few. Under a Hunter's Moon, we parted.

How shall the burial rite be read?
The solemn song be sung?

From *A Paean*,
Edgar Allan Poe

XIV

"You have conquered, and I yield. Yet henceforward art thou also dead—dead to the World, to Heaven, and to Hope! In me didst thou exist—and, in my death, see by this image, which is thine own, how utterly thou hast murdered thyself."

From *William Wilson*,
Edgar Allan Poe

It was night in the lonesome October when I went over the high wall of fieldstone, avoided an armed patrol and began to make my way through the miles of landscape garden toward the main house at the Domain of Arnheim. I could not be certain of the exact location of that edifice, but a recent visitation with Ligeia—who now seemed to have access to the kingdom by the sea—had left me with marching orders for the ascent of the Wissahiccon River. I broke into Landor's cottage that night and slept there, Ligeia having mentioned that Annie might have been confined to the place for a time. I did find there a Spanish comb such as she had once worn in her hair at Prospero's castellated abbey. I kept it, of course, and in the morning I pressed on.

The magnificence of the landscape gardening would, at any other time, have proved distracting. But I was blind to beauty now. Every night—and sometimes days, as well—came a fresh dream or waking vision, of Annie, of Ligeia, of distant Poe rushing toward his doom. Such a coming together of power and of disturbances told me that something in our relationship was building toward a climax.

Onward.

The visions of the local scene had all pointed in one direction: Ellison and his rivals had concluded that it would be better for them to join forces than to fight each other. My supposed benefactor was now in league with the men he had sent me to chase more than halfway around the world. Von Kempelen, here at Arnheim with them, would transmute a large amount of lead into gold. This hoard of precious metal would then be turned over to Ellison, as payment for vast properties—including Arnheim itself—considerable jewelry, and some other items of great worth. Immediately thereafter, all parties to the agreement would witness the destruction of the gold-making apparatus. No further production would occur to cheapen the price of gold and devalue the new hoard.

Onward.

The colors of autumn were all about me, as I moved my gaze from the sky-blue lake where the most recent vision had occurred. It involved killing Von Kempelen afterwards, so that the process would not soon be repeated.

Onward.

And so at last I reached the center of the Domain, the Paradise of Arnheim, and there I was overwhelmed by a gush of melody, an oppressive sense of strange sweet odor, and a dream-like intermingling of tall eastern trees, bosky shrubberies, flocks of golden and crimson birds, fountains, lakes, flowers, meadows, silver streamlets. For longer than I should have, I stood overpowered by the sensory assault, and then I entered there.

I took my way cautiously, but I encountered no patrols. Before me, upsprung from the midst of botanical grandeur was a great mass of semi-Gothic, semi-Saracenic architecture, glittering in the red sunlight with a hundred oriels, minarets, and pinnacles. Amazing.

As I drew nearer, I realized that the place was moated. I circled it, several times, keeping well-concealed by the profuse shrubbery. Seeing no other means of entry I selected a likely causeway and dashed across it.

Save for a barely perceptible crack down the front of the place, the masonry looked in excellent order.

I passed through a Gothic archway and approached a heavy wooden door. I tried it and found it unlocked. I entered.

There was much old woodwork, somber tapestries on the walls, and an ebon blackness to the floor. I crossed the room quickly and carefully, without making a sound, blade loose in its scabbard, pistol loaded, other surprises hidden about my person.

I stepped into a hallway and passed along it, inspecting each room that I passed. Seabright Ellison was in the third one to the left.

Seeing no need for a dramatic entrance, I merely walked in. It was a library, and Ellison in a maroon dressing gown of silk was seated on a dark, bulging lounge reading and smoking a cigar, a glass of what was probably sherry on a side table to his right.

He looked up and smiled as my shadow fell upon him.

"Perry," he remarked, "and right on time."

I was not about to play it his way and ask what he meant by that. I simply responded with my most important question:

"Where is she?"

"Here, and quite comfortable," he replied. "No one here would harm her, believe me."

"She is being held here and forced to do something against her will."

"I assure you she will be well-paid for her efforts," he said. "For that matter, you are owed considerable recompense yourself for your activities on my behalf."

"I believe I recall your offering a bonus If I killed Griswold, Templeton, and Goodfellow for you. I'm willing to do it now. Is the offer still good?"

He paled slightly, then grinned.

"I'm afraid it expired several months ago when I came to an agreement with these men."

"You're partners now?" I asked.

"More or less, yes."

"And Von Kempelen's here?"

"So he is. You *have* been doing your homework. Would you care for a glass of sherry?"

"So long as you'll keep talking."

"Of course. What can I tell you?"

He found me a small brandy snifter, from which a few drops were ordinarily inhaled. He filled it halfway.

"You say you'll pay Annie," I stated. "But you're still forcing her to do something she doesn't want to."

"For her own good, as I can demonstrate."

I took a sip.

"Demonstrate it, then."

"I spoke of her share in a great fortune, so great that—"

"I see. And Edgar Poe?"

He rose. He jabbed the air with his cigar and paced through the smoke.

"What of Edgar Poe?" he asked. "If he has become a friend of yours—and Annie's—I'm sorry. Truly. But the unique relationship among the three of you could not go on forever."

"Oh, could it not?"

"It could not." Ellison nodded, as if I had simply been agreeing with him from the beginning. "Because Poe no longer exists—not in this world, our world, the world of practical affairs. He must go his way as we go ours. He has chosen the dreamer's way—I did not choose it for him, nor did you."

"The separation is your choice, though."

"Not a bit of it, my boy. No, not a bit. Dreams and the world of practical affairs can never mingle long."

I took a final sip of the sherry and put the glass aside.

"I want to see her."

"Of course," he said.

He walked across the room and made a small gesture. I followed him.

He opened a door and we passed into another larger room, also filled with books and pictures. He continued through it, but I paused before a painting in a niche to the left. It was a portrait of a woman with curling hair and large dark gray eyes. She wore an old-fashioned bonnet and an Empire robe with rounded neck and shoulders, possessed of a floral design. I halted and stared at those mysterious eyes, the dark masses of hair.

"Come on," Ellison called, halting on the threshold.

"Seabright Ellison sounds almost like a stage name," I said. "You ever do any acting?"

His eyes narrowed.

"Perhaps. Why do you ask, lad?"

I studied him in turn. The painting was a larger version of one which I possessed in miniature—my only picture of my mother, Elizabeth. I doubted he could know I owned it.

"The lady looks somehow familiar," I said.

He shrugged.

"It came to me as part of an estate I bought. Just fit that piece of wall."

My head spun. Nothing I had encountered since meeting the man had shocked me as much as this.

"Oh," I said, and turned away.

He passed through the door and into another high-ceilinged room of books, armor, and art. I took a quick step back and ran my thumb over the painting's dusty brass nameplate.

Elizabeth Arnold, I read there, and I hurried after.

It *was* my mother's name, though I'd hardly needed that confirmation of the actress' identity. If he were really the man who'd abandoned her. . . .

But this was this world, not my original one. *Ceteris paribus,* he was Poe's deserting father, not mine. But all things were not equal between this Earth and my Earth, which meant I could never know for certain whether he were truly, intentionally sacrificing his own son in this enterprise. Or if my own father had been a person similar to him, back home.

"Lovely place," I said, catching up with him. The doors had ceased after those first two rooms and now we passed through Gothic archways hung with red or blue cloth. I began realizing that this gallery passed along the entire side of the building.

"You don't remember your folks, do you?" he said, after a time.

"I don't think so. I was pretty young."

We came to the end of the gallery and turned right. A short length of hallway took us past an entranceway to a courtyard about which numerous armed men lounged, eyeing each other from opposite ends of the place.

"Athletic teams?" I suggested.

He chuckled.

"Yes. Mine and theirs. We brought them along to keep each other honest."

"So you had to go in together to meet Von Kempelen's price?"

He nodded.

"The man drives a hard bargain."

"If he were me he'd have brought his own athletic team, to keep the other two honest."

He clapped me on the shoulder.

"Spoken like a true soldier," he observed. "One of the reasons I hired you. You're going to have to tell me all about your odyssey when this thing's done."

"What is Von Kempelen's edge, anyhow?"

"He's got something we want," he said.

"And after you get it how does he walk out of here?"

He took a deep draw on his cigar and let it go. He showed me a lot of teeth then, but said nothing.

"Care to see his lab?"

"I want to see Annie."

"She's probably there."

"What happens to her," I asked, "when this is all over?"

"She's the greatest natural psychic in the world, you know."

"What does that mean?"

"A powerhouse like that is worth money in a lot of other endeavors."

"What if she doesn't want to work?"

"She's becoming dependent upon certain chemicals. She'll work for them."

I felt tears come into my eyes.

"I'm glad you're not my father," I said, on impulse.

He stepped back as if I had struck him. My hand was on the hilt of my blade. I let it drop. I still needed him.

"And I'm not Poe's father either," he said through clenched teeth.

"Never said you were. Do you have any children?"

He turned away.

"None to speak of," he said.

I followed him in what I took to be a northerly direction.

"You hate me, don't you?" he asked, after a time.

"That's right."

He paused at the head of a wide stone stairway. He turned and leaned back against the wall.

"I'd like to clear that up before tonight."

"So that's what you meant about my timing?"

He nodded.

"Tonight's the night. But you must have known that, at some level."

"I guess I did."

"I get to keep all the gold," he said then. "But I had to surrender a lot of my holdings, including most of this place."

"And Annie?" I asked. "She's a part of the price?"

He nodded again.

"But I'm going to want you on my side tonight, Perry, when it's time to pick up the pieces. Yes, I promised them Annie. I'd have promised them anything to get the work done. But afterwards. . . . They're going to have to be happy with the real estate, the jewels, the foreign holdings. I get the gold, you get Annie, the hell with everybody else."

"You're too Byzantine, Ellison," I said, "too Machiavellian. There's no way I could trust a man like you even if I wanted to."

He sighed. Then he stared downward at his feet. A full minute must have gone by. Either he really had at one time been an actor or there was a great internal struggle in progress.

Then, "All right," he said, and he reached beneath his dressing gown and withdrew a silver flask. He unscrewed its top, removed it and waved it under my nose. It smelled like whisky.

He filled the top, which was the size of a shot glass, and he tossed it off in a single swallow. Then he refilled it and extended it toward me. I accepted it and did the same.

"I crossed over by accident myself, during a strange storm," he said, "apparently in exchange for my counterpart. So I knew it could be done. It took me a long time to figure how it might be managed—

which is how I first came to know Griswold and Templeton. We worked together to discover the means. But they'd gotten greedy on a recent deal." He offered me the flask again. I declined. He took another slug himself, capped it, and put it away. "So I've no qualms about reneging on part of a deal with them. If the lady really means that much to you, she's yours."

I sat down on the top step, massaged my brow.

"Consanguinity makes these things easier," he said at last.

"Damn you, sir," I said.

"I'm not asking filial piety, just cooperation," he said. "We'll finesse these bastards and come out on top. I'll get my gold, you'll get your Annie and they'll still be rich enough not to complain too loudly. It'll be better than death."

"Your troops look pretty evenly matched to me."

"I've reserves they don't know about," he said. "They show up on cue, the balance gets tipped, nobody fights. We all back away from each other, snarling and go about our business."

"What about Von Kempelen?"

"What about him?"

"He gets to live."

"Why?"

I remembered the old popeyed man who'd given us a cup of tea back in Paris and shown concern for our welfare as we scrambled away over the rooftops. True, he was venal. But he was not a killer, not a madman, not a predator. But I couldn't say this, and even if I did, it would mean nothing.

"Because that's how I want it," I answered him.

He made as if to reach for the flask again, thought better of it, let his hand fall.

"It'd mean my watching him for the rest of his life, to see he doesn't try the gold trick again."

I felt the left corner of my mouth quirk upward.

"Think you can afford that?" I asked.

"Damn you, sir," he quoted. "If that's what it takes, you've got it. Shall we shake on it?"

"No."

He dropped his cigar to the floor and stepped on it.

"All right then," he observed. "Between you and me, now, everything must be staged. We block out the action, we agree upon our cues. We have our entrances and our exits. . . ."

We entered the deep cellar, illuminated by torch and candle, a bit later in the day. The setup was somehow reminiscent of the arrangement on the worktable in Von Kempelen's Paris apartment, only on a much vaster scale. There were several ovens cooking things. There were jars and vials and alembics and retorts. But the majority of the chemicals occupied large vats, arranged about the floor in some pattern I did not understand. A massive quantity of dark metal was stacked upon a tarpaulin at the room's center. Annie, in a simple gray frock, stood beside a vat holding a pair of rods which extended from it. She looked our way as we entered, let go the rods and came to me. I held her.

"I knew you'd come," she said, "today."

Von Kempelen looked our way.

"I know you," he said. "You was with the little man—and the monkey."

I nodded.

"I get around." Then, "Come on, Annie, let's get out of here," I told her.

She looked to Von Kempelen.

"Go ahead. You can finish charging it later," he said.

I took her out of there and up the stairs and through the halls and gallery and out into the garden, leaving them there below.

A long while later, as we lay amid beauty and sunlight, regarding golden trees, I remarked, "So the process involves mesmerism?"

She nodded, she yawned.

"It's the secret ingredient in such transmutation on a large scale," she explained, "a special kind of mesmerism."

"Oh," I said. " 'Special?' In what way?"

"Other-worldly energy," she replied. "There will be a vast flux of it when the door for Poe's return is finally closed."

"And that takes place tonight, during the work?"

"They would like it to," she said, "but it shan't. I haven't been keeping it open all this time for their benefit."

"You've lost me."

She smiled.

"No, I haven't lost anyone yet. Not even Poe. I plan to give them their gold and get him back, too. The three of us will finally be together, here."

"I am not a scientist," I said, "and my training as a mesmerist is far from complete. But even without knowing the mathematics that must prop such matters, I'm sure of one thing: The universe doesn't give you something for nothing. What's the price?"

She smiled again.

"Mr. Ellison does not know that I am aware of his secret," she said. "He is from that Earth. Therefore, I can exchange him for Poe and *then* close the door.

We will be reunited, and Mr. Griswold will be extremely grateful."

"I'll bet," I said. "This was his idea, wasn't it?"

"Yes."

It was like looking into a maelstrom—things changing constantly as I watched. Would her stratagem prevail? Had Von Kempelen a secret army of homunculi awaiting the appropriate moment, somewhat after midnight of a gold October 7th, to make their move on *his* behalf? I was probably the only one involved without a contingency plan.

So I kissed her, and, "Tell me more about mesmerism," I said. "When the force is as strong as ours there must be special measures for keeping it under control."

"Oh, yes," she answered. "We must construct our own tools. . . ."

On that night of all nights in the year, well after midnight, we made our ways into the cavernous cellar of the manse at Arnheim to commence the transmutation.

The private armies of Seabright Ellison and the men he had dubbed the Unholy Trinity faced each other across the length of the laboratory. There were perhaps forty on each of two sides. Each man bore a rifle and wore a brace of pistols; and there were plenty of edged weapons in sight. I wondered what it would be like with ricochets flying all over the place. Civilians. . . . I'd sneaked in and dug a hasty trench earlier—not too far off to my left—and covered it over with a piece cut from the tarp holding the mountain of lead bars. I'd anticipated something like this; and at the first evidence there'd be gunfire I intended to grab Annie and dive into it.

Von Kempelen was connecting hoses from tank to tank, rods from the final tank to the far side of the stack of lead bars. Annie was seated in a shiny black chair which looked as if it had been constructed from slabs of obsidian. A glass helmet covered her upper head, and she leaned against a strip of gold which ran up its high back. She was given two rods to hold, both of which extended to the near side of the lead heap.

Von Kempelen whispered some final instruction to her, then nodded to Ellison and the others. A certain tension, apart from the psychological, immediately filled the room. I took a step toward Annie and felt an increase in the forces she was manipulating. There followed a gurgling from one of the vats. Whatever forces were emanating from Annie, they began to pulsate. The other vats began to resonate.

I seemed to hear a high-pitched whining, and suddenly my head ached. Covering my ears did not make any difference, though everyone else was doing it, also. Then it went away and half-distinct shapes swam through the air—strange fish, strange sea. . . . Again, the pulsing intensified. It was almost something one could lean against. I felt somewhat more conversant with the phenomenon now, following my exercise of the previous afternoon.

The sound came and went in an instant. Minute explosions of color then filled the air, above the vats, about the gray stack. Annie's hands were white with strain upon the rods before her.

Then came the rippling. It was as if I watched the men across from me—and everything else about me, I suddenly realized—through a shallow, flowing stream. Nothing was changed, yet everything was changed. Everything in the cellar seemed to be vibrating.

Then the points of light—mostly golden this time—returned, to linger within the rippling.

I took another step toward Annie. Some pressure was building. The gray bars flashed yellow for a moment, within the rippling. A moment later the flash was repeated—golden this time, lingering. The pile seemed to change shape, shrinking each time the brightness came into it, expanding as it departed.

I glanced at Ellison, who was smiling. The frequency of the vibration increased. The gold-gray/implosion-explosion sequence came faster and faster. Then the gold portion of the cycle was lengthened, the gray shortened. There was a jogging effect, with the actual scraping, grating sounds of the bars rubbing against one another as some intrinsic factor altered the size to maintain the mass. Several of them were tumbled from the stack.

I looked to Ellison again and he seemed framed in fire, but totally unmindful of it.

Then the vibration stopped, and I beheld a mound of gold. Everyone in the room seemed to inhale sharply at the same time. Lovely, buttery, heavy, gleaming. . . .

I looked from the gold to Annie to Ellison and back. And again. Nothing happened. Nobody moved. Something had to happen. There had to be a counterstroke, a movement, a balancing—

Annie screamed. The light which hovered about Ellison faded.

That which Annie had screamed was, "Poe is dead!"

There was a grin upon Griswold's face. Annie released the rods, pushed back her crown of glass.

Something like a great sigh swept through the chamber, and there came a rattling like an earthquake in a brickyard.

The pile grew and lost its shimmer, turned gray and fell apart.

Griswold screamed and so did Ellison. But no one fired a shot.

Annie repeated what she had said, very softly, but the words were clear. As if in echo there came a tremor and all the lights shook in their sockets. "Poe," she said again, "is dead," and overhead the building creaked. There came a fall of dust all about us.

Eyes turned upward, and a series of growling, cracking noises ensued.

"At the termination of this sentence I started and, for a moment, paused; for it appeared to me (although I at once concluded that my excited fancy had deceived me)—it appeared to me that, from some very remote portion of the mansion, there came, indistinctly to my ears, what might have been, in its exact similarity of character, the echo (but a stifled and dull one certainly) of the very crackling and ripping sound which Sir Launcelot had so particularly described. It was, beyond doubt, the coincidence alone which had arrested my attention; for, amid the rattling of the sashes of the casements, and the ordinary commingled noises of the still increasing storm, the sound, in itself had nothing, surely, which should have interested or disturbed me. I continued the story. . . ."

And then there came a pounding within all the walls, followed by a creaking sound. The entire chamber seemed to move sideways, and more bars fell from the pile of gray. Ellison glanced about quickly, began a retreat toward the stair. A moment later the

trio opposite him did the same. There came a crash
like thunder.

"Poe is dead," came a whisper which filled the
entire room.

"'And Ethelred uplifted his mace, and struck upon
the head of the dragon, which fell before him, and
gave up his pesty breath, with a shriek so horrible
and harsh, and withal so piercing, that Ethelred had
fain to close his ears with his hands against the
dreadful noise of it, the like whereof was never before
heard.'

"Here again I paused abruptly, and now with a feel
of wild amazement—for there could be no doubt
whatever that, in this instance, I did actually hear
(although from what direction it proceeded I found
it impossible to say) a low and apparently distant, but
harsh, protracted, and most unusual screaming or
grating sound—the exact counterpart of what my
fancy had already conjured up for the dragon's
unnatural shriek as described by the romancer."

A massive fall of stone crashed upon the stairway,
blocking our exit. For the first time, various of the
men began to scream. Weapons were discarded as
they pushed forward, seeking to escape. Annie raised
her arms and swayed from side to side. As if in sympathy, the entire structure around and above us did
the same. There followed a series of terrible crashes
from overhead, and the ceiling collapsed in a half-
dozen places. Some of the men were screaming in
agony now, as they were pinned beneath débris. Now
it seemed some passing wind lamented Poe rather
than words; and from somewhere there came to me
a smell of smoke. . . .

❖   ❖   ❖

She had gray eyes, and brown hair lay disheveled upon her brow. Her hands were delicate, fingers long. Her blue skirt and white blouse were sand-streaked, smudged, the hem of the skirt sodden. Her full lips quivered as her gaze darted from him to the castle and back, but her eyes remained dry.

"I'm sorry," he repeated.

She turned her back to him. A moment later her bare foot kicked forward. Another wall fell, another tower toppled.

"Don't!" he cried, rising, reaching to restrain her. "Stop! Please stop!"

"No!" she said, moving forward, trampling towers. "No."

He caught hold of her shoulder and she pulled away from him, continuing to kick and stamp at the castle.

I caught hold of her shoulder. The whole damned roof was coming down, and fire was falling in on us, along with rafters, stone, wood.

"Annie! Stop it!" I cried.

She didn't even seem to realize I was there. Somewhere high above I heard a wall give way. In a moment, I felt, the entire silly-ornate structure would be down here in the cellar with us.

"Annie!"

She wailed and the earth moved beneath our feet. So I clipped her on the jaw and caught her as she fell. Then I called upon that bond established back in Spain before I'd entered Toledo.

"Ligeia!"

I saw her limned in light as I raised Annie in my arms.

"I am waiting," she said.

"Here is my half of the way. Meet me at the middle, pray."

The corridor of silver shot forward to join with its counterpart. As I walked it to the place where the lady waited I heard at my back a long tumultuous shouting sound like the voice of a thousand waters.

I kept going.

XV

Months later I discovered to my total surprise that I had been named in the last will and testament of Seabright Ellison, inheriting from him a small stipend and the residence known as Landor's Cottage, where Annie and I now reside as I labor at the assembly of these memoirs.

Our friends, such as Dirk Peters, have come to visit us from time to time. Neither of us has forgotten Edgar Allan Poe, who has left two worlds the poorer for his passing. We would that he could share with us the park-like splendors of this place where, on all sides, the violets, tulips, poppies, hyacinths, and tuberoses entangle amid the tall trees, among lily-fringed lakes and meadows.

And at times we open a different door, to the rear of that pleasant dwelling, stepping out upon a foggy beach where the sea flows warm as blood and dark shapes pass. From there we've journeyed many a midnight mile to realms both rare and strange, whose ways would not be open had our dear brother never been:

> By a route obscure and lonely,
> Haunted by ill angels only,
> Where an Eidolon, named NIGHT,
> On a black throne reigns upright,
> I have reached these lands but newly
> From an ultimate dim Thule—
> From a wild weird clime that lieth, sublime,
> Out of SPACE—out of TIME.

From *Dream-Land*,
Edgar Allan Poe

American freedom and justice versus the tyrannies of the seventeenth century

1632 *by Eric Flint*

Paperback • 31972-8   **$7.99** ____

"This gripping and expertly detailed account of an episode of time travel that changes history is a treat for lovers of action-SF or alternate history...it distinguishes Flint as an SF author of particular note, one who can entertain and edify in equal, and major, measure."

—*Publishers Weekly*, **starred review**

1633 *by David Weber & Eric Flint*

Hardcover • 7434-3542-7   **$26.00** ____

The greatest naval war in European history is about to erupt. Like it or not, Gustavus Adolphus will have to rely on Mike Stearns and the technical wizardry of his obstreperous Americans to save the King of Sweden from ruin, but caught in the conflagration are two American diplomatic missions abroad. . . .